Having S

ALSO BY KAE TEMPEST

FICTION

The Bricks that Built the Houses

NON-FICTION

On Connection

POETRY

Everything Speaks in its Own Way

Brand New Ancients

Hold Your Own

Let Them Eat Chaos

Running Upon the Wires

Divisible By Itself and One

PLAYS

Wasted

Glasshouse

Hopelessly Devoted

Paradise

Having Spent Life Seeking

KAE TEMPEST

JONATHAN CAPE
LONDON

1 3 5 7 9 10 8 6 4 2

Jonathan Cape, an imprint of Vintage, is part of the
Penguin Random House group of companies

Vintage, Penguin Random House UK, One Embassy Gardens,
8 Viaduct Gardens, London SW11 7BW

penguin.co.uk/vintage
global.penguinrandomhouse.com

First published by Jonathan Cape in 2026

Typeset in 11.1/15.2pt Calluna by Six Red Marbles UK, Thetford, Norfolk
Printed and bound in Great Britain by Clays Ltd, Elcograf S.p.A.

The authorised representative in the EEA is Penguin Random House Ireland,
Morrison Chambers, 32 Nassau Street, Dublin D02 YH68

A CIP catalogue record for this book is available from the British Library

HB ISBN 9781787335370
TPB ISBN 9781787335387

Penguin Random House is committed to a sustainable future
for our business, our readers and our planet. This book is made
from Forest Stewardship Council® certified paper.

For you, if you have picked it up. Be gentle though.
I hope it finds you.

And while I am completely engulfed in my sadness, I am happy to sense that you exist, beautiful one. I am happy to have flung myself without fear into your beauty just as a bird flings itself into space. I am happy, dear, to have walked with steady faith on the waters of our uncertainty all the way to that island which is your heart and where pain blossoms. Finally: happy.

Rilke

Day One

October 2026

ONE

Rothko Taylor was up a ladder in the wind. Eyes sore as peeled grapes, blinking in the cold. It was the kind of wind that rattled the ladder and butted their arms. They'd been reaching for the gutters so long they had a crick in their neck that shot down through their shoulder and into their back.

Thirty-six years old. Single. Living in a van on a site that was flagged for development. Working as a handyman in a seafront hotel that felt like it was minutes from collapse. Six months out of jail and the world had moved on.

Today was their last day on the job, and they had a feeling of endings. The past was accelerating towards them out of everything they looked at.

Since coming home, they'd been maintaining their existence, one menial chore at a time. Real life was still something other people did. But this afternoon – hands clamped round the struts of the creaking ladder, getting pushed around by the freezing wind, they could feel themself approaching the surface. Because they were clean. And free. And alive. And the thanks went pulsing through their system so hard, they had to shake their hands at the wrists to expel the gathered energy. It made the ladder rock beneath them.

'State of it.' They caught themself. 'What are we like?' they asked Donovan, who was curled up under the picnic table, trying to sleep his way out of the wind.

For six months, Rothko Taylor had been holding themself to a pressing routine. They stuck to it, no matter what, seven days a week. They equated routine with possibility and self-control. Lost in dead chaos for years, the idea of an ordered life in the physical realm was balm for the wound.

So, each day they woke at 6 a.m., were washed and dressed by 6:40, and they left site at 7:15, before the streets got busy. They kept to the same side of the road as they walked their ten-minute route to work. Each morning, they reached the seafront and turned right to the battered old hotel. They never turned left into town. Only sometimes looked towards it. A loaded glance, as if to prove their significance to an otherwise indifferent scene.

At the end of their working day, they walked the same route home. Never wandered into town, not even for a look. They got safely back to site, washed up and had their dinner with the others if the others were about. Or they enjoyed their simple meal alone, while watching internet documentaries about people who'd achieved against-the-odds success in their van until they fell asleep.

Today, the worry was that the end of the job meant the end of the routine. The feeling of it was like vertigo and they gripped the ladder tighter. They hated the thought of having hours to kill. Nothing kept them safe like daily targets; glad little boxes they could tick against oblivion.

Donovan pawed at his nose and barked twice as the wind lifted a dustbin lid and hurled a bag of rubbish across the road. 'Don't know what you're on about.' Rothko looked down over their shoulder at him. 'Lovely day for it.'

They had nothing lined up workwise and that worried them. Person like Rothko knew they needed something, otherwise it might not be long before they woke up in their old life again. Didn't bear thinking about.

'Protect me. Please,' they whispered to the grubby weather as they struggled with the guttering. 'Just got to get through today, haven't we, boy?'

But how did a person go about getting a job? They had no idea. It was Roxanne who got them this one.

Roxanne and Rothko had been padded up in Downview, years before. They had both come from the same small town and knew a few of the same small people, and considering the jail was miles from Edgecliff, the two of them ending up with each other had a feeling of destiny to it. It had been Roxanne who had shaved Rothko's head the very first time, when Rothko finally allowed themself to admit they wanted their hair cut short.

Padmates for three years. Roxanne had grown to love Rothko like one of her own.

The span of the stretch was so vast, it was hard to hold in their head. A few of the more memorable faces swam up from the soup of time. Bobbed at the surface. Sank back down.

They'd shared with all kinds over the years. A lot of them had been maniacs. But some had become friends. A few had become lovers. What friendships there were had been intense, but usually ended when the people left. Roxanne was the only one who had stayed in touch. She said to call when Rothko made it out, and so they had.

And here they were.

It was Roxanne who had told them about the site where they were living and given them a place to stay. It was Roxanne who had heard about the job, and got them in with Meryl, the lady who owned the hotel. She'd done so much for them already. They couldn't face asking her to help them out again.

They didn't want her to know that even after all her kindness, they were still the same fucking person.

Shame crunched them up. They straightened their shoulders against the press of it. They didn't want to be someone that always let you down. That couldn't be trusted to sort their own shit out. And in fact, they weren't going to be. Not anymore.

They finally dislodged the clump of leaves, bird shit and slimy crisp packets they'd been fumbling with and threw the grim handful to the floor. They tipped a stream of filthy water out of the wonky gutter. It soaked their wrists and sleeves, gushed down through the cracks and they had to swing to the side to dodge the torrent. The ladder bounced. They wrestled to steady it. Water down the back of their coat.

Just to be touched. Just to be touched and held. By someone who knows how to handle a body like mine.

In jail, you couldn't think backwards, and you couldn't think forwards, you just had to stay in the minute. Rothko had sucked up so much of that kind of time, they'd got to the point where they could rely on it. But out here, time was a menace. It wouldn't stay still. Somehow the weeks raced by, and the nights never passed, and it all went forwards and backwards at the same time and as for keeping it in the minute, their whole life was out there, shouting at them from the corners, and it was doing their nut.

You can go home now, the screw had said. So, of course, they had gone back to Edgecliff; there wasn't anywhere else for them to have gone.

But there was nothing left to keep them here. Except maybe the van and the people on site. Roxanne. And Fletcher, of course.

They let themself into the hotel lobby and wandered

slowly through the bright reception. Noticing the details. The floral-print wallpaper, the tall glass vases filled with coloured beads, the butterscotch armchairs, the stacked pamphlets for adventure parks and miniature villages.

Start again somewhere where nobody knew their name, or try and make a new life in their old town?

They waited for a sign of some sort.

They stood very still and listened to the room. Quiet hum of electricity. Their own breath. Donovan's paws on the lino. Then, a sudden rainfall hammering the conservatory roof. But they weren't convinced it was the sign they had been looking for.

They headed through the door marked Staff Only to the back kitchen. Donovan skipped to his favourite patch on the rug, turned around a few times and laid his body down gently, tucked right in next to the boiler cupboard. Rothko flicked the kettle and warmed their hands on it as it boiled. 'Happy now?' they asked Donovan, who had started rolling his head across the rug, getting a scratch behind his ears, growling in satisfaction.

It was funny to think they'd only known each other six months. Rothko already felt like they couldn't live a day without him. They'd found each other the day Rothko came home. Donovan had been living in the derelict garages that backed on to the site. They watched him scratching his massive brown head on the rug, tongue dangling out of his jaws, stripes of silver and gold flashing around his haunches, and remembered how he'd looked back then: ribs showing through his greasy coat, full of shame and courage. How he'd dropped his head and put his ears back at first. But not long after meeting, the shy old dog had followed Rothko home, and not long after that, he'd curled up and gone to sleep with his head in Rothko's lap. And Rothko felt a peace they hadn't known in half a lifetime. To have been chosen. To have been trusted as *safe*.

Six months. Chipping away at damp plaster. It had kept them from chipping away at themself. Was only meant to be a five-day painting and decorating job but then all these little things needed doing and they'd found themself gainfully employed. It had been good while it lasted. They'd eaten a lot of biscuits. Not had to talk to that many people.

Good for Meryl that she'd found a buyer. Mad old place was running her into the ground. They'd rip it all down more than likely, build a block of flats. Seemed a waste of all that work, but then what did Rothko know.

Years ago. How many? Felt like two hundred thousand. They couldn't have been much older than seven. They'd spent that crushing summer following their mum around the architectural salvage place where she'd managed to score a job fixing up old chairs.

They'd been her eager shadow. Vying for another shot of her overproof attention. Hours hanging round that place, waiting for her to finish her shift. She had distractedly taught them how to use sandpaper, how to mix paint. Eventually, she'd set them up with their own job to keep them busy, mending a decrepit wooden rocking horse. 'You can do it if you stick to it,' she'd told them every time they grew frustrated.

They hadn't thought of that horse in years but somehow today, there it was. Still rocking.

Of all the lessons they wished they hadn't learned from their mum, Meg, Rothko had to give her credit for the rocking horse. Because they *had* stuck to it. And eventually managed to get the splinters smooth, and to paint two monstrous eyes on the poor thing and fix a new rocker for its clumpy little hooves.

That had been a good summer. Meg hadn't tried to kill herself for at least six weeks. And Rothko had learned an important lesson. One so important they'd forgotten it completely until this very moment, nearly thirty years later: how much good could be done to a wrecked old thing that was bound for the tip, if it got into the right pair of careful, patient hands.

They stood in the staff kitchen of the old B&B, staring at the kettle as it started to boil.

'Right then.'

Time for them to see if they were the person they wanted to be.

They had a lot of plans. But here they were, on the crest of a change that was going to break with or without them, and they didn't know if they had it in them. 'Not going back,' they told the teabag cupboard. But it didn't believe them.

They washed up their cup and opened the envelope addressed to them on the table, found that Meryl had left them a note along with their wages. *R – sorry I sold you out of a job. Think of it as redundancy pay. Thanks for everything. Meryl xx*

Rothko took the cash out and counted what was in there. More than they'd expected. It just kept going. Twenty after twenty after twenty. Two weeks' wages, plus a thousand pound.

They sat down. Counted it again. And then again. They put it carefully into their wallet. Put their wallet into their pocket. Then took it back out. Checked the money was still in there. Found that it was. Put the wallet back in their pocket and sat very still on their chair, thinking.

It must have been money from the sale.

They looked around the kitchen in a daze. Those shelves they did, and where the skirts were rotting, they took them out and replaced them. Sorted the leak in the back of the dishwasher that was going down under the boards. They'd pulled the floor up and sorted those joists. Painted those walls. Even managed the ceilings.

It was amazing to them that Meryl had noticed how much they'd done. They had thought they walked around unseen. That people dreaded bumping into them the way they dreaded bumping into people.

They took the pen from the spiral spine of the notebook they kept in their top pocket, flipped Meryl's note over and wrote on the back in small capitals. '*Received with many thanks. Best of luck with your endeavours. RT*.' They placed the note back in the envelope and arranged it nicely on the table, displaying the keys on top. Studying the composition of the still life. Deciding to rearrange it. Studied it again. Opened the note back up and left an *x* at the end. Put it back in the envelope and put the envelope back where it was. Adjusted the keys once more, a little to the left. More central. A little to the right. No. A little to the left again. Then got up, in no great hurry. One slow stride at a time.

'Come then,' they beckoned Donovan, but he was already on his feet, giving himself a hearty shake. He followed behind, only stopping for one look back at his favourite patch of rug, whining a soft yawn.

Rothko paused at the front door. The clock above the desk was ticking. The light on the photocopier was flashing blue. Nothing else moved. They tapped the wall twice with a flat hand, spoke to the quiet room: 'Thanks for having me.' And they let themself out into the piercing weather, checking their inside pocket for the reassuring shape of their wallet.

The rain had come. They looked out of the open door at it. Didn't look very appealing. But resolved, they slammed the door behind them and stepped into a wall of it. Found themself soaked before they'd reached the corner, where for the last six months, they had turned left and walked heavily back to the van.

But this was an occasion, wasn't it?

They stopped still. Looking both ways. The rain was pounding their forehead and rushing their cheeks.

Back to the van. Or into town?

They wanted to walk down the high street, look in shop windows, see the pretty things on display all lit up nicely. Push through the doors of a warm pub. Stand with their foot on a brass runner at an old oak bar. They had a thirst on for an afternoon pint. Imagined the feeling of striding in, being greeted by old friends. Warm sunny beer frothing in a glass. They could have a pint, couldn't they?

One pint didn't mean . . .?

Their throat was sore for beer from all this thinking.

Other people managed it. Maybe they were fine, now.

End of a long day, end of a big job. End of a long stretch. These were milestones worth marking after all. Couple a pints without going back to the bad . . . to the . . .

Rothko made a break for it and turned right, into town.

It was time to go and see what they'd been missing. They struck out towards the site of their creation.

It felt like every day that had led them here was walking with them. They could see themself at ten years old running this very same stretch of beach, down to the pub, looking for Mum. The thought of it was sharp and they waved it off with a batting hand. 'Stop it, now. Come on.' It all could have been so much worse. And with that thought, all the people they had known who'd had it worse came close, mouthing words Rothko couldn't hear, then faded. Rothko opened their palms to catch the raindrops, watched the water bouncing out of the cup of their hands. Focused on what was really there. 'Thank you,' they said to the rain as it bounced. There was so much to be grateful for.

Some days, they reckoned, a person just can't hide from it anymore. It all catches up with them and today was one of those days for Rothko Taylor.

Rothko.

Dark hair and crooked teeth. A curly kind of smile that thinned the lips and pointed the chin. Dimples a mile deep. Impressive eyes, true as mud. Their hair needed a trim, it had grown longer than they liked around the back and sides and now it curled. They'd bleached it in the summer, it was growing out dark and clinging to the rain. They took a flat cap out of their pocket and slicked it down over their head. Broad belly, broad back and broad shoulders. Big arms. Strong with a pliant, animal strength. Slim wrists, scarred knuckles, graceful hands. Wrinkles at the corners of their eyes like pages turning.

Donovan, their friend and dog, was similarly solid. A massive brindle mutt with a huge flat head, and rolling shoulders. Lion-sized paws. His fur was thick and shiny. He'd never caught a squirrel, but Rothko loved how hard he tried.

Together, they paced the bitter beach. A lone figure on a desolate plain, dog at their heels, navy blue pea coat billowing behind them. Grey hood pulled up. Digging in against the weather. They reached the point between two breakwaters where the wind dropped out and enjoyed the sudden feeling of suspension. It was like they were floating. Donovan snapped at the waves as they broke and rolled away. Chasing the wind in mad diagonals. Rothko had taken to calling Donovan by any name that began with the sound *Don*. Their favourites were Doner and chips, Don Corleone, or Donatella Versace, depending on the frivolity of their mutual mood. It was good having a private joke with someone. A clean, bright brick in the wall of their connection.

'Come on then, Donny Hathaway. This way.'

Eager little barks. They were happy together.

The rain cleared so abruptly; it was like a signal had been given. Rothko looked up to catch God in the act. Saw the pale sun there, washing its face in the clouds.

The money sang in their pocket.

They could go private with this kind of money. Start on T.

They dug their feet deeper into the stones.

They thought of Fletcher. He lived in the van next door to Rothko, and he was probably Rothko's favourite person. Ever since they'd arrived on site, Fletcher had been kind to Rothko. Even though they hadn't known each other very long, they had developed a natural friendship. Something easy passed between them. A likeness that didn't need to be explained to be enjoyed. Fletcher had been through it all already, and from what he'd told them, it could be rocky at first while your body got used to it.

They'd been thinking about a name. Felt like that was the first step to working the rest out. They could feel it up there somewhere just above their head.

Rothko was not a name they had chosen for themself. It was a nickname that fell on them at two years old, on account of their irrepressible blushes, which happened all the time. Causing their mum to exclaim, on a daily basis, that they'd gone red as a Rothko.

They'd never really thought until now about the implications of living under a name they had been given because of the obviousness of their shame.

Be nice to spend it on someone.

Just to be touched and held.

The grey apartment blocks stared out at the grey sea. Rothko felt the comfort and threat of being back in the place that raised them.

Released in April. Saw the clouds sink through the pools at low tide. Watched the spring fade, up a ladder with the radio for company. Spent a patchy summer sanding skirting boards in Meryl's courtyard, talking to the stone tortoises. Now the nights were getting thinner. Autumn had her boots off stretching out her toes, and they realised they'd been waiting at the threshold all this time.

It felt like day one.

TWO

The high street was busy after the solemn seafront. Everyone seemed cheerful. People doing people things like crossing the road to the supermarket on the phone saying, *I'm getting teabags and onions and what else was it?*

Things that someone who'd not been locked up day and night in what was essentially a toilet with a bunk bed in it might not even notice, but Rothko couldn't stop marvelling at them all, looking out from under their soggy cap.

That one: yoga mat, expensive hair, scowling like she was ready to kill. That one there: collar up, wheely shopping bag full of blue-top milk and white bread, studying two lottery tickets, right in the way of all the people trying to pass. Rothko crossed their fingers for him, *hope you win.* And over there: high ponytail, big body pushing back against tight clothing, itching and re-itching a patch of skin on her forearm. And inside the chemist, the queue through the window: grey tracksuit, counting something on hard fingers. Black bomber and pointy sunglasses eating Maltesers. White snakeskin trousers fiddling with an eyebrow piercing. Scrolling the phone. Waiting for prescriptions. And all around the kind of daytime seaside drunk that made it feel feasible. Even romantic. Young couple in 1930s knitwear, drunk, touching each other's cheeks in the window of the chippy. Old geezer with a sparrow's face, drunk, trying to put his gloves on. Burly people with tins, pushing their babies along in prams while their little yappy dogs got tangled in their leashes. Be dark soon anyway. And fuck it, it was Saturday.

Rothko passed a group of teenagers doing a choreographed dance routine into the mirrored windows of a closed-down bank. Rothko could not believe what they were seeing and stopped still, but nobody else seemed to have noticed anything unusual.

A young man in a smart beige mac walked towards them, he was looking directly into Rothko's face. Shouting, Rothko assumed, at them. 'Honestly, the fuss she made about getting it done. I couldn't even tell the difference! . . . I *know*! . . . All I'm saying is . . .' Rothko looked behind them to see if the man was talking to somebody there. But there was no one. The man walked past. Laughing.

It was as if nobody existed in mutual space. As if everyone was protected by some invisible membrane of privacy, except Rothko.

What had happened?

At sixteen, the world had been carved in Rothko's own image.

But there were new teenagers in town now. Doing dance routines into reflective surfaces like it wasn't embarrassing.

Real life.

They were looking right at the very thing they'd been clucking for all these years.

But what were they supposed to do with it?

Seemed like the only thing harder than no second chances, was getting the chance and then not knowing how.

They felt old. But they hadn't achieved their age in the way other people had. They hadn't earned it in experiences or relationships. They had just woken up in it, all of a sudden. Old. And unprepared. They watched a blue-rinse lady with her sticks and her shopping bags muscling through the crowd and thought, maybe that's just how it is for everyone.

Beer.

Three kids on skateboards rattled past. Baggy haircuts, key chains. Must have been about sixteen. Rothko was relieved to see them. They made them think of the old days. Sean and Dionne and the parties up the meadows and they re-felt sixteen like falling from a great height and being impaled on a railing.

They needed to call him. Sean. He'd been their best mate before life pulled them in opposite directions. There'd been amends made since then. Sean had been in for visits, here and there. They'd both said the same thing, *we'll catch up once things have settled down.* But the success Sean had made of his life – lovely missus, four kids last time Rothko checked – made Rothko want to keep their distance. They didn't like the jealousy they felt whenever they heard his news.

As if on cue, they walked up on a couple of the old faces and clenched their jaw in a forced smile. Kathy and Jon-Boy. Dogs and blankets. Matted hair. Busking for beer money with a penny whistle by the pawn shop.

Looked like some things had stayed the same.

'Alright mucker,' Kathy called out, waving. 'Heard you was back. Missed your face. Been ages!'

'Hello, hello,' Rothko acknowledged them.

'Got big, didn't ya?!' She laughed, but one of her dogs started barking. Urgent, throaty terror in the pitch. Jon-Boy held the dog back, but the dog pulled and strained. Rothko looked down at Donovan and spoke quietly.

‘It’s alright,’ they soothed him. ‘I’ve got you.’ Donovan’s hackles were raised, he was growling, his eyes wide. ‘Nice and easy. Good boy.’ Rothko pulled him on until they were out of sight. Stroking his neck with a firm hand to calm him.

They could hear Kathy shouting something after them but couldn’t make out the words. They walked on, but it began to press on them, the crowded street. ‘Donny, wait here,’ they told him and ducked into a mini supermarket. Donovan lay down and waited. Looked out from under low eyebrows. Watching the entrance. Calm as marble.

Rothko walked up and down the aisles. Got a few bits and joined the queue but when they got to the front, they realised they had to pay at one of those new machines. They stood looking at it for a long time. Long enough for someone who worked there to wander over. She was friendly, in her fifties, seen it all before type. ‘You ok there, love?’ she asked them.

‘It’s not me, it’s *Terminator 2* over here that started it.’ They laughed it off, until she left them to it, at which point they stepped a bit closer to the screen and read the instructions again. *Please scan your first item*. The queue was mounting behind them. Rothko could hear their blood pulsing in their ears. They froze. Scan where? How?

Eventually a man in the front of the queue said, ‘Come on, mate.’ And Rothko stared at the man, then back at the screen. Pushed at it randomly with clumsy fingers.

‘I can’t do it,’ they said out loud, but not to the man. Not to anyone really.

‘Need a hand, love?’ The shop lady came back over.

Rothko was looking at the words, but they didn’t understand what the words were telling them to do. The people in the queue were moving their baskets from hand to hand. 'No. You're alright. Changed my mind.' They left the things they'd gone in for next to the till and walked out in a hurry. Whole face bright red.

'Come.' They grabbed Donovan's rope and the two of them merged with the churning shoppers. Donovan was alert to Rothko's unease. 'Don't even know what those things are,' they admitted to him when they were at a safe distance and their heart had stopped racing.

A bus pulled in at the stop in front of them. Rothko looked along the windows and saw a grey-faced man with thin white hair combed back, down to his collar, clean shaven, his skin pockmarked and his shirt open two buttons down. Checked scarf knotted at the throat and tucked in. He looked just like him. He looked just like the man that night.

Rothko blinked it away, but the man was still there. Their eyes met and it went on too long. It wasn't him. He was dead. The man on the bus scowled at Rothko and mouthed, 'What?'

They felt their breathing getting weird.

They backed away from the bus stop, ended up sinking against the window of a pet shop, waiting it out. Donovan sniffed towards the entrance: goat ears and hamster piss. Rothko's head was diesel. They studied the fish tanks on display. Thought about goldfish.

If goldfish are kept in small tanks, they only grow a couple of inches. But if those same fish were living freely in ponds, or lakes, or even the sea, they could grow to be huge. The bigger the environment, the bigger they're able to grow. Who had told them this? Was this true information? Probably one of the girls on the landings. Rothko was struck by the empty tanks, stacked up like a block of flats.

They concentrated on their breathing. Forehead against the sticky glass. Looking at the glass instead of through it. They turned back to the street. Kept going. Donovan pulled back to the pet shop, but Rothko tugged the rope around his neck harder than they needed to. '*This* way.' Donovan sighed and came trotting along, nose to the ground. Every now and then, he lifted his head and pushed it against Rothko's side and Rothko was comforted.

Maybe it wasn't wise to have ventured into town after all? Maybe they weren't ready yet. The thought made them sick of themself. Why couldn't they just enjoy a pint after work like a normal fucking person?

Staggering down the high street, looking in the shops. Thinking, *fifteen years.* People on the outside took it all for granted. Automated checkouts. Reusable coffee cups. Rothko hadn't learned about those things. They had learned a lot inside, but not this stuff. Not gas bills. Road tax. National Insurance. Patio paving. Online dating. Lunch with the in-laws. Barbecue tongs. Dishwasher tablets. Fitness goals. The sharing of digital calendars.

Drive them mad that life, anyway.

Why push it with big dreams of starting over? They could just keep going the way they were. Cash-in-hand work and the van parked up. No one to report to but the wind and the rain.

Alright, maybe the smoking. Maybe the coffee and junk food.

Maybe the rage. Maybe the sleeplessness. Maybe the bad moods.

Maybe the voices and hallucinations. Maybe the week-long depressions.

Maybe the body.

Discipline. That's all they needed. A stricter routine.

They wanted so bad to be healthy. But . . . *Jesus, would you give it a rest?* They calmed their brain down by speeding up their body, swivelling on their toes as they pushed, a little faster. This was supposed to be a celebration after all.

They left the high street, took a narrow road that snaked uphill, the wind squealing round the highest windows, in through the doors of an untrendy corner boozer, still called The Shipwright's Rest, and felt immediate respite from people and wind and late afternoon on a Saturday high street. Slow, quiet breaths as the pitch eased off in their ears. All that jagged focus left them dizzy.

A pallid bartender wearing a leather waistcoat over his Morrissey t-shirt, long silver necklaces and an expression of deep concern awoke from a daze as Rothko swung through the doors.

'Yes please, sir?' he asked. Rothko pointed to one of the ale taps, indicating a bitter. The bartender started tugging away at the tap like he was milking the cask. Rothko stood as broadly in their body as they could and laid a tenner on the drip tray, blushing at the inevitable 'Sorry. Miss.' that followed awkwardly behind.

Rothko offered a disappeared smile in reply. Shrug of the eyebrows.

They carried the pint over to a table in the corner. Took their wet coat and hat off and sat with their back pressed right against the radiator, but it was cold.

This was it then. Their first sit down in a pub.

Wasn't quite the golden atmosphere they'd been dreaming of.

The room had the empty, ticking clock feeling of a station waiting room.

At the table next to Rothko, a woman sat alone. Badges on her breast pocket. Some kind of uniform. Sleeves rolled back on her work shirt, tight black polyester trousers. Worn-out black leather slip-on shoes. Flat heels for long corridors. Tough, quiet face on her.

Blank white hair, pulled back in a bun. No shine to it. Brittle as sticks. The colour of an onion. She had craggy, gullish eyes. A soft mouth.

Angel Douglas.

She was tall and she haunted herself. Sat there in her chair like she was her own overhanging branches. Hunched over; legs crossed at the knee. Folded in half.

Her phone started ringing. She looked at it, put it face down on the table and went back to her glass.

She couldn't be bothered anymore.

She'd just popped in for a minute to herself and a couple of gins to level her head.

She couldn't face another bitter little silence from her girlfriend.

Every time they spoke these days it made Angel feel like her head was so full of pressure her eardrums were going to burst.

Hadn't always been like this. But she couldn't remember when it started going bad. Ruby was just there in her life. One day she wasn't. Next day she was. And Angel had been churning out excuses ever since.

Angel had never. Not fully known love. Not ever fully known it. Or maybe she had, and this was it, with Ruby. She had another sip. If it was, Angel didn't understand what all the fuss was for.

It had been a shit day. Fucking horrible day. And tonight,

they had plans. Taking Ruby to the cinema. She'd booked the special seats that are joined up like a sofa. It was all part of the new regime. Twice a month, get out for a drink or something. Even just a walk around together. Not talk about work. Not talk about fertility windows or stages of ovulation or the IQ of a potential donor. Or the baby.

Just be in each other's company.

But what was Angel's company for if not to listen to Ruby talk about those things?

And then today, one of the kids at the facility had stabbed another kid in the stomach with a shank he'd made from a biro. And Angel was finished. The blood all over the floor. The futility of the argument that started it. The whole fucking mess of the whole fucking thing. To move around, free, at the end of a shift like that, to sit in a pub and squeeze a wedge of lime into a gin and tonic, while they stayed locked away, fighting each other because what the fuck else were they supposed to do. She didn't blame them. She couldn't share these thoughts with anyone. No one else at work saw it the way she saw it. Everyone else thought the kids were subhuman, violent scumbags and that a secure unit was the best place for them. All the others, like Mitchell and Linda and Glen and Trish, they finished their shifts and that was it. They went home and got on with their lives. So why did Angel find it so hard to disconnect? The way the others talked about the kids just turned her stomach. And the thought of *stomach* brought back the image of the stabbed kid. And the wound under his t-shirt, like an open eye.

Angel flinched in her wooden armchair. She had to get it out of her system before she got home, otherwise she'd never hear the end of it from Ruby.

She didn't know how other couples made it.

Sometimes she felt so claustrophobic at home, she caught herself standing in the street before coming through the front door and imagining a version of her life when she just didn't walk through it.

Work had been stressful for ages. There were too many kids and not enough staff, and it was pulling her away from Ruby.

She could still see her mum coming home from work, wrung out and exhausted, how she'd sworn to herself that whatever she did, she'd never end up like that.

Her body would be rotten by now. How long does it take? To rot right down? Only the bones. And how much of a person is left in the bones?

Angel still sees her in her dreams sometimes. Decomposed. Flesh coming off her. She'd read up online and apparently it was normal to see things like that.

She would have wanted me to settle down.

The gin is clear and nice like glass or wind or something bright as air.

But all the talk of babies though. The treatments and appointments. It had scared the present right out of Angel. It was sucking her back to the past.

She just wanted to lie down in soft grass and close her eyes and feel close to another human being without it being *for* something.

She was lonely.

Ruby always told her that she needed to open up if she wanted to make new friends. But she'd never been good at making friends. And it only got harder as she got older.

All her friends were Ruby's friends.

They'd all gone to school together. They'd gone to each

other's birthdays and each other's weddings, and had their kids at the same time. They were all straight and white and comfortably off. But Angel didn't have friends from school. Angel had hated school. And hated bumping into the people she'd had to attach herself to at school to keep herself safe. Not that she ever did bump into them. She lived a different kind of life these days.

Why was Ruby calling?

She'd be getting home from the gym. Letting herself in without looking up from her phone. She'd only be calling to tell Angel what she was looking at. Or to ask Angel questions about what she had eaten that day.

Maybe I don't have to go back.

Remember that night Ruby had a few of them round? Angel hadn't wanted to see anyone, so she cooked dinner for them all, because that meant she could hide in the kitchen and she'd made that weird lasagne and the pasta sheets had been raw because she didn't want to use too much sauce because of her belly and they'd all smiled and said *mmm delicious* and she hated herself.

Shame.

Shame like the smell of damp laundry, clinging to her clothes.

That time she got angry because she wanted the beer on the seafront like everyone else but all the bars were too expensive and she couldn't find the right one and she made them walk out of three different places, because they weren't exactly it, and Ruby said *you're always miserable anyway, let's go home* and Angel said *ok fine* but she wanted a beer by the water like everyone else, *just do something nice just for me something nice that I want for a change*. And maybe it was Angel's fault that things had gone the way they'd gone, because Ruby was right, she was a child. *What you want is a mother.* She said it all the time. *You want a mother not a girlfriend.* Because Ruby was older, and Angel's own mother was dead. Had been dead a long time.

And now they had their donor in place and everything was getting real.

She couldn't tell Ruby she didn't want anyone to have to grow up and find out they were just like her.

Shame.

Shame like wet sand in wet clothes.

Shame like the sand at the beach that night in the wet sand with Trish.

Coming home and stuffing all the clothes in the machine, and even now there was still little bits of sand in all their clothes.

Trish from work, on the beach after Mitchell's birthday drinks and they were smoking outside in the dark. *Stop it.*

It wasn't really lying. Ruby never asked. So, Angel never told.

Ruby was ringing again. Angel silenced it and opened their messages.

Still at work. Cant answer. 4got Mitch booked wknd off. here all night. Yawn emoji. Scrambled eyes emoji. *Sorry bout pictures.* Red heart. Yellow heart. Red heart. *C u 2mo*

Nice this gin. Like clean. Tastes clean.

She opened the chat with Trish.

I want u

Angel watched the screen, saw the message had been read.

Can you come?

She dangled gently from the dot dot dot that told her Trish was typing her reply.

Usually, yeh. All over u. Raindrop emoji. Tongue emoji. *Where we linking?*

The gin so clean and bright and sharp like a mirror as Angel smiled for the first time that day. Like a polished mirror, so pretty when you look in it.

Go on then. May as well. Have another.

THREE

At their table in the corner, Rothko watched their pint but didn't lift it. The bartender brought Donovan a bowl of water, placed it between his paws and patted him on the head, smiling at Rothko.

'Is it a girl or a boy?' Rothko noticed a look in the barman's eyes as he waited for their response.

'He's a boy. But he has his moments,' they heard themself saying. Unsure of what they meant by it.

'He's lovely.' The barman offered a breath of approval as he walked away.

Desperate for a piss, Rothko looked for the toilets and saw the two doorways, either side of a table of a group of solid men, engaged in solid drinking who looked like they'd been in for a while.

Ladies. And Gents.

Terrifying terms.

There was none of that in jail.

Rothko didn't want any trouble.

They sat harder on their chair and tried to take their mind off pissing while the drinking men continued at their chat, passing time swapping cruel remarks about each other that betrayed their deep affection. Rothko reached the point they couldn't hold it any longer. So they got up, head down, and pushed through the doors to the ladies. Nobody else in there, thank God. They rushed a terrified piss and afterwards, stood silently behind the locked door, listening.

Satisfied that it was safe to come out, they washed their hands surfing a tide of dread. Too slow. A woman walked in, saw Rothko at the sinks, frowned, walked back out to check the picture on the door. Came back in, still frowning as if needing a witness for her confusion. Rothko tried to sweeten up their body language, but it didn't seem to help. The woman just kept staring at them, face like a blunt pencil. 'This is the *ladies*.'

Her friend came in, saw them looking at each other and said, 'What's happened?'

'Look!' She spoke loudly, pointed at Rothko. 'I don't know what that is, but it aint a woman and it shouldn't be in here.'

Rothko did not want a fight. They felt their pulse begin to darken their vision.

The woman's friend backed out of the way as Rothko shuffled for the safety of their table, but as they arrived, they found a small, strong man in a heavy jumper lingering. Looking down at Donovan.

Rothko clocked him, warily.

'Lovely dog.' He cracked a quiet grin. 'Just gorgeous aint he. How old?'

Dog chat. What a relief.

Rothko knew how to have this conversation and relaxed into it. 'Think he's ten, coming on that way. Maybe older.'

'He's doing good for ten, aint he?' The man admired Donovan. 'Mind if I say hello?'

'Go for it mate, he's friendly.' The man crouched down, cooing and clicking as he ruffled the big dog's ears. Donny leant his head heavily into the man and the man was charmed. He looked up at Rothko and seemed to recognise them.

'Aint you Meg Taylor's girl?' he asked. Rothko felt the tug of her name. 'Rothko? I remember *you*.' He stood up from where he had been crouching with Donovan and leant against the wall opposite Rothko, face overflowing with whisky and sentiment. 'Haven't seen you since . . . ages!' He held out his hand to show how tall Rothko used to be, and laughed at the size Rothko had become. 'Errol,' he explained. 'My name's Errol, you must remember me? I used to stay above The Whale with your mum, back in the day.'

There was something of an old collie about Errol. Twinkly eyes digging their way out of a face full of wrinkles. Bouncing gently on the balls of his feet. Gazing at Rothko like Rothko was the lost painting of a master.

Rothko smiled a bittersweet kind of smile. 'Course I remember you. Course I do.' They saw a flash of themself again, scared of her face changing. Waiting in her room for her to come up from the pub below. Flipping through her records, spinning on the spinny chair they used to love so much. Looking out the window at the dustbin alley, at the people getting on it. Trying to figure out exactly what it was that made them act like that. Later, when Rothko was in the bad days, trying to find a place to sleep in a room crowded with loneliness. Taking shelter in the feeling coming off this man, that even in the darkest pit of the night, he was doing what he could to keep watch.

'You look well.' Errol crossed his arms and leaned further into the wall, 'I always liked you,' smoothing his scraggly beard. 'You were a little cheeky one.'

Rothko smiled and nodded and smiled and nodded and waited for it all to be over. Their body was still repairing itself, after the toilet woman's words.

'Are you back now, then?' Errol was keen to connect.

They reached for their beer, 'I am yeah.' Turned it on the table a couple of times but did not lift it. Errol got the message and heaved himself away from the wall.

'Well. Welcome home.' And he lost himself in admiring Donovan again. 'He's well behaved, isn't he?'

Rothko gazed at their dog, gratefully. 'He is, yeah. Thank you.' Donovan held them in his calming presence. Errol bent down again to offer him a firm goodbye pat, then he swaggered off to the bar.

Rothko watched their pint as it watched them.

This had been a bad idea.

They should have known that they weren't ready. They should have just stuck to the routine and gone back to the van. They'd made a fool out of themself coming here. Everyone was looking at them. They wished they hadn't put an *x* at the end of the note back to Meryl.

Donovan slept with his ears open to Rothko's body. Aware of the decision to leave before Rothko was, he started to stretch. Rothko noticed Donovan stretching and climbed back into their jacket as if they were only leaving because Donovan wanted to go. The pint was on the table, untouched. A witness: that Rothko Taylor had been to the pub and had not had a drink.

They stopped at the door to exchange nods with Errol. 'Do you still see her around, my mum?'

'Now and again.'

Rothko didn't want to think about her. But there she was, laughing in her scratchy way, digging through her tobacco pouch, dropping her things on the floor.

There she was.

'Well, next time, would you tell her I'm home?'

Errol nodded, gravely. Accepted it as duty. 'Will do, mate.'

Rothko raised their hand for goodbye, but the panic of it made them clumsy, and they got trapped between the swinging doors as they pushed out to the street red-faced.

'Fucking idiot,' they swore at themself. They bumped into Donovan's body and tripped over. 'Fuck.' It was futile. 'Stupid fucking.'

The past was everywhere.

Meg and the past.

FOUR

Meg Taylor came to. Itching all over. She was in a narrow room with a plastic curtain at the end. Everything white. Except the floors. The floors were grey. A low sink stuck out of the wall at the far end. Beside it, a stack of cardboard bedpans was piled on a white shelf. They looked like cowboy hats. Big scary machines on wheels stood in the corner, like doormen.

Meg fucking hated hospitals.

She could hear her pulse in her ears. She focused on it. Full of admiration for the mechanics of the whole thing.

'Not so useless after all.' Her words smudged together when they sounded in the room.

'What was that, Mum?' She rolled her head towards the voice. It was a woman. She was sitting next to the bed, in a plastic armchair, looking at her phone. 'What is it you're saying? Do you need something?'

Why was she talking to her like that?

The woman reached out but stopped short of making physical contact; instead she held on to the side of the bed, staring kindly at her mum. 'You're in the hospital.'

It was like she was talking to a disobedient pet.

Meg tried to tell the woman that she wasn't stupid, even though she knew she was, but her words came out without definition. The woman was struggling to hear her.

'It's alright.' She was shushing her.

Meg fought through the weight that was pushing against her thoughts, making her speech all sludgy. 'Where's Michael?'

Sarai Shepherd dropped her head into her hands briefly. Sighed and looked up again. Michael had been her mum's twin brother, but he'd died before Sarai had been born. Which was almost four decades ago. She watched her mum's screwed-up face, scanning memories, looking for the present. He had only been twenty. They'd had his portrait in a frame on the living room wall. Looking sad in his uniform.

Meg had been mixing time for a while now; events in life were no longer linear, but simultaneous. It was as if once something had happened, it happened forever, existing with and above and alongside everything else that had happened. Going forwards and backwards at the same time. Some days, Sarai saw a kind of mysticism in it, other days, it felt effortlessly sad.

'Michael's been dead for a long time. It's me, Sarai. You've had a fall. And you're in the hospital.'

Meg was blinking. Folding her lips in. Ezra hated it when she did that. He always says it makes her look like a chimpanzee. *Chimpan-zee-zee-top.* That's what he calls her. Because of all the hairs on her chin. She's got more of a beard than he has. It's funny. She likes it when he laughs.

But she was right, this woman. Of course. Michael was dead. She saw the details in flashes. The uniformed shoulders that carried him. Standard bearers from his regiment. The shine of the polished wood, the smart brass plaque, the smell of lilies and white roses under the vaulted roof. Handsome flag draped over it. 'The Last Post' and brave words. Her father shaking all their hands. No one said *suicide*. No one even said it.

She had to get back to the house. Ezra would be angry.

She just wanted to get things right. But there was so much to remember. What he did and didn't like to eat, and when. What he did and didn't like to watch, and when. What words he did and didn't like to hear her use. What time he wanted to wake up, what time he wanted his paper, his coffee, his egg. When to bring him the phone if it rang and when to tell the people calling that he wasn't there. When to get out of the house and when to be home. If things went his way, it was his hard work and good thinking that did it, but if things didn't go well, it was her that was putting him wrong. There was so much to hold in her head.

I know what you are.

It was Sarai? Of course it was.

Things just got away from her sometimes, that's all.

Don't know why I put up with it.

'You've had a fall, Mum.'

'I know,' she snapped. 'I'm fine.'

Sarai smiled at her and went back to her phone. Skim reading the headlines of articles.

Meg looked at her, with some concern. Her eldest daughter.

She seemed so glamorous to Meg. So well put together. Lipstick done. Mascara done. Forty years ago, she'd been the size of a grape, getting bigger in Meg's belly. And then she came and Meg was so sad she couldn't lift her. Felt so bad and scared and Ezra saying *what kind of a woman doesn't know how to pick up a baby?* But what if she hurt her? And she wouldn't stop crying. All the time she was crying that terrible sound that meant what kind of a woman. But look at her now. That lovely hair, the ends all neat and swooshy. She looked so pretty to Meg. She looked just like Meg's mum.

Watching her sat there in the chair beside her bed, Meg noticed the way the light seemed to catch in her eyelashes and Meg thought she was a miracle.

When Sarai felt her mother's eyes on her, she put the paper down. Meg admired her. Her beautiful broad frame. Her big, deep eyes. She had such a serious look about her. No messing around with Sarai. Prominent features. She was wearing baggy fashion trousers made of parachute looking, kind of silky material, and a real nice soft-looking hoody. Light grey one. All designer, Meg had no doubt. Designer trainers too. Silver anklet. Such clean clothes. All looked so lovely to Meg, and so soft.

'You need more care than you've been getting.' Her posture sank, and Meg saw that beneath the meticulously maintained hair and make-up, Sarai didn't seem to be coping very well. 'And we've got to talk about you living somewhere with more care. That means leaving the flat. And going somewhere people can be on hand to look after you.'

Meg narrowed her eyes. The beauty went out of the image before her. 'I'm not leaving the flat. That's our flat. We live there.' She was almost shouting, fear in her voice. 'I won't let you. I don't want you to lock me up in one of them places.'

'No one's locking you up anywhere. We've just got to talk about it.'

Meg pointed at her, jabbed a crooked finger. 'I'd never do this to *you*!' She screamed it. 'I'd lay down my life before I'd let . . .' and she was wriggling herself up in the bed so she could glower at Sarai better, but then her frown cracked and under the fear Sarai saw an old sadness looming. 'Don't take them away from me.'

Sarai was tired. Her voice was tired. The anger left Meg and she reached out the pointing hand to stroke her daughter roughly on her knee. 'Can you show me the video again?' Sarai's heart wobbled in her chest. The ups and downs of it had her completely wrung out.

She found the video and the two of them came close to watch it again. Sarai's youngest, Hayley, striding out to the centre of the school hall. 'Look at her little face. So proud, and her voice! Isn't she good?' Sarai blinked tears away, as they both watched Hayley taking a deep breath and announcing every syllable: 'Welcome to our show.'

Meg held Sarai's hand as Sarai held the phone and when it finished, she wanted to watch it again. She seemed smaller and softer and more loving than ever. As the video played for the third time, she gripped Sarai's hand tighter and whispered, 'Don't send me away.'

'I won't, Mum.' Sarai pulled herself together. Went back to her phone, clicked on something and read for a while, straightening her hair by shaking it. Meg watched her hands. Remembered her at five months old, incredible to think it was the same person.

It was, wasn't it? The same person?

'God knows what's going to come of all this.' Sarai scrolled through the article, despaired of the world in sighs.

Beyond the room people were moaning and coughing and it made Meg shudder.

'I can't wait to go home,' Meg told her. 'When can I go home?'

'You can't go home just yet, Mum.'

'Why can't I?' She stared at Sarai with sudden distrust. Frowning so hard, it shrank her face to the size of a fist.

'You've had a fall.' Sarai was so tired. 'They thought there might be swelling on the brain, but there isn't. So, it's good news.' Meg cut her eyes at Sarai, dismissive of lofty ideas like *good news*.

She reached for a tissue and coughed into it. 'Where's Rothko?' Sarai watched Meg scrunching up and straightening out the knotted tissue. 'I want to see Rothko. I hate these places.' Meg peered around, 'No one's ever nice to me in these places.' Her voice grew thin and spiteful. Sarai felt like she was suffocating. 'Rothko's nice to me. Not like you. Too much like your dad, you are.'

Sarai got up. Kissed Meg on each of her skinny cheeks. Rearranged the card she'd brought in on the table beside the bed. The kids had made it. Colourful picture of stick people in the sunshine.

'You're not leaving, are you?'

'I'd better be getting off now, then.' Sarai got her things together, stopped on the way through the curtain that separated Meg from the rest of the ward and gave her mum a stiff smile. Meg's brows were knitted, her skin was bruised and thin. She'd broken her fall with her hand and her wrist was bandaged. 'No touching up the doctors, alright? I'll be back tomorrow.' Sarai pulled the curtain back behind her as she left.

Meg stared into the middle distance. Minutes passed.

'Love you,' she called after Sarai, but she had gone.

Sarai stood outside the hospital and pushed the back of her head against the wall. Felt the gristle of the bricks against her skull and exhaled for as long as she could.

It was dark and the night was filmy, a mist had rolled in off the back of the waves.

When she thought of her mother, the tenderness she felt was colossal, it washed up inside her like the fucking sea. And she felt she understood her, and she wanted to let her know how much she loved her. But then she saw her, and it always went the same way; it always left her feeling too small and too big for herself at the same time and trapped in a personality she didn't recognise as being hers. Rendered down to nothing more than an accessory, to whichever version of Meg she happened to be inhabiting at the time.

The idea of her mother was one thing. But it never held out.

She couldn't shake the image of her sitting there so weak and thin. Her little sparrow's wrist all bandaged and her sorry eyes, glinting for dread. It crushed Sarai. It crushed every bone in her body till her ribcage felt like rubble on top of her lungs.

She watched the road. Headlights phasing in the rain as the cars sped past.

Years ago. Her and Rothko in the back, Mum and Dad up front and she was screaming at him as she drove. Back from a party. Someone's wedding.

Ezra trying to placate her. 'She asked me to, and you didn't want to anyway . . . what's wrong with it? I like dancing.'

'I could see you liked it, yeah,' she sneered at him, as if he was something she couldn't bear the smell of.

'She's got to be eighty years old! Meg? You can't be serious? It's what people *do* at weddings!'

'She was all over you.'

Meg was speeding, and Sarai was staring at the headlights blazing towards them from the other side of the road. Forcing herself to keep watching them, even as they blinded her.

'Teasing her like that. It was embarrassing. She thought it was her lucky day. All night. It's disgusting. What do you think people are going to be saying? About *me*?'

'No-one's going to say anything!'

Meg kept pushing the car faster and faster.

'Slow down,' Ezra asked her. But she didn't.

'Why do you keep doing this to me?' She was screaming. 'What's the matter with you that you have to behave like this?' And Sarai could see her dad had started to be afraid. 'You want to humiliate me, don't you?'

'No,' he said quietly.

'Look at me.' Meg's head turned away from the road, looking at Ezra, and the car speeding faster and Ezra not looking at her. Ezra looking away. 'Look at me!' Shouting at him. 'Is this what you want?'

'Slow down,' he asked her again. But she didn't. 'I'm sorry. I should have thought about you. I didn't think.' Sarai watched Ezra turn to Meg and reach for her arm. 'Please, I'm sorry. You're right. Just stop the car?'

And then Meg slamming the brakes and pulling the car off the road into a gravel layby that loomed out of the night and the sudden jolt of it was scary and everyone was thrown. The engine turning over. Ezra, whimpering, 'I can't take it. I can't take it anymore.'

And Meg looking out at the road. '*You* can't take it?' And laughing a bitter, sarcastic laugh.

That's when Sarai unbuckled her belt and got out of the car and started running.

'SARAIAH!' Meg shouted after her. 'GET BACK IN THE CAR.'

But she hadn't stopped. She just wanted to run. Meg jumped out after her and chased her down the side of the road. She was running as fast as she could, but Meg caught up to her and grabbed her, lifted her. Sarai struggled to escape from her mum's arms but her body was weak with anger. 'It's a road.' Meg held her tightly, spoke into her head, hair, neck. 'It's a fucking main road. Why would you do that?' Sarai tried to twist away from her. She was tall but Meg kept her in her arms, half dragged half carried her back to the car and shoved her in. She pushed Sarai's face into the car, more violently than she realised. Then Sarai relented, stopped struggling. Meg climbed into the front and locked the doors.

And as the car regained the road, she felt Rothko. Sitting there on the other side of the back seat, not looking at her but giving her something only a sibling can give. Their presence. Sharing it. All of it. The good things, and the too-big things that were sad and couldn't be changed. They both looked out of their own windows, Meg turned the radio on, too loud. And Sarai felt Rothko reaching their hand across the back seat, finding her hand and holding it. Not saying anything at all. Just giving her palm a warm squeeze. So warm she could still feel it.

She looked down at her hand, and squeezed her own palm. But it wasn't the same.

And that time in the carpark of the saver centre. How Meg had left them with a magazine, locked the doors and said *won't be a minute*. How she'd smiled through the window with her gone-away smile, *stay there.* Rothko on one side, Sarai on the other. Watching the families pushing their shopping. They waited three hours for her. And in the end when Meg came back it was the monster one not the mum one that got in, glaring her smile back over her shoulder and saying in her gone-away voice, *did you have a nice time, girls?*

FIVE

Out in the night, the encounter with Errol in the Shipwrights still ringing in their system, Rothko was walking fast back to site, trying not to be visible. It was a solid thirty minutes before they came to a stop. Breathing heavy. Sweat underneath their cap. But at least the rain had stopped. They undid the padlock on the steel doors and swung the gates. 'Home, Donald.'

Lights on at Roxanne and Cookie's, smoke puffing up from the flue in the roof, but apart from that, there was no one about.

To the uninitiated passer-by, the site where Rothko had come to live didn't look like much. A non-space waiting its turn in the process of development, surrounded by half-built lots, piles of anonymous black shingle and the smell of construction. But behind the padlocked gates was a special kind of paradise.

Roxanne and Cookie had been onsite since the early days. Rox was no frills. Long lank hair that clung to her forehead. The years had been cruel to her and the heavy drugs were loud in her face but she was as kind as she was lost. Mechanically gifted. Constantly fixing old engines. She had skinny limbs and a little pot belly. Glasses. Hardly any teeth. Cookie, her love, could be heard a mile off. Loud bouts of laughter. Cackly. Sweary. Curvy. Twinkly. Furrowed and open. Dangly earrings. Leather trousers or sparkly dresses. Mothers to several children between them who visited often. They lived in the dented horse box they'd done up like a country cottage. Wood-burner, tweed armchairs, meticulously organised apothecary drawers where Roxanne kept her nails and screws. Each wore a chain around their neck, attached to which was a vial of the other's blood.

There were four vans of various make and model parked up in the yard, including Roxanne and Cookie's horsebox, with Velma's static caravan at the end. Washing lines hung between the van roofs. They had a vegetable plot, multicoloured planters. A pizza oven made of clay. Benches round a fire pit. At the far end of the yard was the factory building. It had been a ropery once, and now it held their common spaces; downstairs was a massive room, big enough to hang a trapeze and a couple of hammocks from the lofty rafters. They had a sound rig, a place to dance, three sunken old couches, a screen and a projector. And then upstairs was the kitchen: stainless steel industrial countertops, left over from the days when the factory was functioning. Large wooden table in the middle, huge windows, views of the town. Light moved through the room all day.

It was a long way from cell B2,15 where Rothko had done the last four years.

After a while, a person had to get used to being shipped out. Rothko had played by the rules; had no rucks, had even grown trusted enough to get work as a listener, which meant they could cross all the different barriers of the jail, and go cell to cell to listen to people tell their problems, in the hope they wouldn't kill themselves. And Rothko was good at that. But even so, the screws could spring it on them whenever they wanted. Rothko understood the game of it. Anything to keep you in your place. Soon as Rothko looked like they were getting too comfortable, the screws would put the slip under the door and that was that. You'd be gone in the morning. No matter the bonds you'd formed or the sense of safety you'd finally found. No reason given. And nothing you could do. You'd have to pack up and ship out and go through the whole process of having to establish yourself all over again. It meant a person could never get comfortable. Cat A prisoners like Rothko got sent all over, it was like a cherry on the cake from the courts.

Most of the people Rothko had got close to in jail had never known safety in their lives outside; for those people, life on the landings had been their first experience of structure, or support, and taking it away so suddenly from people who had lived so long without it felt particularly cruel to Rothko.

There were seven currently living on site. Transient people, from all over the world, who had, in one way or another, been burned by the fire out there. Rothko spent the first two months onsite in a state of tense fascination, awkward and impressed. Until they got used to it, the absence of violence had felt more threatening than its presence.

Velma had the static at the end. She was the oldest on site. Looking her seventies dead in the eye. Strong body carried softly, thick white hair that she wore in plaits. Velma could most often be found chain smoking high-grade in a dressing gown and combat boots and tending to the plants. Her caravan was crowded with statues of birds. Bead curtains. Doilies. Herbs in pots. The blessed virgin looking down from every corner. Velma had lived about a hundred and fifty lives. She maintained a gentle kind of pity for the world.

Next along were Dill and Eugene in the blue school bus. Dill occupied a place of authority in the yard because he had opened the site years before. Well-built and quick to judge. Tight tops and fake fur coats. He had deep brown eyes, a five o'clock shadow and a neat moustache. His boyfriend, Eugene, was a generation younger. Incredible cheekbones. Long eyelashes. A regal beauty with the glowing skin of a person obsessed with hydration. Their bus was cosy: Persian rugs, fringed lampshades, framed photographs of moments from their longstanding love affair. A banner flew from the bonnet, the name of their van, *Boyfriend Material.*

Rothko's van belonged to a man who'd gone over a few days before Rothko had got out of jail. Eugene had been the one who found him. His name had been Headache Mo, and that was pretty much all that Rothko knew about him.

Rothko had tried to make it their own. The bed and the burner were in there already, but the rest Rothko built themself. One thing life in jail had taught them was how to make a small space pretty with not much to play with. They used to tear strips off jay-cloths to make curtain-ties with big bows, or to wrap around half milk cartons for pen pots. Out in the yard, Rothko couldn't believe the possibilities that were open to them now they only had to go two steps to find an old brass lampstand or a pile of timber offcuts. They had no hesitation about sleeping in a dead person's bed. They'd had to do it lots of times in jail. New quilt and pillowcases. They flipped the mattress. Burned some sage and knelt for *thank you.*

Finally, there was Fletcher next door. Big soft body. A dancer's inclination to deep stretches. He could have been sixty or sixteen. Sincere smile that shrank his eyes. Sensitive and non-committal. Nice shirts, tailored trousers. Shoes, boots, jackets. Occasionally braces. Rothko had never known someone so dapper.

Fletch lived in the old ambulance. He'd laid scaff planks as floorboards. Had a record deck. A fireplace. A tiled kitchen. He even had a bathtub outside the van, sheltered by a trellis where he'd trained creepers and vines.

He was a session bassist. When he wasn't touring, he taught kids music theory and piano. He lived for music. He'd rolled up to the factory for a party one night five years before and never left. A joyful human being with trouble clinging to every limb.

Rothko dropped onto their bed and closed their eyes against their racing thoughts. One night out without a drink didn't mean they had it in the bag. Each tomorrow was a new threat but before they could indulge in further fears, sleep was dragging at them, pulling them down beneath the covers, holding them in its weighty arms until their breathing went all fluttery and they lost their thoughts to rest.

SIX

Meg didn't like how hot it was on the ward. It was stuffy and flat, and she needed a breather. She just needed some air. That was all. Big deep breath and fill her lungs up.

She wasn't going to lay around forever waiting to be told what to do.

She was still entitled to her own thoughts, after all. She didn't like the way they looked at her, these doctors. Took one look at her medical record, saw IV drug user, and decided she wasn't worth a scrap of decency.

She found herself sat on the benches outside the hospital. Dressed. Bag in hand. Waiting.

It was cold and the pavement was as slippery as the sky.

He'd be here any minute.

He must be coming on the bus. Ezra was too tight for a cab. And he knew by now that she didn't like riding on the back of his motorbike.

She stared at every person that passed without curiosity.

Meg had a body like forked lightning, as jagged and thin and punishing. Ripping through the vagueness of the evening. Her spirit was air. When she walked, her feet barely touched the ground, and as she sat waiting on the bench, she bounced her toes incessantly. The years of hunching over the works on hard floors had rounded her back. She sat waiting. Holding herself tightly. Folded forwards. A woman on a bench outside a hospital, seen by no one that passed.

She smoothed her hair. Once she met Ezra, she paid more mind to what she looked like. She shuddered to think of before. When she went about in whatever she fell out of bed in. An unset break bulged the cartilage in the bridge of her nose and gave her a lopsided look, like she was always halfway through a question. Her fingernails were buffed and neat, painted beige. Nude they called it at the salon, but she'd bitten round the edges. Her lips were thin and disappeared when she smiled, and the wrinkles were deep as fault lines in her beautiful face.

Sarai was coming to fetch her.

She shouldn't have taken it upon herself to wander out here like this.

A bus pulled up; she studied every figure who got off.

She should go back and wait inside. She just hated these places so much. Didn't like being round so many sick people.

Down the street, a raspy woman with a sharp face was shouting at a tall man in nice clothes. He gripped his laptop bag and held it away from the woman, behind his body. Meg could see his face; he wore the bemused expression of a pampered person. 'Just because I smoke *crack*,' the woman was half-shouting. 'Doesn't mean I stole this bicycle!' She was pushing a bike by the handlebars and the man was trying to get past her down the road, but she was stopping him. 'It's *mine*. I never stole it.' Face like a pothole with teeth. The man tried to pass again. 'Wait.' She softened. 'Excuse me, sir. Have you got two pound please?' Meg couldn't hear what the man's response was, but she could hear the woman reply to whatever he'd said; a single desperate 'Please?' And it was such a hard *please* that it hurt Meg all over. The laptop man squeezed through the gap between the woman's bicycle and the wall and hurried off and the woman climbed on to the saddle, muttering. She stood up on the pedals, easing them back and forth to stay in place. She looked out down the road and started moving. A teenager was jogging along behind her. Looking like she needed to go to bed. Skin grey and hair greasy. The woman wobbled past Meg on her bike. The teenager slowed as she passed, and Meg was disturbed by the way the child stared at her. Straight into her face. It flooded her with restlessness.

Rothko.

No one was coming to get her.

She got up and started pegging it, away from the woman and the teenager and the hospital and the bench. Past blocks of flats and cul-de-sacs, past the park and the railway line and the bridge that went over the carriageway. Other people's lives carried on.

Are you going to behave yourself? Or have I got to learn you?

Not anymore.

Memories ran up and down her skin as she rounded the bends. Walking hard without direction. Down the high street where the people hunkered down, drinking on the benches. Their dogs were curled up beside them, chewing happily on plastic bottles.

She was made of Edgecliff.

These pubs, this scrubby football field, this concrete air, the endless waves that slowed your life to waiting round for everything to change.

It was late evening when Sarai got the phone call from the hospital. She went out to the garden in her socks to escape the noise of the telly. It had been raining, and her feet were getting wet but she didn't go inside to put shoes on. She just stood there with the phone pressed into her ear. Cold water soaking through the fabric of her socks.

The man on the phone was nasal and monotonous. 'I understand you're upset. But we're not a secure unit. We're a hospital. If someone wants to leave, there's nothing we can do to stop them.' Sarai hated him.

Meg kept going, walking automatically. Turning down roads she knew by heart. The ghosts of dead days and dead nights flocked behind her. The neighbourhood felt like a set. But the show had been over for years. Hard how life moved on. Streets that had belonged to her were the scene of someone else's story now. She ended up at the train station. Found herself lost in the echoes as the announcements came and went. She looked up at the screen by the platform gate. So many trains departing. Arriving. So many places to go to or to come from.

Couples passed in gusts of laughter.

She felt loneliness; a wafty sphere that emanated from her middle and touched everything she looked at. Inanimate objects reverberated with significance. The open barrier of the ticket gate. The intricate iron latticework that fringed the platform roof. The Army billboard that said *Be the Best*. Everything suddenly prominent. Out on to the platform, staring down it. The world thinned to straight lines and dark tracks that went into the night forever. She kept staring until it spooked her.

A train pulled in, slow route to somewhere else, and she stepped on. The sky fell all the way down to the ground and the night was the rain and the rain was the night.

People were in Saturday spirits. Just gone half seven and for the weekend revellers, things were getting interesting. Meg squeezed between two sets of four-tables occupied by a group of high-pitched prosecco women, spilling out of strappy tops, yelping with pleasure, crowding the aisle. Clapping as they yelped like a troupe of captive seals. They ignored Meg as she squeezed past, not one of them moved their elbows or bags or legs to make way. She took the seat by the window behind them and tried to think through the noise of their shouting. Voices indiscriminate. Beachy, salty accents. All of them, hoarse with drink. The confidence of people who have never been defeated.

Out there, beyond the tracks in the dark, she could feel the town even if she couldn't see it. She knew the place by heart. The gap in the fence by the overgrown field. Dead grass and the rain easing off. Walking up the old road behind Ezra, home. Sarai standing up on the back of the pram, and Rothko asleep in the pushchair.

Where were the babies?

They were safe at home.

She'd left them with Ezra.

He was good with the babies. It was only her that he wanted to destroy.

Rothko, squatting on her hams, to study a procession of ants. Her little earnest voice like a light going over the rocks of Meg's soul, *why do they walk in a line, Mum?* Little arms reaching for cuddles at bedtime, Meg lifting her up, *hold on tight.* Koala child with her arms and her legs wrapped round. Cracking her eyelids open, secret little looks, just enough so she could watch Meg's face from half an inch away, touching her cheeks with her own. And then someone was at the door, and when she opened it, Rothko was sixteen, with a face gone white as split bone, and those haunted eyes, all pupil. *I want to come and live with you.*

The walls of the train were pushing close. The women

were still yelping, wetly, feeding each other slabs of fresh attention, then diving back down to hide beneath the froth of their complete unknowability. It disgusted her. They disgusted her. The whole world disgusted her.

She stood up, gripping the headrest of the seat in front. 'Can't you shut up?' She shouted it, hard voice of a person who has no need to fear the worst, having known the worst. The women were making exaggerated faces of hilarity at each other. They pulled themselves away and turned to stare at the intruder. Falling towards each other with the force of how funny it was, how random.

She barged herself through the aisle they were occupying, shouting as she went. 'You better shut up. All of you.' Staring at them from the doors, waiting for the train to stop. 'None of you have got a fucking clue. Don't know the first thing about what it's like to have to . . .' the train finally pulled into a station, and Meg pushed her face out, into the air.

'Nutter.' They called after her. Faking laughter until it was real. 'Miserable old bag.'

Meg stood the other side of the glass. Shouting back at them through the window. 'You think you're clever, do you? I'll smash your nasty little faces in. You think I'm something to laugh at?' Thumping her hands against the window and the whole carriage rattling with the force of her desolation. Her warped face glaring through the window, jittery and bleak.

The women were glad when the train pulled away and they could go back to pretending that their own robust functionality had nothing to do with the fragile dysfunctionality of chaotic strangers like Meg.

'What was that all about?' They fussed at their jackets and dresses, re-settled themselves and changed the subject.

*

Meg stood on the platform with a racing heart, fiddling with the bandage on her wrist. The problem with some people, she reckoned, was that they didn't know what it was like to get smacked in the face.

It was a funny place to have ended up. She'd never actually been here before. Only ever passed through on her way to other places. Cherry Hill. More desirable than Edgecliff, even though it was just a couple of towns along. People moved here with dreams of simpler living. They wanted old fashioned shopfronts, retired neighbours, white people at the checkout.

She headed down the cobbled roads towards the seafront. Until there it was.

The beach went on forever. Chalk and slate and stone that crumbled upwards, into long grass. It was dark but she could see the shapes of things in the lamplight.

Big waves charged the breakwater. The sea was foaming at the mouth. Meg stood square on and let it wash up in her lungs.

She'd got herself away.

Last time she'd been away from Edgecliff, it was that holiday to Spain. She was pregnant with Sarai. They'd walked through the square in the evening, arm in arm, which was the way he liked it. Walking in the square they passed two couples they had got to know drinking at a wooden table. Ezra had grown friendly with these couples, but she hadn't been sure. *Nonsense* he'd said. *They're nice people.* And *what would you know about nice people.* She had been wearing a simple cotton dress. It was light purple, more like pink. It was very hot, and they weren't up to much, walking from the pool to the bar to the village square. One of the men had shouted to Ezra, 'So we'll see you both later for dinner then?' and Ezra had slowed to a stop and said, 'Yes, looking forward to it.'

'It'll be evening then,' the man had said, looking at Meg. 'You can get changed out of your nightdress.' And she had looked down and laughed, it did look a bit like a nightie. Everyone had laughed.

'This?' she said. 'I've had this for years.'

And Ezra had led her away, saying, 'Yes, we can tell by the stains down the front.' And the whole table erupted to laughter, and Ezra was pleased with himself as they walked back to the hotel. Meg didn't say anything. There hadn't been anything really to say.

The spray leapt over the seawall and onto the prom. She watched two kids daring each other to go close to the edge and race away from the spray before it soaked them. Their mother, carrying bags in front, turned around and shouted at them to get away from the edge.

Meg kept going, into the wind. She could see lights further up the prom. She headed for what looked like a grand old pub, opposite a little harbour. Big windows swelling out of Tudor beams.

Inside The Last Hope, the carpet was greasy, and the walls were noisy with pictures of the harbour in its heyday. Black and white fishermen taking in the nets.

In the pub, the old men sat alone, and the young men sat with women. Meg stood at the bar, waiting her turn, and watched a young couple. The woman was beautiful, little black dress and green Dr Marten boots, hair up, but she kept pulling at the hem of her dress and she covered her mouth with her hand when she talked. The man was in a white shirt, baggy tracksuit bottoms, and he talked over her head to two men at another table. Broad build, big gestures, persuasive smile. The noise was a general low rumble, cut with the hard crack of pool balls being struck on the table in the corner. It was coming on ten and they were playing 'Under the Boardwalk'. Ezra loved this song. She could see him, ducking his head and singing the bass part. Enjoying how annoyed she pretended to be at his silly ways.

But Ezra didn't love that song anymore. In fact, he hated it. Just like he hated every song that made him think, even fleetingly, of his difficult first marriage.

'What can I get you, my darling?' The bar lady shone her way. She was in a white t-shirt with the sleeves rolled up that she'd tucked into dark blue jeans. She had red braces. Red lipstick. Black hair. Short straight fringe. Rockabilly type. Sailor tattoos all over her arms.

'Rum and coke please, love. Large one. And have you got rooms here?'

'We have rooms, not sure if we've got any vacancies. Hold on, I'm rushed off my feet.' She gave a nod to the round yellow frizz and blue eyeshadow that was pushing for attention. 'I've seen you, gorgeous. You're next, ok?' Then she turned back to Meg. 'If you go out and round the corner, there's another door. That's the B&B in there, there should be someone on the desk if you ring the buzzer. She'll check you in if there's anything. Tell her you've spoken to Viv.'

'Thanks, love.' Meg began to relax. Something about the energy of the bar lady reminded her of happier times.

'Want your drink first or after?'

'Probably both,' Meg told her. Viv smiled.

'One of them days, was it?'

'Something like that.' Meg handed her a score, Viv took it.

'Thank you, my darling,' noticing the bandage and the bruises round her cheeks.

'Pint of cider too while you're at it.'

Viv fixed the drinks and gave Meg her change with a rocky little smile. Her eyes were playful and considerate. She watched Meg choose her table and sit down carefully, at the back of the room, facing the door.

Tired out by the whole fucking thing.

She had a long slow sip of her rum. That was more like it. Warm like summer. Much better. Warm like her feet on the stones in the summer. She drank like she was kissing.

Ezra would be getting worried by now.

Good. Let him stew in it.

SEVEN

Banging outside. Quick dull thuds. Three in a row. *Fuck time is it?* It was dark. Rothko squinted their eyes open. Reached for the lamp.

'Roth?' It was Sarai. She kept knocking. 'No hurry. I've only been stood outside the gate for twenty-five fucking minutes.' Rothko wriggled down to the end of the bed so they could unbolt the door. They pushed it open, hair sticking up, t-shirt and pants. Looking grey and jangled.

'I'm up, I'm up.'

Sarai poked her head in. Scowling. 'What's the point in having a *phone*? If you don't *answer* it.'

Rothko burrowed back into the bed and pulled the covers up over their ears. Upset at the awakening. 'I was asleep. I've been at work all week.'

Sarai closed the door behind her and gave Donovan a rub on the neck. Donovan lifted his giant head appreciatively and she sat down beside him on the cushioned bench that ran along one side of the van. The big dog rested his heavy jaw on her lap and tucked himself into her hip. '*Twenty*-five fucking *minutes*,' she complained, scratching his head as he started to snooze. The reassuring weight of his head on her thigh and the metallic smell of his hair, like earth. Van dog. It calmed her down. She looked around. 'It's nice in here.'

As with most of her compliments, it could have been an insult.

'Had to get your address off Dad.'

They remembered the intense commitment their dad had to keeping up with everyone's addresses and sending cards on special days. It was sad. To think of him looking for the right pen. Seemed a solitary way to say *I'm thinking of you*.

Sarai was warming her hands under her thighs, jiggling her legs. Donovan was trying to get comfortable while his pillow was moving. Using a paw to steady her. She laughed at that. She was softening.

She eased herself out from under Donovan's head and went over to the stove. She checked the kettle had water and set it to boil. She pulled the curtains back, peered out into the purple dark. Imposing blocks of new builds surrounded the lot on all sides. Streetlights shone in over the wall and lit the yard up yellow. It seemed friendly and together. Flowers planted in old bathtubs. A skate ramp for the kids. She hadn't imagined it like this when she'd heard from Rothko that they were back, and living in a van off Turpin Road.

She was looking for teabags in the food cupboard, but all she could find was an empty jar of peanut butter, two tins of peaches and half a pack of watch batteries.

'Water?' Rothko sat up, out of the bedcovers, sticking out a hand. 'Please? From the jug.'

Sarai filled an ornate glass with a gold rim with water from the pewter jug on the side. Put it into her sibling's outstretched hand. A feeling of childhood passed through her. Breakfast with Roth before school. Pouring the milk over their cornflakes. It was a finished feeling.

'Teabags are in there.' Rothko pointed to a patterned jar with an ornate clasp. Sarai admired it. She was struck by all the little touches; bright fabrics, sepia-toned photographs of suited butches from the twenties in gold frames. She was half comprehending a slippery truth: that Rothko had spent the last fifteen years of their life in a room no bigger than this one. That definitely hadn't been as beautiful.

She got it.

People needed beauty.

Especially the ones who'd soaked up more than their share of ugliness. So the rest of us didn't have to.

Rothko was gulping water and wiping their face. Waiting for Sarai to tell them what she was doing in their van. They noticed her looking at their things. They weren't used to having visitors, and Sarai could feel their nervousness. They felt like she was judging them.

'Come here, then.' She reached for them. They had a static way of hugging each other that kept distance between their bodies.

Sarai let go and went digging through the mini fridge. Nothing but a bottle of chilli sauce and a plastic tub of vegan cocktail sausages. She closed the fridge and slouched against the countertop.

Rothko had forgotten the pressure they felt being around her. Everything she did felt like it had a hundred hidden meanings.

They scratched at their chin and wondered how to ask her about her life without starting her off on a monologue about how tough everything was. Decided not to ask her anything, and as the minutes backed up, time was heavy traffic. Until finally, Sarai had made two cups of tea and was settled back on the bench.

'Mum ended up in hospital. They found her on the street. She was out of it. Not dressed properly.'

'Don't sound like her.' Rothko's sarcasm was infuriating.

'*Any*way,' Sarai put a stop to it, 'she's walked out of hospital. And I don't know where she is.'

Rothko worried for their sister, still trapped in a relationship with Meg. They'd learned it hard by now, that their mother was incapable of love. That she couldn't think about anybody but herself, or feel anything above her own pain. She talked a good talk, knew how to tell people exactly what they needed to hear, so they'd give her what she needed them to give, but the core was hollow. She thought she could do it all her way. Rothko remembered how she used to sneer at the people in the meetings. She was always above it: the stepwork. The slogans. The sharing. She'd nod along stone-faced. But afterwards, alone with Rothko, she would laugh unkindly about how easily people were led. This is how she never gave herself over. How she tricked herself into protecting her addiction. How she managed to keep putting it above everything, even as she said she wanted rid of it forever. It had all of her attention. She devoted herself to keeping its secrets. It always came first. Above her kids. Above life itself. But by some perverted twist of fate, she was still alive. God knows how she'd managed it.

Sarai had found a temporary peace in her relationship with Meg. She'd learned to disengage. To not give beyond what she was willing to give. To expect nothing in return for kindness. It was a frustrating relationship, of course. One-sided in a lot of ways. But Sarai was devoted in her loyalty, to the point of self-harm. It made her husband shake his head at the end of the day, when the kids had gone to bed, and they could drink their brains to sleep together. Saying, *my concern is babe, the part of you that thinks you deserve to be treated like that*.

Meg had lived four years in assisted housing, fifteen minutes' walk from Sarai's. The terror that she might be dead at any minute had mellowed to acceptance that she might be dead at any minute. Sarai knew she couldn't save her mum. She wasn't trying to. She just wanted to give her the respect she deserved. She knew Meg was doing the best she could with each day she had. So, she went round twice a week. It did her head in, but the way she saw it, it was the least she could do.

'When was this?'

'Just now. They just called me. I didn't know. What else to . . .' Rothko saw their sister buckling under the weight of care. How impossible it was, looking out for someone who wouldn't look out for herself.

'They want her to go into a home.' She made her can-you-fucking-believe-it face, eyebrows raised, chin down, lips drawn into an exaggerated frown. 'They can't even keep her in a bed overnight, and they want me to just, what, just hand her over? They just want the money. It's a fucking racket.' She slurped at her tea.

'Do you think it could be a shock thing? Like a shock response? Some kind of episode? Like. You know. A *psychiatric* thing? Brought on by the confusion? Like, waking up and not knowing where she is?' She wrapped both hands around her mug. 'Should we be *worried* is what I'm saying? Has she been kidnapped or something?' She registered Rothko's surprise. Stopped them before they could start. 'No. I'm *serious*. Listen. Has someone decided to granny bash her and rob her fucking benefits?'

'Don't think that's what's happened,' Rothko said, trying to calm things. 'She's probably just gone somewhere to score.' They meant to reassure her, but she felt trivialised.

'You do hear about it. Elderly people. Get taken advantage of all the time!' She shook her hair back. Infuriated at the idea.

Rothko couldn't bear the way their sister was so doomish about everything.

It must be exhausting, they thought, looking at her, to always be so upset about things, when you could just not care.

Sarai, on the other hand, hated Rothko's affected indifference. Found it false and selfish and another signal of their inability to take anything seriously or think about anyone apart from themself. She was so sick of how hard she had to work all the time to be constantly coming up short, while Rothko seemed to float through life, satisfied with going nowhere.

'When did you see her last?'

'Today, I was at the hospital.'

'And how did she seem?'

'She seemed alright. It's just hard. Because her memory's gone.'

Rothko took it like a slap. 'What do you mean, her memory's gone?'

'I mean exactly that.' She held her wrist, massaged it as if it ached. Her eyes shone the frenzied dark of the child Sarai, the one that Rothko used to seek for protection. They sat for a while, their shared history washing up and drifting out. 'She doesn't want to go into a home.'

Rothko rose from the floor and hugged their sister tightly but Sarai's face was trapped in the hug, so she wriggled out of it. 'You're pulling my hair,' she complained, and Rothko sat back down again. Rejected. 'You want to get your heating fixed,' she said, shivering loudly. 'Freezing in here.' Rothko took the hint and knelt to build a fire in the burner. 'Should we call the police? Is she a missing person or what are we thinking?'

'She'd never speak to you again if we did that.' they said quietly.

'If she's fucking *dead* then she'll never speak to me again anyway.'

'Don't call them.'

'Well. I'm running out of ideas.'

Rothko occupied themself completely with the placement of the kindling.

'I just can't let it happen, Rothko. A stranger, wiping her arse. She'd hate it.' Sarai crossed her legs. Spun her anklet around so the clasp was at the back. 'I want to take her in. At mine.'

'Does she even know who you are?' If Meg didn't remember what had happened, then it was like she'd gotten away with it. And left Rothko right in it. Left them on their own.

'Course she does.' But Sarai's face told Rothko she wasn't convinced. 'She asked for you.'

They were unmoved. 'I don't want to see her.'

'I know but Roth, it's not about *you*.' Sarai was still spinning her anklet. 'You know what they do to old people? In places like that? Fucking horrible. I just can't bear the thought of it.' But the thought of it pushed from the corners.

The kindling was going, Rothko placed a couple of small logs on top. 'Should warm up soon.'

They glanced at each other. 'I can get a carer to come in the morning for an hour, but that won't be enough. She needs company, and someone to make sure she's not cold, or uncomfortable, or falling out of bed. That she's on top of her meds. That she's eating and drinking. That she's clean. She'll just watch telly and that's it really. You don't even need to.

Talk or anything, really. Not at the moment. I thought, you could come and stay at ours. For free. While you're getting yourself together again. Better than staying here isn't it? Get to spend time with the kids? Be a family.'

They were sure their sister meant well, but what she'd just described sounded less bearable to Rothko than skinning themself with a potato peeler.

Sarai waited for an answer. But Rothko wasn't giving much away. 'You can't just leave this on me.'

'I'm not.'

But Sarai had already decided what Rothko was trying to say, she didn't need to hear Rothko say it. 'It's out of *order*! Do you know how much effort I put in to visit you every week? No matter where they moved you to. No matter what was going on for me, or my kids, or my husband. I made sure to be there for you.' Rothko frowned into the growing flames, ignored her with an injured sigh.

'You're shaking your head. You're sighing. You're obviously trying to tell me something. Why don't you just tell me.'

Rothko felt suffocated by her presence. Sarai felt infuriated by Rothko's meekness.

'It's just like it always is.' Her voice took on the throaty sheen of an ancient gripe. 'Me doing *everything*.'

Rothko snapped at her. 'Well, don't do it, then. If you don't want to. Don't do things and then moan about it later. This isn't my fault, for once. Is it?'

'I've never been able to rely on you. You've never been there. When it comes down to it . . .'

'Hang on, hang on a minute.' Rothko sat back on their heels, raised their hands to stop it going somewhere neither of them wanted it to go.

'It's just *scraps*. You think you can throw me the scraps

as if that's enough. It's not *love*.' She grew more expressive, more animated in her gestures as she continued. While Rothko shrank, enclosed themself. Became stiller. 'What if *I* just decided that I couldn't be relied upon for anything? What then? Who would the hospital have called if they couldn't have called *me*?' She stopped for emphasis. Landed on the words. 'What if *I* was just like *you*? Do you get it? I CAN'T be.'

Rothko didn't want to hear it. They threw the door open and fell through it. Sarai heard something heavy being pulled over and the clang of it hitting the floor, a wordless blast of sound, then repeated dull blows of various intensity, like Rothko was kicking something. Then nothing. Just breathing.

Donovan watched the door, ears up, until his person came back through it, stamping round the small space, looking for things they couldn't find. Eventually, they settled on grabbing a towel and a washbag. Checking their pockets for their tobacco tin and nodding to themself as if something had just clicked.

'You know what?' they said, keeping their voice calm as they could. 'I'm just going to leave you to it.' And they headed out the door. Donovan stared after them for a couple of seconds, before he pushed himself to his feet and ran to catch up.

'Leaving, are you? What a surprise.' But all she heard in reply was the silence of the van. She was alone. 'Fuck's sake.' She walked around as if she was about to do something, but she didn't know what to do.

Sarai could have laughed at the whole outburst, if it hadn't made her feel so fucking annoyed. She looked out the window, watched Rothko cross the yard towards the factory doors and disappear through them. 'Are you serious?' But apparently, they weren't coming back. 'Fine, then.' She got her things and went to the gate as Eugene came out of the school bus.

'You want some help getting out?'

'Yes please.' She sighed a giving up kind of sigh. Stood with him as he opened the lock. His movements were fluent, and he smelt fresh like a posh hotel. Like sophisticated perfume. She wanted him to like her.

'Thank you.' She wished she'd done it all differently. 'Please can you tell Rothko I said to call me?' she asked him as she left.

'Sure,' Eugene replied as he closed the gate behind her. But she couldn't tell if there was a question mark at the end of the word or not.

At The Last Hope, the lady on reception was folding towels with the radio on. *Unbreak my heart, say you love me again.* She was so neat it felt aggressive. Tall with an Eastern European accent and deep, fierce eyes. She moved in fast skips as she led Meg up the stairs to the bedroom and she explained where breakfast was and how to turn the radiators up with a steady, blue focus that made Meg feel old and clumsy. Meg thanked her and they exchanged knowing smiles and she left, and Meg was alone in a clean, quiet room with an en-suite bathroom and a faded pink bedspread.

She lay down on the bed and felt everything sliding off her shoulders. The train station platform, the prosecco women, the never-ending hospital, the cold wait on the lonely bench. It all slipped off her and she felt herself getting lighter as she sank deeper into the bed. She could hear the pub downstairs and people laughing. She was relieved to be behind a closed door. She felt waves and waves of despair and relief, welling up and crashing through her. Nothing made any sense. But she was alive. Safe in a warm room. She'd been down in the dirt but she had got herself out of it. She had a drink now and then, sure. But she didn't touch the rest of it.

Please Ezra, I'm nothing without you. I'll stop crying. I will. I don't deserve you. You're right. I'll do better.

She had never once, never not once, been away on her own, done this. Got off a train and checked into a room. Lay down on a bed on her own, all for herself, not for anyone else. Not for a punter or a session or a use-up. It pummelled her with something she didn't know the name of. It felt like regret but also like arriving at last in her own skin, in her own blistered body.

Something about it felt like before. Like childhood. Like the pub she had grown up in. Her mum and dad had their big room at the front. Little Meg and Mikey in bunkbeds at the back. He'd let her have the top one and she could see out the window from her bed; she could see the muddy creek in the moonlight. The shuffling drunks at closing time, singing themselves home. The big horse that pulled the rag and bone man's cart that came stamping past in the mornings. Sitting on Mikey's bunk with her little box of ribbons. Mikey on the floor trying to learn his guitar.

She stared at the bedside lamp. Peach lampshade with a frilly edge. She ran her finger through the frills, slowly back and forth, till she was pinned down by an ugly sleep.

EIGHT

When they were sure Sarai had gone, Rothko took a long shower. Tried to wash the day off. The freezing gutter-water, up the ladder in the wind. The end of the job. The high street. The checkout machine. The pointing woman in the pub toilet. Errol saying *welcome home*. The dreamless sleep they'd been snatched out of too fast. The row with their sister who they hated letting down. And most of all, the shifting presence of Meg that crept behind every encounter, and made the whole world feel achy and solemn.

They could hear the others in the kitchen. Talking and cooking and laughing together. They hated themself for not being able to be a part of the good time. They didn't want anyone to have to see them.

They knew this feeling and they knew when it came on like this, they had a very small amount of time to get the fuck away from people before they did something bad. They hadn't had one like this come on since getting out. They should have been stricter with the routine.

They just needed to walk it off. That was all.

They needed streets beneath their feet. Fast movement through vast space without restriction. They needed to be up high, looking down on the mess of it all. That would sort it out.

*

Donovan beside them, pacing the backstreets and alleyways, climbing. Even here, so far inland, Rothko could still feel it, the deep low breath of the sea out there, drawing them on.

They'd come home.

Squat rows of houses and quiet estates, shining in the drizzled night. They took the old roads to the old days. Not thinking about where they were going, till they realised where they'd ended up.

Devaney House. Dionne's block.

Funny. It was just a building, on a street. A common space that must have belonged to so many other people since Rothko was kicking around. But to them, it was a temple.

They wanted to go back, grab all the years they'd lost and drag them into the present. Protect the kid they used to be. Keep them safe.

Donovan noticed their energy and growled beside them, gently. 'I'm alright,' they told him, stroking his big flat head. He wasn't convinced. 'You're a good dog.'

They blinked up at what used to be her flat. Lights on behind the curtains.

Dionne.

Still so much to flinch about all these years later.

They wondered if she still lived round here, and if she even remembered them. They had thought of her often over the years.

They could see the younger Rothko, sixteen years old, checking back behind them while they bombed it down the pavement. Face all smudged with dirt and crying. The black smoke curling in the streetlight.

They took one more look. The same old low-rise blocks, four storeys high, built around communal grass. The same old patch of red tarmac behind the bent railings. Pair of janky swings with the chains all knotted. That same old yellow slide coming out of the caterpillar's mouth. They used to sit and blaze on that slide with Dionne in the middle of the night, watching the light from the TVs shifting out the windows.

It was all still here. But nothing was the same.

They kept on. Glancing back at her block every few paces until they got to the steps that led up to the meadows. And each time they turned back to look at it, her flat hit a little softer. Played a different note in the scale of significance. Until eventually they could hardly hear it anymore.

They jogged up the endless flights of narrow steps to the open space; the wide hills that formed the borders of the town known as the meadows, where Rothko came of age.

There it all was.

It all looked so much bigger than it used to.

Rothko's perspective had been so restricted in jail it had affected the way they thought. Everything had shrunk to tunnel vision, tunnel language, tunnel dreams. Up here, the wide-angle was dizzying. They could see for fucking miles.

Rothko climbed to the highest point so they could stare down at the lights; they just wanted to see the town for what it was: strips of houses built in rows. It looked harmless. Little lights in neat patterns, stretching from one darkness to another. A place you could leave anytime you wanted.

Edgecliff.

It was an *I could have been something* kind of town.

It was an *I'm going to give them what I never had even if it kills me* kind of town.

But it was becoming an *I love it, you get so much more for your money* kind of town. Like everywhere was these days, or at least that's what people told Rothko.

Most people from here left young or never at all.

Most people moved here when something had gone wrong.

It was a fresh start kind of place.

A slow end kind of place.

Hopes and the lack of hopes and the hopes that got away spoke from the ornate cornices, the union jacks and chipped plasterwork. Something grand and falling apart.

Rothko could see the map of their whole life out there.

Their eyes kept getting drawn to the nice part of town, where they'd lived with their dad. They couldn't see the house from up here, but they knew where it was, and they found themself looking for landmarks.

Their dad had left town not long after Rothko had gone away. He lived with his new family now, out in the sticks. Two boys. Seemed to Rothko that Ezra finally had the life he'd always wanted. A better, simpler, happier family. Which meant he could be a better, simpler, happier man.

As the years went by, Ezra had made a point of getting on the phone once a month. His kids seemed confident and affectionate when they were summoned to the call, to talk about computer games and rappers Rothko had never heard of. Ezra sent photos in and detailed their achievements in his letters. Rothko stared long and hard at the photos; at the eyes and the chins and the way they held their shoulders. Looking for something in their faces that was Ezra's and not Meg's. To try and separate the parts in their own face better. But what could you tell from a photograph? The boys looked cheerful and sporty and well-adjusted. Nothing like Rothko at all.

Ezra's wife Julie was bubbly and possessive. She was his third wife and so far, obviously his favourite. She was working as an estate agent, and Rothko had learned from Ezra's last letter that they were looking for a holiday home in Spain.

Good for them, Rothko thought. Funny how some people managed to move on, from the very same past others couldn't climb out of.

Ezra had always sent money on Rothko's birthdays. Handwritten prayers in gold envelopes on high holidays. Hebrew on one side, English on the other. It was his way of maintaining a relationship. They each carried a part of the other through life, a vague damp shape without dimension or name.

And what about Meg? Rothko could feel her and it still hurt.

Those first six months after the sentence, when Rothko needed her most, Meg vanished into that life and eventually overdosed. Rothko knew her well enough to know it wouldn't have been an accident. Meg being so well versed with the living death of the whole affair; with the blood and the needles, alone on the bathroom floor, bent double with the glass rim of the pipe burning a print into her forehead as she left herself behind.

When Rothko really needed her to be there for them, Meg disappeared into her pain.

That OD sent her to a treatment centre and they kept her in six months. So, for the first year of Rothko's time inside, Rothko and Meg had no visits. They sent some letters back and forth. *I can't feel sorry for you forever.* A couple of hopeful phone calls from the clinic. Meg's voice all bright and full of life in a way it hadn't been for years. *I know baby. I know.* Tears and funny memories. *Yes, of course you must protect yourself. But . . .* Making promises. This time it was different.

But it wasn't different.

She was only out two months before she threw herself back in, another eight months passed in shadow, and by the time she'd clawed her way out of the suck of that abandon and declared herself ready at last to be there and wanted a visiting order – it was too late for Rothko. *You can't just do what you like all the time, then get angry with me when I feel bad because of the things you've done.*

Meg was working hard at making things right. She wanted to be free of it, or that's what she said in her letters. But Rothko had enough time on their hands to rethink the scope of their life. And if it was Meg's fault, it wasn't their own. *I can't forget things just because you have.*

They gave up giving her chances.

Some days the anger helped time pass.

They didn't know if she'd relapsed or what kind of hell she was living in. All they knew was that they couldn't save her. And that it wasn't their problem what she did anymore.

It was good to have someone to blame it all on.

Rothko didn't have much in their life that gave them any real sense of achievement, especially in the first few years when they were still adjusting. *Don't give up on me, please. You're all I have.* Sending Meg's letters back unopened was the closest they came to a feeling like power.

They saw the shape of her face in a screeching vision. Sudden as smashed glass. There she was. The thin, jutting jaw, the doomish, liquid eyes. All they had wanted to do was take care of her.

Mum.

It was a hard word.

Crack smoke in a phone box. *Give us a smile, then.*

Waiting for her to notice they were waiting for her to notice.

Their mum had never needed much of a reason to shit on everything that was good in her life, just to prove to herself how tough she had it, being her. Her capacity for self-pity was only ever matched by her capacity for self-satisfaction.

Vanity and shame, two sides of the same coin they all took their chances on.

They watched the town roll on below.

There it was.

Sarai and the kids were over there, in the nice bit. Not far from where they'd grown up.

It was hard seeing Sarai. It had made Rothko feel dirty and stupid. They might have come from the same people, but they had never really been coming from the same place.

They picked out the old familiars in the rows of lights. Chip shop behind school. Fairground on the seafront where they worked on the donkey rides for about two minutes one summer.

Other people had done things with their lives. Rothko had just sat in a room. Watching it pass.

They could see the younger Rothko still out there. Sitting on the walls, kicking the bricks. Bopping along behind their best mate Sean, off to get a draw.

Back then, life felt like it could have gone a million ways. But from where they were standing now, it looked like it could only ever have gone the way it went.

They caught themself spinning into thoughts that didn't serve them. 'Pull yourself together,' they whispered to the grass they waded through. They were out now; they could be a normal person. Just like these lot, with the lights in the windows and the dinner in the pan. Looked nice, that life. And they could have it if they wanted it.

They didn't have to go back to dirty floors in dark rooms with claret all over the walls.

They watched Donovan run himself ragged chasing foxes,

the shadows of foxes, the air where foxes had been until it was time to head back to the van, dragging the past like heavy boots.

Rothko was the youngest child of Ezra and Meg Taylor.

Where Meg was wilderness and romance, Ezra was practicality and drive.

She had wanted grand, true music and soulful encounter. He had wanted solid routine and the respect of his peers. But crucially, both wanted to be needed.

And so, they made a family.

Like many other couples who exist in polar oppositions; they necessitated each other for a blazing moment, before they each saw themselves reflected in their partner's eyes, and couldn't bear what they'd become.

Ezra Mason Taylor was born and bred Edgecliff. The only son of Morris and Rose. Two textile workers in the garment trade who went regularly to synagogue. Skilled and industrious people, children of the war. They had moved to Edgecliff to change their lives. Leaving London's East End, for a new beginning: running a Jewish boarding house catering for an affluent clientele. The landlord was the same high-spirited man who had built the cinema and restored the little theatre in his desire to encourage a new wave of Jewish visitors to leave the horrors of war in the past, and take up the peacetime trend of trips to the seaside.

Morris was a solemn man, a drinker and a dreamer who despised his dreams for having never come good. Rose was community minded. Sober. Always immaculately dressed. Her survival tactic was tried and tested – no matter what threatened her, she just stayed quiet until it went past. Usually, it did.

She took care of the meals and the bar and the front of house. He took care of the groundwork and the cleaning.

Neither made it far beyond sixty. Rose of a stroke, Morris with his liver. The only things that Rothko could remember of either of them was being held in strong arms and kissed with a wet moustache, and the warm, oniony smell of Rose's kitchen.

All Ezra ever wanted was to make something of himself; the kind of something that his mother would have boasted to her friends about.

His father had scared him. Not because of violence, or any meanness in him. He was just a broken spirit, and for a child, full of energy, that was a hard thing to see. Morris was constantly exhausted. Devoid of personality until he'd had a couple of drinks. And then overwhelmed by it, once he'd had a couple more.

Ezra swore to himself that when he grew up, if he ever set his mind on something he would rather be the type of person who would fail trying to get it done, than the type to never try at all and blame the world forever.

Ezra's defining trait was his restlessness. He pushed himself harder than anyone he knew. It was this striving that gave him his purpose, over and above what the striving did or didn't yield.

Ezra had achieved a great deal in his life, but as soon as one peak was climbed, he found himself at the bottom of another and it always came back to the same old restlessness.

Relationships came and went. The minute things were about to get serious, he left. Without explaining why.

It was hard for a man like Ezra Taylor to ever feel satisfied.

Margaret Elizabeth Wrennal, or Meg, had grown up down by the river in London. Deptford Creek. Her twin brother

Michael was older by half a minute. Her dad, Frank, was a pub landlord, and the family did very well. From the look of it, they had it made. But behind closed doors, Meg's mum, Lizzie, couldn't bear the constant cheating, or the pressure to perform the happy wife for the punters in the bar. Frank had the doctor prescribe her Valium. And when Meg was eight years old, her mum was found drowned in the bath, with an empty pill packet and a bottle of wine. Terrible accident. Everyone was very sympathetic.

Frank kept himself busy in the pub. He was beloved by the regulars. Behind the bar, he could be the man he wanted to believe he was. Big Frank. Generous and fair. Upstairs with the kids, though, seeing himself lashing out at them for no good reason, his stories were harder to believe.

After Lizzie's death, Michael shrank inwards, barely said a word. Meg pushed out, to the air and the muck. She spent her days down by the river. Feet in the sludge. Looking for thrown-away things that other people didn't want.

That's where she met Gordon. Or Uncle Gordon. As he told her to call him.

He was nice to her. Packets of fags. Bottles and cans. He never laughed at her like the rest did, even when she said what she wanted from life. To see different places and do something good in the world. To make life better for people.

All she had to do in return for his kindness was go limp and pretend it wasn't happening.

She thought that he was loving her.

It felt good to be loved.

But word got around that little Meg Wrennal would let you do it for a packet of sweets and a bottle of cider. After that, they wouldn't leave her alone.

The way Meg saw it, they were going to laugh at her

whatever she did. It was easier just to let them do what they wanted.

She liked sitting by the river on her own after, happy with her little bag of sweets.

But when she saw the way they all treated Michael for it, she learned to hate.

Her brother Michael had always been a gloomy kind of boy, but the loss of his mother pressed heavy on him and he had never grown past it. Now he had to fight all the time because of what people said about his sister. Lacking direction, he joined the army. It did him good; getting away from the place that told him who to be meant he could start to be who he was. Seemed like he was thriving. His letters to Meg were confident and full of jokes. His example gave her the courage to get away from the pub and her dad, and the neighbourhood boys.

She worked in shops and waited tables. She was trying to be the kind of person that Michael told her she could be. But she lost her focus in the parties, liked it when she took it too far with the drink and the little white bags and what came after, and soon enough she found herself involved with a married man. Much older than she was. He put her up in a flat in Soho, on the understanding that when he came to call, she belonged to him. He hated the attention she attracted, while at the same time he craved the validation that it gave him.

She made friends with the sad glitterati of the West End. The girls who danced at the late bars and the boys who fixed the drinks. But the emptiness of that life was draining.

Three years she was his property. Sometimes he'd send men round, for Meg to pay his debts. Until the night she woke alone to stomach cramps so bad she couldn't breathe. There was so much blood she was sure that she was dying. He told her he was on his way, and not to go to hospital without him, but he never showed up, and she miscarried alone. *Too late now,* he complained days later. Annoyed that she didn't want to fuck. *No point getting upset about it, is there?*

The depression was like a coma. How many months had passed? At some point, she noticed that Michael's letters had stopped landing on the mat. But even so, when the phone call came, it didn't feel real.

He'd only made it as far as twenty, before he went the same way as his mum.

And deep down in Meg, the grief piled up. It was in her guts and in her organs; it was blocking the airways from the inside out; she struggled to breathe through the pain of not being good enough to have kept any of them alive. Not her mum, not Mikey, not even the little baby.

Michael had been the best part of her character. And she had made him ashamed. Made him wish they weren't related, so people would leave him alone. The thought of him drove through her bones all day. Until it dawned on her, that sometimes you did get to choose whether what you suffered was your end or your beginning.

Sick of belonging to whoever picked her up, she turned her back on London and washed up in Edgecliff. Trying to be a person.

She pushed her pain down as far as she could push it. She stayed with a friend and worked in a tearoom and set herself on the hope that one day, her soul might start speaking to her again.

Meg met Ezra in the pub two weeks after she'd arrived in town. It was nearly the end of 1985 and a storm was blowing in from the sea. The winds were so heavy the landlord had locked the doors. The TV behind the bar played the local news with the sound down, pictures from Tottenham of Broadwater farm; a young family looking down from the top-floor window, blazing cars all smashed to bits, lampposts pulled up from the concrete, and a line of running bodies silhouetted against fire, while from the stage by the toilets, a local singer was murdering Joni Mitchell. They were all in for a long night.

Part of what attracted Ezra to Meg was the feeling of wildness that he felt coming off her. She didn't fuss about how she looked, and she didn't mind what she said to people. She was just who she was. He'd never known anybody so unguarded. And she knew about things he didn't know about. Writers and bands and impressionist painters. She had the dirty glamour of London all over her, and she seemed so free to Ezra. If he saw her as his ticket out of drudgery, though, he had misunderstood her. She wanted the very life he was desperate to escape.

For Meg, it was the solidness of him. He seemed unshakeable and sure of things. Not showy or impressive like the other men she'd had. She could feel it, that Ezra wasn't violent. And he didn't seem the type to punish others for his own shortcomings. She liked that he could laugh at himself. And that he didn't seem to judge her. He just let her be.

They went for long walks at low tide. They listened out for birds. They sat by the fire in their favourite pub. They went to the cinema in the afternoon and watched black and white classics with all the old ladies. It hadn't been like this with the others.

Two months after meeting him, she left the room she was staying in and moved in with Ezra, to the poky little bedsit that he rented above the greengrocers. They ate dinner together in the kitchen, looking out of the third-floor window at the sunset. Before he knew it, he was calling in sick so they could spend all day in bed, and Ezra Taylor had never pulled a sickie in his life.

A year passed in a slow kiss.

When they finally came up for air, Meg was pregnant, and Ezra was working three jobs to move them into a place of their own. Dead set on getting them out of the bedsit.

Delivery driving first thing in the morning, then washing machine repairs in the afternoons and after that he balanced the books for local businesses. He was studying accountancy. He wanted security. A future they could all believe in.

Meg didn't want any of that though. All she wanted was a life of nothing special. For him to be hers and for her to be his. And for that to be enough for both. But it wasn't enough for Ezra.

And anyway, she was changing.

Ezra had never lived with a person who suffered their distress so openly. In his experience, you got on with what you had to get on with and if things were hard, you kept it to yourself. And he didn't like the way she was drinking. His dad had been a drinker, and seeing it in Meg brought things back to him he didn't want to think about. So Meg started hiding it.

They both wanted it to work so badly. But you can't want love into existence. So, they got married.

After Sarai was born, a depression landed on Meg that swallowed the house. It was the worst she'd ever known it. Ezra could feel everything slipping away. He didn't know what else to do but push himself further into providing.

Meg's dark moods ran so dark, Ezra felt smothered. Then out of nowhere, the bright moods ran too bright, white hot, and Ezra feared the fallout. So, he retreated. And he blamed her for the distance between them. He couldn't understand why she wouldn't get up or get dressed or stop crying. All he knew was how to put the effort in, he felt like she just wasn't trying hard enough. Like maybe it was a lack of discipline that had her talking to people Ezra couldn't see.

He'd always told her he didn't care about her past. But it started creeping into all their arguments. How many men had she had? He kept asking. She'd never hidden anything from him. But she couldn't see what good could come from dwelling on what couldn't be changed?

More than one hundred? Less than?

Every other thought Ezra had was of a queue of men, waiting their turn.

By now, he had achieved his qualifications and found good work. At twenty-eight years old, he had a wife and a kid, and he'd managed to move his family into a better home than his parents had ever been able to afford. The late nights and early starts and long hours on the clock had all been worth it. The facts of his life stacked up to happiness. But he didn't *feel* happy.

He was sure that Meg would snap herself out of her funny moods eventually. That she would look after the house the way his own mother had, despite her gruelling job and her difficult husband. But they were all going down under a wave of mess and disorder and he didn't like what that said about the kind of person people might have taken him to be.

He got a better job out of town. Became a commuter. Up and down to London every day.

That's when it started with the other women.

The guilt he felt drove him back to Meg with a new tenderness. For a moment it seemed like they'd really turned a corner, and she found herself pregnant with Rothko.

During the pregnancy, Meg had been so completely absorbed by what was happening in her body, that Ezra had found himself jealous and abandoned. He grew careless. Started dropping hints about his other women. As if a part of him wanted to get caught. The part of him that needed his wife's attention so badly, it didn't matter what he had to do to her to get it.

But when she pulled him up on the inconsistencies that he left around for her to find, he grew defensive; told her it was her fault, that she'd driven him away. That any man in his position would have done the same. That it was just sex, after all. It didn't mean anything. And that anyway, he promised her, it was all over now. No more lies. They had their family to think of.

The kids were getting bigger every day. Nice house in a seaside town. She wished her mum had lived to meet her children. She had it good. She knew she had it good. She loved him. But it was like he couldn't even see the surging mess she spent her days defending their home against; paid no mind to the constant battle she fought with the cleaning, the making, the chopping, the scrubbing, the exhausting, endless toil of a day that began with somebody screaming for her and ended with grudging sleep, stolen in minutes rather than hours.

Sarai needing constant attention, her *yes, I can see you, I'm watching*, unable to play by herself, needing Meg there to notice at all times, as if out of a fear that without being seen by her mother she wouldn't exist. Then the baby, crying for contact, crying for changing, crawling towards every danger; hands outstretched; the incessant mouthing, eating, pulling at her. The fingers, the swamp of their consummate bodies, the sores, the scratches, the shitting and pissing and puking, the hunger, their hair needed brushing, their chins needed wiping, their clothes covered in mud or food or paint, the walls groaning under the weight of the washing, the dishes stacked up, dirty things covered in dirt, everything phlegmy, all surfaces sticky to touch, mashed potato all over the floor. *It's just normal*, he told her, *what kind of a woman can't cope with this stuff?* It's just life, *normal life*. It proved it to Meg, what she already knew: that she wasn't cut out for it, didn't deserve to be happy and never would be; that she was too dirty, too stupid, too wild for a nice life, embarrassing how she'd got carried away, let herself think that little Meg Wrennal could ever have really been loved. And if he had come home just once and just seen it, for once, just seen how much she was doing.

But he didn't see anything. Silent. Pretending not to be silent, so that if she was to ask what was wrong, it would be her that had started it.

And he was getting mean.

Of course, he had noticed her stiffening under his touch. She said she'd forgiven him, but she was the one that was always bringing it up. He couldn't put a foot wrong without getting it in the neck. Each time he came home, she seemed to despise him that little bit harder. No smiles for him, no special words, no jokes between them anymore, no little laughs snatched over the heads of the chaos they'd created. Suddenly, they weren't a team. He had noticed. He was aware of that. But he thought it was her fault for always having the hump with him. Rather than his fault for giving her cause for it.

She was trying so hard, but he was never satisfied, pointing out what she had undercooked, or how she had overdressed. Comparing her to his other women in coded half-said things and making her feel she was losing her mind. In her desperation to be what he wanted her to be, she completely lost track of who she was. She was dreaming of her mother in the bath again. A recurrent dream she thought she'd left behind when she met him. He was always angry with her. Always upset. Always shouting. Always poking at her. She was terrified of upsetting him. She had been a powerful free spirit, how had she ended up reduced to a wreck of a person. Obsessive and anxious. Hiding her empties. Followed by things that weren't there.

Fearing she would lose her mind for good if she stayed another minute in his house, she walked out.

Rothko was five years old. Sweet little bruiser. Built like a tree stump. Sarai was eight and already grown up. Meg left them there, in Ezra's warm house with his warm dream to hold them. She believed him when he said she wasn't worth the time he'd given her.

She stayed with friends at first. The plan was to get herself together and get a place of her own and then the kids would come and live with her. She thought they'd work it out. Share custody. There were lots of ways it could have gone. Couples did it all the time. But Ezra was out to punish her, to make her pay for leaving him.

He threw the full might of his drive into the court case. He came across as professional and respectable, while she was clearly unstable. A drinker. Couldn't even be relied upon to take her medication. And she didn't have the confidence to meet his campaign with a charge of her own. She didn't want to bring up the affairs, or go grubbing in the gutter for scandal, telling tales. Snivelling to the judge in the family courts. She just wanted to live in her own body, without feeling like that body belonged to a man who hated her for having a mind that didn't work exactly the way he thought it should. And she was tired.

He got sole custody. She got the drinks in.

And a year later, he got a court order that denied her visitation rights.

In Edgecliff, it wasn't too far to fall from drinking to drunk. Or past drunk to the harder, thicker, dirtier afflictions that linger at the edges of the session.

Ezra moved his girlfriend in a few months after Meg moved out. Wendy was so different to Meg. Kind to him and interested in the things he said. Together they set their sights on happiness, which had always looked the same to Ezra. Clean house, smiling wife, nice kids, good job. But something dark had fallen on his dream.

And slowly, Meg Taylor became a regular face. Cackling in the morning over urgent plans, with a can and a roll-up in her skinny fist. She got a room above the pub she did most of her drinking in, odd jobs here and there to supplement the dole.

After a good long drink up, one swampy night in Edgecliff, Meg had found the top of a pool table in the street and dragged it back to the pub on a couple of skateboards. Her and the lads she drank with got it down to the basement eventually, and it meant they had their own little after-hours drinking den.

It just kind of happened. It wasn't remarkable. The sniff was all gone, and someone had the pipe out. It came her way and why not? May as well enjoy your life. Most days, there was nothing in her head but screaming.

NINE

Rothko was heading home. The shops were closed. Everything was still. The empty road was lit by streetlamps that shone on clouds of quiet rain.

Pitched up in a doorway, Rothko saw a woman, jagged features, heavy posture, sadness all around. Pain sprouted out of her like two enormous wings. She saw Donovan and lit up.

'Alright?' Rothko greeted her, slowing.

'That's a nice dog.' She admired Donovan.

'Ah yeah, he's lovely.'

'I used to have one. Similar. What is he, Rottweiler/shepherd?'

'He's all sorts. He's a mixed bag.'

'He's very handsome. Is he friendly?' She didn't have any shoes on, and her feet were badly swollen. One of them, Rothko saw, looked infected. She wasn't long off losing it.

'Yeah, he's a sweetheart. His name's Donovan.' Donovan heard his name and came over to investigate. He sniffed the air around the woman's extended hand. She gave him a calm stroke. He stood very close to her, side on, offered her his back to rub. She combed his fur with her fingers, he turned and nuzzled her.

'Ahh. He's very nice. Lovely dog,' she said, laughing. 'Aren't you nice.' He howled in agreement. They all enjoyed that. Time passed. Donovan was gentle with her. She blew warm breath into his face, he sneezed and shook his chops, poked his nose towards her nose. The rain was soft. Her things were soaked. Her face was covered in sores and cuts and her eyes were raging with life.

'What's your name?' Rothko asked.

'Constance.' Rothko nodded but she didn't ask for theirs. She went back to watching Donovan.

'He likes you.'

She laughed. 'I attract all the dogs, my darlin'.'

'How are you?' Rothko asked.

'Me?'

'Yeah.'

She shrugged. 'Cold. Been tough tonight.' She smiled at Donovan. 'Never mind though. You get used to it.'

'How much to get in tonight?'

She thought about it. 'I need another nine, ten pound. But I can't get down there tonight, not with my foot. And what time it is. They don't let you anyway, unless they seen you out three nights in a row. You can't get in anywhere. There's so many of us at the moment they don't know what to do with us.'

'Is it more than usual?'

'Feels that way.'

Rothko went to their pocket. Slipped three twenties off the stack of notes in their wallet and offered them.

'Get a bag then, or a bottle or whatever, and a couple of nights out the rain, will you?'

Constance eyed the notes. 'You sure, mate?'

'Can you get down a health centre or something? For the foot?'

She shuddered. 'Oh no. I *hate* hospitals.' She shook her head. 'Just can't do it to myself.'

'I don't like them either. But really, it don't look good.'

'I know, I know.' She looked down at it. 'I will get down there, yeah.' Rothko, still holding out the notes, waved them towards her. Constance took them, put them in her pocket. 'Thank you.' She raised her face to the rain. 'Thank you!' She smiled and Rothko saw the child in her. Donovan wagged his tail. Constance stuck her hand out and Rothko held it, tight. Saw how red the knuckles were. The veins all dead. It rained on all of them and they released each other's hands.

'You're welcome,' Rothko said. Looking in her face, but it was hard to read now. Her eyes were distant. She had the money in her pocket and that meant what it meant. 'Night then, Constance.' Rothko kept going. 'Courage to you.'

'God bless you, my sister. Good night,' Constance called after them. Rothko swallowed the pip and kept going, until they heard her voice call out. 'Oi, mate?' Rothko turned. 'Mate. Are you a girl or a boy?'

Rothko smiled and said slowly, 'I don't know. Maybe I'm both.' And they raised their arms in a wide shrug that took in the street, the rain, the pointlessness of the whole thing.

Constance nodded. Cheerful. 'Good for you!'

Rothko paced back towards her. Earnest again. 'Listen. Constance. Listen to me.' Their voice reared up in their chest. 'When they ignore you. Or. When they look at you like you're a piece of shit, like you're less than nothing. I've got to tell you.' Rothko bristled with intensity. 'They wouldn't last a minute. If they had to go through it.'

'Yeah, alright, mate.' She waved it off.

'Not one day. Out here, like this.' Rothko pointed at the wet blanket. The ripped cardboard.

Constance was frowning. Toothless mouth open in a brief trance. Scarred and swollen, dirty, grinding life, heavy in the eyes. Then she started laughing. A deep, textured laugh that got deeper and deeper, unfurling into a fleshy cough. Rothko shrugged again. Walked away.

'You're more of a nutter than I am.' Constance shouted after them as they turned the corner. She watched the space they had occupied for a while, her fist smiling around the notes in her hand.

TEN

Angel Douglas was trying to sit up, but the weight of the room kept pushing her back down. She was lying on the bed, head propped up against the wall. She was naked with the quilt wrapped around her legs.

Trish in her white Calvins was stretched out across the two-seater. Her legs hung over the armrest and one arm was folded behind her head. The other held her bottle of port squashed up into her boobs. The TV was on.

Was it day or night? Angel had lost track of everything.

The bed was right next to the window, but the curtains blocked out the world. Heavy, dusty satin. Dark blue. Trish had got them from the Wednesday market. Every so often, Les on the clothes stall got a house clearance in and Trish went treasure hunting, a black fedora, a flugelhorn and a pair of satin curtains. All for a tenner.

Angel could hear the clanking of dishes in a sink from next door. Explosions from the TV. Machine gun fire. Someone shouting *what? What's the fucking matter now?*

The ceiling was bulging. Patches round the light fixture. The plaster roses had gone brown at the petals. The damp springs gave beneath her as she turned on the mushy bed and reached down for her beer.

The artistic gymnastics was on, Trish paid extra for the sports package.

'Want another one?' Trish asked, without looking at her.

Angel checked the level of her can by shaking it and said, 'Go on then.'

Trish went to the bag under the coffee table, opened her a beer and brought it over. Angel finished the one in her hand, set the can down on the floor and accepted the fresh one. Trish budged her over with a look. Angel shuffled her belly and hips towards the window and Trish sat down on the edge of the bed. She held one leg up to her chest, chin balanced on her knee, the other leg dangled off the side, toes resting on the floor. Eyes on the screen. She was so pretty, Angel thought. So detached and unimposing. Not like Ruby.

Ruby's friends ran all the bars in town. Ran the restaurants and galleries and second-hand clothes emporiums. Nowhere was safe. They were all tired of their own lives, and desperate for a bit of gossip to validate the depravity of their sensible choices.

So, that afternoon, after the Shipwrights, they snuck off to where they couldn't be seen. Holed up in Trish's room, like they did once a fortnight. Plus they found moments together behind locked doors at work. Angel knew Trish liked her more than she liked Trish. It was so satisfying. To go along with being someone else, in the eyes of someone else who thought she was a different person, which meant she could be a different person.

Trish didn't know that deep down, Angel wasn't really anyone.

Only Ruby knew that.

On the TV, it was the parallel bars. The athletes were doing miraculous things.

'I used to do gymnastics,' Trish said.

'Doesn't surprise me.' Angel's voice was heavy. The words

came out as one word. They'd been at it for hours. She fought against the pressing weight of her brain but wasn't sure of much. She hadn't had a session like this for a good long while. But Trish and her pretty shoulder blades, caving in beneath her. She wanted to grind her down, just ruin her, just push her face into her thighs and crawl for her and have her on her knees like she was still alive enough to feel like this.

Ruby in the bathroom, sitting on the closed lid of the toilet while Angel shaved her armpits in the bath, saying *I don't think I'm learning anything new with you, sexually. I don't feel we're growing . . .*

'I wanted to do ballet, really. But we didn't have the money for it. So, I did gymnastics instead.' Trish held her leg up to her chest tenderly and allowed herself a little sigh. 'I loved ballerinas.'

'You'd have been a good ballerina,' Angel told her, and she meant it. 'Perfect for it.' She could imagine Trish, young. She could see the part of her that had been present even then. The fiery stillness in her eyes and the smooth, long way of walking and the sweetness in her, not yet gone bitter. On the TV, a man was doing a handstand in the air, supporting himself on two wooden hoops.

'Mad thing to be the best in the world at.' Angel admired it. 'So. *Specific.*'

'I used to love it.'

'Did you do the competitions?'

'I could have done. But . . . Funny time.' Angel had never asked, but she knew something had happened to Trish young. She was so childlike sometimes; it was like she stopped developing at eight years old. Angel had been around long enough to know what that usually meant in a person.

'Can you still do it? Any of it?'

'Damn right I can, baby.' Trish laughed. Standing up to try and sink into the splits. 'Sometimes,' she said, stopping with her legs spread, unable to go an inch further, laughing at how hopeless it was but holding the shape. 'Sometimes I think, if I'd stuck it out.' She tried again, failed again. Tried again, a little lower. Made a face of pain. They both laughed. 'If I'd have stuck it out, I'd be retired by now.' And she tried to push deeper into her splits, but her feet stuck on the rough carpet, and she swayed there in her pants, catching her balance.

'I stopped going when I was nine, I think. But I missed it so much. I ended up joining the netball team like halfway through secondary school. But they caught me going down on my teammate after practice.' She was giggling about it. '*Jeyda*. Ah, if you ever saw her, Angel, she was beautiful.' Still holding the stance. 'Mrs Lyle. That was it . . . Hated her. Caught us in the changing rooms.' She stamped her foot with the effort her laughter required, as she remembered. 'Stood there long enough to get a good look, didn't she. Then she kicked us off the team.' She slid herself back to standing, went for her bottle. 'Fucking homophobes.' She drank thoughtfully. 'Everyone was homophobic back then though, weren't they.'

Angel rolled from her side, onto her back. 'I was homophobic.' Tone dull as she confessed it, holding herself when she spoke. Hand under her armpit, close to her heart. 'I spat on someone once. On a bus.' Trish winced. Angel nodded. 'For kissing her girlfriend.'

Trish watched her, compassion in her frown. 'Sweetheart.'

'Wish I could tell her I'm sorry.'

Her heavy body sank into the heavy bed and Trish felt Angel's heavy eyes as they settled on her and the whole room dropped beneath the weight of it. The breath dropped in her mouth, she turned back to the bed and moved slowly, carrying the weight. She climbed up to sit across Angel's hips and look down the length of her body at her and Angel reached up and pulled her close, crushed her to her chest and turned them both over and Angel felt Trish beneath her like shifting sand, like the falling side of a sandy cliff, like trying to climb a falling wall, or run up falling dunes, her eyes dark pools of quiet rage, she was so hungry for sensation and they ground themselves together, dug deep down, one into the other, pushed and led and crushed and gripped and gave and finally relinquished because why not feel? Why not fucking feel in all of this.

Until lying there together after, looking quietly into each other's faces, the feeling in the air of time having run its course, each knowing it wasn't long before Angel had to go back to her girlfriend. They had to be contented with the moment. No weekend plans, no friends, no moving in together, no beach walks at sunset, no buying tickets to gigs, none of that, no, just this moment. Foreheads close, the darkness warmed by bedside lamps. Trish felt it and decided. Why hold it back? It couldn't do more harm than this was doing to her heart already.

'I love you.' She whispered it.

Angel held her eyes and stared deeply into them, and what Trish read there was that Angel felt the same. But couldn't say it back. Because of Ruby. Angel gave Trish her dreamiest expression, as if what this was to her was the tortured connection of a star-crossed couple, who rested together, inches apart, breathing each other's expelled breaths, in the agony of their last hour together. But what Angel was really thinking, as she looked into Trish's eyes, was how simple this person was. How easy and dumb and ugly and soft, how compliant, how uncomplex, how childlike and usual, and stupid. How ruined it all was now. How boring. How sickening, after the fact.

It must have been chucking-out time, Rothko realised with concern. They kept their head down as they passed a group of lads. 'You'd never have the guts.' One of them was saying. 'You'd never have done it!'

'I would have done it. I was about to! If you hadn't . . .' The lads came closer. One of them, early thirties, receding hairline, no coat despite the cold, in a short-sleeved shirt two sizes too small, taking his biceps for a night on the town, saw Rothko and stopped walking. 'Molly!' Gradually, his stopping stopped the others, and the group assembled vaguely. 'Molly Taylor! It's *me*! Lee Maguire! Remember? I used to buy draw off you!' Rothko stopped walking, looked at him. Some kid from school, probably. Maybe someone's little brother?

'How's your *life*?' Lee asked, excited. High-pitched. 'Been YEARS, aint it?' His friends turned around to light cigarettes and find something better to look at. Lee came a step closer. 'You out now, are you? I've not seen you about, I would have thought I'd have bumped into *you*.' Lee checked around him, lowered his voice. 'I heard about what happened.' Rothko had no recollection of ever having met this person before.

Donovan whined, responding to Rothko's unease, and pushed close to their legs.

Lee saw his mates were moving away. 'You still serving up?' he asked.

'No. No.' Rothko shook their head. Walking off.

'Well, it's good to bump into you again!' Lee said. 'Have a good night, darling.' And he bowed his head grandly and caught up to his boys. Rothko could hear them all talking in loud, boozy voices as they walked away in the opposite direction.

'Who was that, you bellend?'

'That was Molly Taylor.'

'It weren't, was it?'

'Why? Who's Molly Taylor?'

'Remember that crackhead, years ago, bashed up the old grandad? In his own house? Went to Edgecliff Green, in my brother's year?'

'Is that *her*?'

And another one laughing, saying, 'I got a blowy off her mum for a tenner once.' And the whole pack of them laughing. Cracking up.

'Jase, you disgust me. You're fucking disgusting.'

'Say what you like, boys, I'm telling you; it's better when they don't have any teeth.'

Rothko sped up, entertaining detailed fantasies of running back and beating the shit out of all of them. Cracking their heads on the pavement. Kicking them all in their faces until they didn't have faces left.

No point getting upset. They could almost hear Meg saying it. *People like that live the most miserable lives that it's possible to live. Because they don't even know how miserable they are.* How she used to wink and tap the side of her head and then point her finger at Rothko and say, *they think they're having a good time. But* we *know. Don't we darlin?*

Rothko broke into a run. They hadn't run for a long time, and it was uncomfortable, but they kept going, pushing themself harder, until the anger that was grabbing at them started to let go. Eventually, they reached the site. Red faced. Donovan matching them, stride for stride, and they stopped against the heavy gates, catching their breath.

They hadn't followed those boys and started a fight.

No.

They'd run the other way.

They felt like there was another person inside them, buried beneath all that time, digging their way up to the surface and trying to get their attention. Like this person was *them*, but not as they were now. More like how they used to be when they were just a kid. There was a sweetness to the feeling. Sweet like it used to be with Dionne. She was probably the only one that had ever seen that sweetness in them. Except for maybe Fletcher.

They wondered if Fletch was home from his tour yet. They had a feeling he was back this weekend.

They'd missed him. And they wanted to see him. He made everything funny and fine.

ELEVEN

Back in the yard, Donovan ambled to the factory kitchen, looking for dinner scraps and a warm place to lie down. Rothko saw the light on at Fletcher's and knocked.

Fletch swung the door open, stuck his head out. 'Captain Rothko with a crossbow.' Deadpan Dizzee Rascal reference, as always.

'Ello mate!' Resting their sweaty head against the cold steel of the van, watching their breath mist in the night. 'When did you get back?'

'I just got here. I'm fucked. What you doing?' His voice was hoarse.

'Nothing.' Rothko wrapped him in a hug.

'You been alright?' Fletch asked their shoulder.

'Yeah mate. All good.' They left it a second before they said. 'Missed you though.' And Fletcher laughed his rolling bellow as they let each other go.

'Awwww. Aint that nice. I missed you too my mate.' Hoarse as he was, and scratchy, his voice was still full of music and Rothko was relieved to be around him again. He was so at ease in himself, it put Rothko at ease.

'What you doing? You going bed or . . .?'

'Bed? Never. Just unloading the van. Come in, come in.'

Rothko followed him inside. 'How was it, then?'

Closer, in the light, Rothko saw that Fletcher looked weary, road sick, the hollow glare of motorway food and no sleep. 'It was good, yeah,' he said. 'Glad to be home, though.'

It smelt musty in the van, trapped air and stale incense. There wasn't much room to move with the pedalboard and cases. Fletcher was in the process of stashing his bass in its special place, a purpose-built shelf above the cab. He reached into the rider bag for two beers. Passed one to Rothko, and then remembered, and threw Rothko a posh bottle of green tea blended with fruit juice instead. Rothko gave it the eye. 'It's delicious,' Fletcher sold it to them. 'What can I say, I've been gentrified. And I like it.'

They sat down at each end of the bed. 'It's not cold though. They've been on the motorway since last night. Like me.' Rothko turned the bottle around in their hand. 'Looooong drive.' Fletcher collapsed against a pile of cushions, stretched his legs out. Feeling the stillness of the ground after three weeks in transit. The smallness of the room after the company of bandmates. Somewhere in the distance, something happened, and people cheered.

'What was it like?' Rothko asked. 'I'd love to travel like that. See all them cities.' Fletch thought about it; the hours in the van, staring at his messages. The waiting around in dead spaces. The drinking. The grey meat and brown lettuce and watery coffee. Budget drugs from clingy promoters. Tinny music from a phone in a windowless dressing room. The buoyancy of a willing crowd. The sludgy resentment of an unwilling crowd. The still, expectant flatness of record-collecting men. The ringing ears and blown amps. The chasing of sex in the bar after. Then back in the van, sick and exhausted. Waiting for the drive to pass to do it all again.

'It was good,' Fletch said. 'Lots of people. Dancing. So . . .' he tailed off.

'Must be mad, that.'

'We just done twenty shows in twenty-two days.' Fletch poured a bucket of breath out of his lungs.

'Is that a lot, then?'

He laughed a tired wheeze. 'Yeah, boy,' he said. 'It's a lot.' He rustled a curl of his hair in a floating hand. Rothko watched their returned friend. Impressed with him. He seemed so complete and at home in himself.

'Can I ask you something?' Fletch waited for more, eyebrows raised for *yeah, course*. 'Did you always *know*?' And Rothko looked at Fletch and then didn't look at Fletch with a pain in their eyes that was unmistakable. 'That you, like . . .' They tailed off. Fletcher saw how they grabbed at their knees, pinching little handfuls out of their jeans. Rothko caught themself creating and laughed. 'Sorry,' they said. 'I mean . . .'

Fletcher's face opened towards his friend. He'd been half expecting a question like this, and he reached over to give Rothko a slow shove. 'Yeah,' he told them. 'I always knew.' He resettled on the bed. Bent one leg up towards his chest, rested his arm across his knee. 'Funny thing is, I went to the doctor at sixteen. Which, believe it or not, was a long time ago, and things back then were just. Impossible. So, I made myself forget about it. I stamped it down, down. But little by little, it kept rising up.' He levelled his hands and moved them up the course of his body from down by the floor, towards his chest, up towards his mouth. 'By the time it got to here, I just had to let it out. I couldn't hold it anymore.' Rothko nodded. Listening. 'I was twenty-six. Twenty-seven. Twenty-eight and it just kept rising. I thought I was too late. I thought the hormones wouldn't work on me. That my life would fall apart if I said anything to anyone. That it was better to be miserable forever than risk upsetting my family. Losing my job. Losing my friends. But I just couldn't keep pretending.'

'How did you know it was time, though?'

Fletch rubbed at the back of his head, smiled into the past. 'Mad to think about it now, it's like I was a different person. I'd completely turned my back on myself. I was just . . . numb. Like, completely disconnected from my body. Just going through the motions.'

Rothko shook their head in disbelief. Because what Fletcher was describing was so unlike how Rothko thought of Fletcher, and in fact so much more like how Rothko felt about themself.

'I think what really did it was that I lost three people who were close to me in the same year. My mum died, then my nan died, then one of my best friends died who I'd known since forever. And I just thought, life's too fucking short. I just. I just didn't want to go to my grave, having never even lived a day of my life.'

Rothko felt the ache of tears, tried to firm it. 'So, what happened?'

'*I* happened,' he said. He studied Rothko. 'and I was finally, after almost forty years of living. *Alive*. And the depression.' Fletch shook his head. 'The *thing*. The secret I carried around all my life,' he pointed his beer at Rothko, 'had finally started to lift. And I could stand up.' Rothko met his stare, and they looked into each other's eyes. Fletcher saw the pain there and nodded. 'Why do you ask, mate?'

Rothko dropped their shoulders beneath the weight of what they didn't know how to explain, their slump was so sad it made Fletcher correct his posture in encouragement. 'It makes me,' they began. Fletcher kept very still and waited while Rothko searched for the words. 'I just feel it very deep in me. And I. It's like. I think . . .' They started again. 'I just look at you and I think. I don't even know how you did it.' They went quiet, chewed at the side of their thumb. 'Isn't it hard? Being . . .?' but Rothko couldn't even say the word. Too afraid of it and enthralled by it and what if it didn't belong to them?

Fletcher laughed kindly and said, 'What, trans? No mate. It's not hard. It's harder *not* being trans, if you are. Know what I mean? It's harder lying to yourself and feeling all tied up in a body that isn't yours. But no, being trans is amazing. Same way, being cis is amazing. Because being alive is amazing. When you're alive, it's great. You can fuck, you can dance, you can go to work, you can go to the fucking post office, you can sit in a room on your own. And it doesn't hurt.'

The soft air in the van expanded the moment.

'I mean, you're still you. You're still annoyed by the same things. You don't just magically stop being a dick about things that you've always been a dick about. You, for example, You'd still be awkward and oversensitive. But you'd also be *more* you. Don't know if that makes any sense?'

Fletcher shifted so he was facing Rothko. Then Rothko did the same.

They felt like children, sat opposite each other on Fletcher's bed. Legs stretched out. It was cute. Rothko tried again. Spoke slowly. 'Can I ask, what are you, then Fletch? Like? Trans man, is that it? Trans masc?'

'Yeah. You're allowed to say it, it's ok.'

The words were new in their mouth, salty and wet as eating an oyster for the first time, scared of it, scared of getting it wrong. 'In jail, there were lots of people that I thought were like me. Plenty of butches on the wing. Kings and Daddies they called us. Lot of girls said we were their men. But it didn't mean . . .' They got lost and couldn't find their way to the end of the sentence. 'Do you know what I mean?' Fletch waited it out with them. 'But there wasn't anyone who was really like me. Who felt like I felt. Like. I've been carrying the thing around all my life, too.' They shone their eyes on Fletcher. 'I never knew what was wrong with me.' It was a relief to say it. But it was sore. 'I wish I'd known. I feel like if I'd have known the name for it at fifteen instead of thirty-five, my whole life might have turned out different.' Rothko's face fell.

Fletch took a moment before he spoke, waited for Rothko to meet his eyes. 'There's nothing wrong with you,' he said in his deep, kind voice. 'It's not like: Rothko is ill. They have dysphoria. They need curing. The cure is transition. Surgery. Testosterone. Then they'll be normal and happy.'

Rothko looked at Fletcher's face. Fletcher drew his words from the ground beneath the van. 'Those things might be things that you want and need, maybe. At some point. But also, they might not be. And it's no problem not to know.' Rothko was turning red. Tears stung the corners of their eyes. 'You're not ill, mate. You're beautiful.' Fletch tucked his legs in, held his knees in his arms. 'It's the world out there that's fucking ill. The world that says people like us don't exist or are wrong or not natural. That's the thing that needs treatment and healing. Not you. My friend.' He rested his chin on the top of his arms. Watched Rothko sitting there, stranded in the middle of their feelings. 'You just take your fucking time. And when or if you want to talk. Ever. Anytime. About any of it or none of it. I'm here for you. Ok?'

Rothko covered their big, rough face with their hands and laughed because they were about to cry. Fletcher stroked his beard with the pad of his thumb.

'Come on.' He tipped his beer up.

Rothko looked up from their hands. 'Do you really think I'm oversensitive?'

Fletcher hid his grin in the last swig and stood up.

'What? Where we going?' Rothko asked him.

'I'm taking you out.'

Rothko groaned. 'Out? Where?'

They'd heard about the nights that Fletch went along to, but they always said they weren't up for it. Made excuses about work in the morning. They imagined those kind of places would be intimidating. *You think everywhere's intimidating*. Fletcher had said when they'd told him that. He'd been trying to get them to come along with him for the last three months, but Rothko maintained that they just wanted to go to a normal bar without it causing problems. They didn't want to *have* to go to a special place for it. *Suit yourself,* Fletcher had always said but knew the time would come. And here it was.

Rothko distrusted the idea of community, having never experienced it. But Fletcher could see, the lack of its nourishment was making them weak.

'I just spent three weeks in a van with straight people sniffing cocaine.' He rolled his eyes and shook it out of his body. Jumped up and down on the spot a couple of times. 'I need some queers in my life. And so do you. There's a big dirty party at the basement tonight.' He squeezed Rothko's shoulder. 'And you aint wriggling out of it this time.'

The Old Days

April 2006

ONE

Rothko Taylor. Middle parting, frizzy curtains, limp and dull. Hair they never brushed pulled back in a tired elastic band, all the stretch gone out of it. Dead little bulb frizzing at the nape of their neck. Their eyes were slippery as mossy stones left behind at low tide. Their skin was the colour of dug sand; the warmth of their dad's complexion deepened in the sun and wind. Sixteen tomorrow and as tall as the boys if they weren't slouching. But they always were.

Sat at the back of the classroom. Waiting for life to restart.

Gold peace sign on a flimsy chain. Fire opal on a silver band that they wore on their middle finger. Big thighs, big arms. Wide hips they hated. Stocky frame. A belly that rounded out over their belt. Their fingernails were bitten to blood, blue biro smudged over the backs of their hands.

Trapped in a small room with small people who wanted small things. They slumped at the desk. Too big for it all.

Stoned.

The pressure in the room was stifling. Everything dragged. Mr Pelton was pacing the desks with his hands on his hips, ticking along at the front like a reliable car. A Rover estate in hiking socks.

They drew a constant line across the top of the page that was open in front of them. The pen followed the line until it became a face, then the face had sunglasses on, sucking a spliff. Headphone cable threaded through the sleeve of their shirt, Sarai's old Walkman in their trouser pocket. Listening to *Liquid Swords*. Resting their head in their left hand so they could hide the headphone that sat in their ear.

They were being watched.

They looked up.

The whole room was looking back at them. Mr Pelton, bushy eyebrows, phlegmy disposition, crossed his arms. Rothko slid the headphone out of their ear and smudged it back into their sleeve. Pelton was mid-sentence, '. . .that you are very busy not doing is much more important than learning with the rest of us, isn't that right Miss Taylor?' the blush crept inwards from their temples and turned their cheeks first, then rose to their forehead. 'You are wasting everybody's time,' he continued, unenthusiastically. 'Some of these students care about their future.' Rothko stared at the desk. The blush was like a seizure. 'Well?'

They could see the sky out there, through the blurry windows. And Pelton with his day-at-the-races stance and his transparent skin and the swollen bags under his eyes and his tired paunch and the black hair sprouting from the backs of his hands. He walked three slow steps towards them. Grey jumper riding up, sweat patches at the armpits. He peered at Rothko's book from a few rows away.

'Why do you even bother coming in?'

Rothko sagged further over the desk and hid their red face in the crook of their arms.

'I don't know what you think makes you so special that you can do exactly what you want. But the rest of the class are suffering because here I am, again, talking to you instead of teaching.' Condescending speech of a thousand schooldays.

'Not even in uniform. Not even written the date.' Rothko sank into their skin, pooled inwards.

'Why are you always giving me shit, sir?' they said plainly, without anger. Pelton reared up.

His voice boomed from his wobbly neck as he pointed a stiff arm at the door. 'That's it. Get out! Now!'

'For what?'

'For swearing at a teacher.'

'I didn't swear *at* you.' They couldn't get in more trouble. They were on their final warning.

'I'm not going to waste more time arguing with you about it. Just get your stuff and get out.' Rothko pushed their chair back. The other kids snickered. The normal girls rolled their eyes. Sean was the only one who held their corner. He winked at them as they stuffed their books into their rucksack.

Rothko stopped at the door, holding the handle. They looked Mr Pelton dead in the eye and said, 'Suck your mum, you ugly cunt.' The classroom exploded into laughter. 'There you go; now I've sworn *at* you.'

Sean was cracking up. Slapping the desk.

'Have a good life going nowhere,' Mr Pelton shouted after them.

And then Rothko was out of the door and walking the corridors, alone.

These people were all too small. But not Rothko. Rothko was going to get out of this place.

Running their hands against the dented steel doors of the lockers. Listening to their footsteps echo. Shoulder to the wall, pushing themself along it, picking at the crumbling bricks.

If Rothko got another suspension, they were going to get kicked out for good. Their dad had said if they didn't start doing better at school, they better start looking for another place to live.

Too late now.

They sloped off, round the side of the building and through the back field to the gap in the fence.

Freedom.

But what to do with it?

They crossed over to the sunny side, aimless but alive to the colours in the air. Down through concrete nothing roads, the music turned up in their ears, strutting for the bass. They rounded the corner to the little strip of shops at the bottom of the flats by the station: chippy, newsagents, bookies.

They pushed against the railings. Waited for something to happen. Nothing did.

In the bookies, the man at the desk was reading a paper, glasses on the end of his nose. 'How old are you?' he asked Rothko without looking up.

'Twenty-five,' Rothko said.

The man sighed. 'You're not allowed in here.'

'I'm twenty-five.' Rothko shook their head in exasperation. 'I get this all the time.' The man, grey head, razed to a silver sheen, wire-rimmed glasses, big hooky nose, studied Rothko.

'Can I go on the slots then or what?' Rothko asked. The man turned the page of his paper. Flattened it meticulously.

'If someone else comes in, you get straight out.'

Rothko took up their stance at the slot machine and played their three-pound stake. On the last twenty pence, they won back eight pound sixty. The coins came rolling out one after another. Hitting each other in the collect tray. Rothko cheered. The man coughed disapprovingly at them. One twenty pence piece at a time, gritting their teeth, they put it all back in and didn't win again.

Frustrated and skint, they hit the machine.

'Oi!' the man shouted. They walked out under a cloud. Stood outside the chip shop for five minutes. Eventually they went in. 'Hello, boss,' they said. 'Can I have some chips and I'll pay you tomorrow?'

Large hands spread over the wipe clean surfaces. Meaty wrists. Sleeves rolled up. White shirt going yellow at the neck. 'No.'

'Go on mate. I come in here all the time. You know me.'

'No,' he said again. Rothko left, stood outside. They could smell the curry sauce, and it was making them hungry.

They were meeting their mum later. She was picking them up at five and taking them out for a birthday burger. Wasn't that long to wait.

They walked over to the bogged grass between the shops and the flats where there was a row of benches and sat down. They put their headphones in and tried to listen to GZA again, but it made them feel restless, so they took the headphones out and listened to the gulls instead.

In the bottom of their trouser pocket, they found a nugget of hash. They picked a corner off it, smelt it. Soapbar. No good. They skinned up anyway. It tasted of tar and made them feel sleepy. Thirty per cent petrol. Two lads came walking past. Hoods up. Hands in their trousers. Dragging their left legs. One tall, one shorter. Both white, hard faced. Moody Moschino jeans and Nike TNs. Rothko looked down at the floor.

'Look,' the shorter one said. Blond French crop. Gelled at the front.

'Alright, geezerbird,' said the other one. Lanky, gormless. Sprouting facial hair. 'What you doing?'

'Nothing,' Rothko said.

'She's puffing,' the little one said.

'Is that a bit of puff, is it?' They sat down heavily either side of Rothko. Close. 'Let's have a zoot please, babe,' said the little one. The taller one put his arm over the back of the bench. Tucked himself in. 'Go on. Be nice.' Smiling. Stinking of Lynx.

Rothko took the small lump of hash out of their pocket and gave it to them. 'You can have it.'

The lads got up, laughing, and walked off. 'Too easy,' the taller one said. 'You make me feel bad.' And they were gone.

TWO

Rothko walked the slow way home. Hands in the pockets of their favourite coat. Dark brown suede but so old it was almost green. It had been their mum's once, but she hadn't asked for it back yet. Shearling collar turned up. Full of romance, doomed to a town without it.

They turned on to their street and narrowed their eyes as they looked first one way, then the other up and down the quiet road. No sign of her. Just clean cars and rose bushes and two women in headscarves trimming a hedge.

They shuffled up the path to the door.

Home.

Or that's what it was called.

The semi-detached three-bed with the loft conversion and the spacious garage on the quiet road of identical houses where people like them had lives like these: jobs, kids, cars, three-piece suite, meat on the table, keep-fit equipment gathering dust, few drinks down the local at weekends. Pebble dash and varnished decking. Fishnets on anniversaries. Clean countertops. It felt like screaming to Rothko.

It was their dad Ezra's lifelong dream made manifest in tall rooms and sash windows, but Rothko barely noticed how the light moved through the house, or the calmness of the street they lived on. Instead, each time they trudged up the front path, all they felt was dread. Loneliness like an open mouth at the door.

Five came and went, but Meg didn't arrive. She was supposed to be picking them up.

They walked from one side of the glossy front room to the other and back again. The walls were painted a fashionable pebble. The carpet was natural jute. The lilac sofa was uninviting. Too firm and square to get a good lie down. Ezra had recently redecorated, and everything that Rothko had found comforting and homely had been thrown out, replaced with clean lines and hard edges.

They looked out of the window again.

Nothing.

They sat down on the floor opposite the window, against the wall. Felt like they were always alone in this house. Their sister Sarai had gone away to uni. It was just Rothko and their dad left now, but he was hardly ever home. Ezra left early and worked late, and at weekends he preferred to stay at his girlfriend Wendy's place, or get out of town completely. He thought staying out of Rothko's way would take the pressure off the relationship. Or that's what he told himself anyway.

They lay down on the carpet and looked at the undersides of things.

She'd promised they were going out. It was meant to be a birthday treat.

It was their own fault for believing her.

They heaved themself up and went out to find her.

Rothko Taylor was not the kind of teenager that adults watched pass by with a hazy smile; they brought no joyful longing for the old days to strangers. A hard, bullied kid who got things wrong. Frowning. Unfashionable, ungraceful. Big, wide steps of a full-grown man with a woman's torso slouched on top and breasts that didn't belong to them. Hands in pockets, scruffy clothes in other people's sizes. Trousers too long. T-shirts that were either too small or came down to their knees. Hand me downs and things they found. Anything to not go shopping with Wendy. Who was eager for what she liked to call girly bonding time.

They bopped past the carpet shop and the garden centre and the tablecloth cafés with the cakes in the windows, until they reached the park with the sheltered benches full of people gouching out, and they cut across it, to the other side of town, where the paintwork flaked and the railings bent, as if someone had been trapped behind them, desperate to escape.

They pushed in through the big double doors of The Whale. It was dark and it smelt like pubs. Raw petrol smell of the smoke and the sour piss smell of the beer and the warm armpit smell of the people.

They saw a woman they recognised at a table in the window with a paper spread out. Legs crossed, leather jacket, long red fingernails, skin like an old pair of boots. Her name was Carleen. 'You seen my mum?' they asked her.

'She's out back, my darling,' Carleen said, gentle as kisses. 'Come and sit down here with me, I'll send someone to fetch her.' And she shifted on the bench for them to sit down. But they didn't want to sit down.

The back door led to the alley that ran down to the sea. Rothko pushed through it to where the bins were and looked around but couldn't see anything. Then they looked down, and there she was. Posted up between the wall and the bin, holding her knees, looking out to sea. She didn't look up but Rothko could see her face was wretched from crying.

'What you doing down there?' they asked her.

She turned her head. 'Rothko?' She looked at her child for a long time before she smiled. But Rothko didn't smile back. 'You're not allowed in here.' She wiped her face on the bottom of her jumper.

'Mum?' It was such a little word, but there was so much to it. It felt like every single thing that flowed between them passed through that word and came out changed.

She pointed down to the sea, smiling in a distant way. 'Look at her go.' And Rothko pushed their shoulder against the wall and kicked at bits of gravel. 'Me and you go back a long way,' Meg began in her once upon a time voice that Rothko knew meant she was speaking for her own pleasure. She crackled with drunken emotion. 'All that blood in your veins,' she glared. 'That's old as people ever were.' She picked her head up from the damp bricks. Her smile had gone and she was on the verge of crying. '*Quiet* life? That's what people want when they can't bear to admit who they *really* are.' There was spit at the edge of her mouth, gathered in white clumps. She raised a crooked finger. 'I gave him *everything*. He *lied*. Took you all away from me.' She shook her head. Hard. Like a dog with a rat in its mouth. 'Left me out here on my own.' Staring, hard, spitty. The weight of it was too much and she went down under it, forehead on her knees, gasping. 'I have *nothing*.' She broke into choking sobs. 'And *nobody*.'

'It's alright.' Rothko crouched down beside her. Put an arm around her and moved her hair out of her eyes. 'It's alright, Mum.' Picked her up so she wasn't bent double.

'It's not *alright*! You look down on me.' She glared. Rothko held on tighter. 'And, and, and, and you *judge* me for being dirty and, and drinking and not like all the other mums with their fucking . . .'

Rothko rested the side of their face on Meg's back and held her tightly. 'Just look at the sea, Mum,' they said gently. 'You're right. She's really going for it today, look.' Meg looked.

'I loved you.' Her sobs were dryer now, wracking through her body. 'I *loved* you all so *much*. And *none* of you ever . . .' But she was calming now and losing the rage. Sadness was sucking her under. She was whirling down the drain of it. Her hand went to her heart. 'He wasn't the person he *told* me he was. And *you*. You were supposed to be my one. But. But.' She broke into panting sobs. 'Stop *attacking* me?' Her jaw dropped open in a silent scream. 'He doesn't know the meaning of the fucking word. He has no *idea* what attacking feels like.' And she crumpled into a puddle of pain. 'I've been *fucked* so many times.' Rothko held her as tightly as they could, screwed their eyes closed to try and change what she looked like. 'People are *cruel*.' She choked on her crying breaths, her body juddering and collapsing as if she were being punched from the inside out. 'I've had glass bottles . . .' She broke off. Crying without sound.

Rothko rubbed her arms and held her tight as they could. But she shrugged them off to point up to the blank windows above them. 'They think they're all better than me.' She looked down and saw herself. 'They aint no better. I was *clean*.' New sobs cut her voice off, and her words came out jumbled and mashed together. 'It wasn't supposed to not meant to be like this it wasn't I didn't mean it I didn't.'

'I've got you,' Rothko told her. 'I've got you.'

'You haven't *got* me,' she sneered. 'Got me? You only care about *yourself*.' Her pupils swallowed the whole of her eyes. Black pits of sore confusion. The bricks were damp and crumbling behind the bins and her hard, shouting voice rang out. 'He *hurt* me. His lovely little family. All of *you*. Like nothing had happened. Like I didn't even *exist*. He was fucking everything that moved. But it was *my* fault? Because *I'm* unfit. And now I'm out here in this fucking filth as if I didn't even EXIST.' Performing. For who? Rothko could never tell. They waited it out and stroked her back as she twisted her body from side to side. Her face was a mess of tears and snot and dirt and her hair was stuck to her skin and she'd not been there when she'd said she'd be there. Instead, she'd been here, doing this. She was too good a drinker for slurring, Rothko knew it was bad when her voice went weird like this. She had promised on Rothko's life that she wasn't smoking it anymore. Seemed like that promise was worth just about as much as all the others.

'It's alright,' Rothko whispered. And Meg broke again. Her hands found Rothko's arms and she gripped so tight it hurt.

'You've got to be careful around a man that gets everything he wants out of life, my Rothko. Be very *careful* around a man like that.' Her eyes boiled over and simmered down, the black of her pupils began to lose its potency. 'My baby. You're just like me. You're just like. *Me*.' She clung on to them with her hands like metal spikes, dug into the tops of their arms so hard Rothko felt it in their bones. She stared into their face as they crouched there with her. Her voice dropped, quieter now. 'Don't let go of me. Please?' She repeated it. 'Please?' Wrapped in a battered red anorak. A can in her pocket. Lines on her face like cracks in the earth.

Rothko tried to pick her up, pulled Meg's tiny arm around their neck and gripped it at the wrist, but couldn't get her to her feet and instead they both fell to the floor.

Rothko scrambled up, annoyed. 'Get up, Mum,' they

whined at her. 'Come on.' Meg lay still. Looking up at the sky. Until finally she nodded as if she agreed with something profoundly, and then she pulled herself up, grabbed their hand and led them back through the pub.

Inside, people were listening to a grey dent in a baseball cap playing the guitar. Skin so pale it looked fluorescent. Stamping his foot to keep time. The strings buzzed as he strummed the chords to 'Live Forever'. Every now and then, people joined in, tailed off, clapped along. Meg started swaying, dancing with Rothko in the sad daylight of the pub. Kissing them on their cheeks, singing, 'Maybe I just wanna be. Maybe you're the same as me.' They wriggled out of her embrace and pulled her arm at the wrist until eventually they left together.

Outside, Meg stopped to look for cigarettes in her pockets. Carleen came out, talking behind her as she pushed through the door. Rothko watched her. She carried a purple pint of snakebite and black in one hand. A packet of crisps and a fag in the other. Her hair was flowing all round her face in little soft curls and her lips were painted glossy red and Rothko liked her. Carleen saw them watching and smiled. 'You found her then, my darling?' she said, winking. Meg scratched the air at her. An impotent punch at nothing.

'Don't you talk to me. *You* get me in nothing but trouble,' she growled.

'What?' Carleen straightened up. 'What have I done?'

'Get away from me!' Meg was shouting. 'Get the fuck away, alright? You owe me *money*. I'm *warning* you . . .' And she was pulling Rothko close to her, and they walked off down the street, Meg muttering into her collar and staring back behind her.

*

They walked at Meg's pace, too fast for Rothko. Past the massage parlour, the barbers, the grow shop, the wide forecourt of the MOT garage with the tyres stacked up in piles, and cut through the built-up, churning lanes of the old West Docks. Down damp streets of what used to be the workers' houses, until they came out by the grubby high road with its strip of convenience stores: off-licence, pizza delivery, second-hand furniture, and turned onto Nightingale Road where Meg had been living for the past few years, in one of the flats in the housing co-op.

She opened the door and bowed for Rothko to go first.

'After you, my liege.'

Rothko took the first door off the hallway, into the small front room with the kitchen attached and flicked the kettle on. Meg stood in the doorway for a long moment, watching Rothko getting the cups out and opening the fridge for milk. There was a back window out to the garden above the kitchen worktop and the shy daylight came in through the thin striped curtains. She pulled her anorak off and chucked it on the couch. Raked her hands through her hair.

'Let's have a coffee?' Rothko asked her, unscrewing the top of a pint of milk and smelling it.

'You're so grown up,' Meg said, going to the stereo and flicking through the stack of records. 'You were just a tiny little thing.' She went for Cream. *I Feel Free.*

Rothko was pouring hot water into the coffee pot and looking for something to stir it with, settled on a fork. Meg spun herself towards them, jutting at all angles. Frayed jeans and soaring hands. Rothko had the kettle. 'This is hot, ok?' they said, guarding it with their body. 'Be careful?' Meg stopped spinning and wandered out of the room. 'Where you going?' Rothko shouted after her. 'You got a coffee here.'

'Just going the karzi,' she called back to them. Rothko set the cups down and waited on the rocking chair next to the speakers, cradling the cup in both hands, holding the warmth.

A long time crawled by. Long enough that the record stopped. End of side A. The music sounded empty without her anyway.

They stared at things. The bright red of the skirting boards. The chipped corner of the kitchen counter. They knew what it meant that she'd disappeared for so long, but they told themself not to know. They stood to flip through the vinyl. Sat down again. Waited some more.

She came back in like there was nothing to notice about the thirty minutes she'd been gone. Smiled hazily at Rothko as she picked up the mug. 'Thank you.' She curtseyed. 'Café au lait.' She changed the record. *Rum, Sodomy and the Lash.* Dropped the needle on the B side. 'Dirty Old Town'. Held the mug tenderly to her temple.

'Be cold now.' Rothko watched her from their low chair, looking for signs of the lie they knew she was telling. The lie she knew they knew she was telling. It was all so exhausting and endless and round and round it went forever.

'It's not cold. It's lovely.' The verse got going and she started swinging herself to the music, and Rothko watched the coffee splashing all over the floor. 'I met my *girl*. By the factory *wall*.'

They took the mug off her and set it down. Unburdened, Meg kicked off her boots, pulled off her socks and started twirling. Scrunching the shag-pile rug under her bare feet and losing her balance as she spun on the spot. Singing every word, arms moaning up and down. Singing into Rothko's face, finding their eyes for emotional impact, until the chorus came to its close and she grew still. She began to cry again, silent intense tears that sank her body towards the ground and folded her face into tiny pieces.

Rothko went through the records. Stopped The Pogues, knowing how they made Meg cry. Picked out Aretha Franklin. The album was called *Soft and Beautiful.* They offered it up for approval.

'Fine.' Meg settled with her back against the wall, watching her child with a look of intense suffering on her face. Rothko set Aretha up, turned the volume down a notch or two and went back to their chair. There was a haunted, slippery feeling to Meg's skin. She was taken by the music briefly, she swayed a little, eyes closed, and as the music played, she seemed to be falling asleep. Her forehead dropped towards the ground. She bent herself over at the waist.

'Mum?' Rothko woke her. She smiled up at them, flat, long smile, eyelids thick.

'Dozing off,' she said. 'Didn't sleep last night.'

'You'll hurt your back like that. Here.' They took a cushion from behind them and went to throw it over, but she waved it off.

'I'm not going asleep.' She stood herself up, leaning forwards by the wall, ghostly and unreal. 'The mess I've made of my face.' She angled her face towards Rothko. 'Do I look like one of them fellers out of Kiss?' And Rothko shook their head.

'No Mum, you're fine.' It was easier to go along with the show than call it what it was and risk the fallout.

'I'll just be a minute.' She drifted towards the door.

'Where you going?'

She turned and wagged a finger at them. 'Put a bit of slap on. Must look a right mess! Not nice for you to see me all cry-y all the time.' She left the room. Quick, airy steps, and when she came back in, twenty minutes later, she was pretending not to be pretending again. But this time she was faster, colder. More erratic.

'What's going on?' Rothko asked her.

'Nothing. I just can't *go* at the moment. Takes me a while.' And she held her stomach and sighed. '*Agony*. Honest to God.' And she believed it. So, Rothko had to believe it. But maybe she saw the confusion in their face. 'It's not fair on you,' she said, sitting back down. 'I just want you to be ok.' Her stammer was getting more pronounced as her emotions intensified, or maybe it was the fear of Rothko naming her behaviour that encouraged her to lose her thread a little. 'I just need to . . .' She struggled to start the next word. 'To. Get away some.' She struggled again. 'Somewhere. Where they can fix me.' She faltered. Tried again. 'I'm not doing.' She closed her eyes. 'Doing it on purpose sweetheart . . . But you . . .' She stretched her legs out in front of her. 'You think I want to live like this?' She started crying again but there were no tears this time, it was just her face that was crying. 'I'm trying my best.' She gagged and spluttered and punched herself in the legs. 'Where's your *loyalty*?' She broke off and her crying became a vacant, unreal laugh. Aretha was singing, 'I wish I didn't love you so.' Meg smoothed her hair back again. Regained composure. Smiled again.

'What a palarder.' She meant palaver, but she couldn't be told.

She went over to the records; lifted the needle on Aretha and dropped it on The Everly Brothers. She danced sadly side to side, looking through the nets, out to the street. Singing along. 'Whenever I want you, all I have to do is dream.'

She floated down to the red leather chesterfield, sat on the edge of it. Bird in a cage on a swing. 'Why don't you come and live with me?' She was staring at them. 'You could have Sky's old room. We could make it nice. Couldn't we? Put pictures up. We could cook dinner together and I could help you with your homework and . . .' She watched it play out around her. 'Come and live with me, I'd make sure you got into school and had your baths and got your dinners.' She was holding herself very upright. Her eyes were wide and hopeful, her face was tense and rigid with the monster it was containing.

'Live with you?' Rothko checked. 'Here?'

'Exactly,' She nodded, sagely. '*Exactly*.'

Rothko's phone went. It was Rosie P from the sixth form looking for a Henry.

They had about a ten draw left. They reckoned they could get away with selling that to Rosie P for twenty quid. She didn't know any better.

Meg was still staring at them. 'Will you think about it?'

'Yeah, alright.'

She seemed satisfied with that. Rothko focused on their coffee before they drank it. Ran their fingers against the grain of the wooden arm of their rocking chair.

Meg's stare was all encompassing. Her attention was swallowing them whole. They didn't like it when she fixated on them like this. Felt so claustrophobic.

They finally found the courage to ask. 'Are you using?'

She shook her head, and frowned, devastated. 'No.' Her face became a stage for a procession of studied emotions. 'No!' Crying again, without tears. 'No, I'm not *using*.' Horrified. Wounded. 'I can't do anything right. You think I'm disgusting . . . don't you? You're always punishing me. I just asked you to *live* here. Why would I do that if I . . .'

'Alright Mum. Alright.'

'It's not alright.'

She wouldn't drop it, now. Rothko knew this one by heart.

She would hound them until they apologised. But they didn't want to get sucked into it, so endless and oppressive. They stood to leave.

'I've got to go.'

'Why?' She feigned innocence. 'Don't leave? You've only just got here?' Her jaw was tense. 'You never come to see me.'

'Mum, come on.' Rothko grabbed their jacket and headed out the door.

'Come on, what?' she shouted after them. 'Why would you start a conversation then leave the room?'

They could hear her out the window as they walked past it, down the street. The breeze on their skin was sudden and fresh and they wished they were light enough for it to lift them up and carry them off over the rooves of the houses.

She'd promised.

It was their own fault for believing her.

Meg leaned over the low table, twitching in anticipation. Felt like five minutes since Rothko was two foot tall. Wobbly little storm cloud with their hair in their eyes. Drifting close behind Meg. Watching everything she did, so they could copy it when they thought she wasn't looking.

The thoughts were too big for her. Impossible to grasp. She rifled through her pockets for what she needed. Concentrated on peeling back the clingfilm, and the whole world shrank to the stone.

THREE

Rothko went down to the front and around the old harbour to get to Rosie P's. Rosie was a kind-of friend of Rothko's who lived with her mum and sister in one of the crumbling Victorian terraces that swayed heavily into the others, on a crowded lane in the old town.

They could still feel Meg's eyes, pushing against them. It always took a few hours to get back to normal after spending time with their mum.

She was the counterbalance to Ezra. As open as Rothko's dad was repressed. With his dissatisfaction and simmering insecurity, his pathological drive to achieve at all costs. At least Meg wore her wounds out in the open where everyone could see. Sure, she'd broken their heart more times than Rothko could count, but they knew she didn't mean to. And when it came to their mum, at least Rothko knew what they were dealing with. Dancing, swearing, nightmare. Causing a scene wherever she went. Full of empty promises and intense affection. A hopeless case that they couldn't escape. They knew where they were from when they watched her go to pieces over some little line in a song they'd never heard before. But they didn't want her to die alone on the floor. And if she was using again . . .

They passed a row of pink and grey stucco blocks, with balconies out to the sea. If they'd have looked up, they might have seen the face at the top flat window, where Angel Douglas leant her forehead against the glass. But Rothko didn't look up, they just kept pounding the pavement. And Angel didn't look down at the street, so she didn't see Rothko. Instead, she kept her eyes fixed on the murky swell as it stretched out into the distance and turned into the sky.

Angel had just got home from school. She went to the other school, the better one. She lived in a bright flat. White walls. Checked lino in the kitchen. Thin carpet in the bedrooms. Angel's mother Eileen kept it clean in daily fevers where she'd empty out the cupboards, turn the furniture, go dusting underneath.

She was in the front room. They had a dark wood dresser with a glass cabinet full of teacups that weren't for using. And on the old-fashioned couch, in floral-patterned dusty pink, her mum was lying on her back. Holding her head. The TV was on. Hollywood. Romance. Julia Roberts. The phone was ringing. Eileen was not answering because it could only be someone she didn't want to talk to. Family she'd pissed off or bills she couldn't pay.

'If that thing rings one more time, I swear I'm going to throw it in the sea.' It kept ringing. But she didn't move.

Angel was eating a packet of crisps, slowly, and looking out through the glass of the balcony doors at the sea beyond. Whenever Angel felt unsure, she slowed things down. Walking, speaking, cleaning her teeth, whatever it was. She placed one whole crisp in her mouth at a time, without breaking it. And waited for it to dissolve completely before reaching for another one. She didn't allow herself one suck or chew to hurry the process along.

She was still in her coat. She'd been unzipping her jacket,

one notch at a time since she got home from school an hour before. Still in her uniform. Pleated skirt, long socks, pinchy little shoes.

Eileen eased herself up, groaning as she swung her feet down and found her slippers. Holding her body in the places it hurt. Sides, back. Head. 'I'm banjaxed.'

Angel pushed her forehead into the glass and watched the sea move until she felt dizzy.

There were birds sitting on the tops of the waves. Riding up and down.

'Shoes,' Eileen demanded as she bustled to the kitchen. Angel heard her clanking the pans around and putting her music on.

Absorbed in the process of freeing her feet from her shoes without moving the rest of her body, Angel kept her eyes fixed on the seafront where she saw two women on mobility scooters approaching each other from opposite ends of the prom. They stopped to talk. One of them had souped their scooter up with chrome attachments and big handlebars like a Harley Davidson. She wore a fringed leather jacket, covered in badges. Angel would have liked to have had a mobility scooter. The other woman had her dog on her lap, all wrapped up in a tartan blanket. The dog was peeking out from under the blanket, hiding its ears from the wind. Angel would have liked to have a dog that sat on her lap. Dogs made mess though and they ran in the house and knocked things over, and they always tried to jump up and slobber on your face. Angel liked it when dogs jumped up. But her mum didn't like things like that.

It was raining again. It looked so nice to her the way the rain fell into the waves. She was trying to hear the sound it made through the double glazing by watching it, but there was too much noise inside.

Angel wished she had somewhere she belonged the way the rain had the sea.

Mariah Carey was on the stereo. It was thundering through the flat. Angel put her shoes where they belonged, and found Eileen in the kitchen, sleeves rolled up, eyes closed. Gesturing. 'I know you're shining down on me from heaven. Like so many friends we've lost upon the way.'

She sensed Angel at the doorway and turned to her, tears streaming, and held her in a brief dance.

Angel's sole purpose in life was to be whatever her mum needed her to be, moment by moment. If she could keep her mum happy, the two of them would be alright. Angel had learned to read her mum's moods and feelings better than her own.

Eileen broke the embrace, laughing, and went back to the stove where she had a pan bubbling. 'Sit down and eat your dinner now, you're getting skinny.'

Angel went out to the hallway, still unzipping her coat one notch at a time. Only three more notches to go. She was almost there, couldn't rush it, right at the end. Or she'd have to start all over again.

Eileen was shouting towards her, above Mariah Carey, above the TV, above the phone that was ringing again, 'She was a waitress, Angel! A *waitress*! Gave her demo to a customer!'

Outside Rosie's, in the rain, Rothko rubbed their hands together, fast, and shook them at the wrists. Rang the bell and turned to watch the street behind them as they waited at the door.

Rosie spoke with a lisp that Rothko suspected was put on; a kind of mock-fairy little-girlishness that Rothko found unnecessary at best, and at worst, straight up disturbing. She had long strands of green and pink running through her hair. She wore little tops and massive jeans that trailed down over her trainers; they were always ripped and wet at the bottoms. She was one of many girls who had a thing about Rothko. Who enjoyed their attention, or who found them interesting in a way that boys weren't. It rarely got to sex with these girls, it was more intense than that; hanging out for days at a time, speaking on the phone for hours, sleeping in each other's arms fully clothed. Maybe a couple of kisses goodbye when the day came. But then they'd get a boyfriend, and Rothko wouldn't hear from them for months.

Rothko was a person you could call for drugs if you didn't know anyone you could call for drugs. They didn't make any money, but they got theirs for free, picking up for people and taking bits off the top. They enjoyed the status it gave them. A pass to exist around people.

Rosie squealed when she saw them, opened her arms wide and they hugged hello. 'Squish me tighter,' she said, hanging on to them.

There was another girl hanging out at Rosie's. Rothko had seen her around and nodded at her.

Dionne Troy was sat on the floor, leaning back against the bottom of the couch. The curtains were closed, *Scream* was on the TV and the room smelled like Nag Champa.

Dionne was wearing a grey hoody with a black and white picture of the log lady from *Twin Peaks* on it and a little black flowery skirt. Her legs were stretched out in front of her. Her feet were bare, she had a plaited blue thread around her ankle, and her toenails were painted turquoise. Dark scars mauled the brown skin of her legs above her knees and around her thighs, each as thick as a little finger. She looked at Rothko. Eyeliner curved up from the corners of her eyes. High cheekbones. Half a smile rising from her lips. She looked like a pharaoh. Everything about her was assured, except the scars.

She had a pack of tarot cards in her hand, and she was studying the pictures as she shuffled through. She shoved herself over a bit and Rothko sat beside her, their back against the bottom of the couch. They lifted their shirt and rested their hand on the warmth of their belly in a gesture of confidence they had learned from observing their best mate, Sean, but realised that doing it made them feel exposed. So, they pulled their shirt back down and put their hand in their trouser pockets instead.

'What you saying?' Rothko asked Rosie.

'I'm *heartbroken*.' She stood in front of the TV, holding a bottle of Amaretto. Curly pink straw sticking out the top. She sucked on it. 'Mark. Just last week he was saying that I could have one of the puppies.' She scrunched her face up. 'He's such a prick.'

Rosie passed the bottle down to Dionne who settled it next to her and carried on looking at the pictures on the cards. 'These pictures are buff, man.'

'We're asking the cards if I should stay with him.' Rosie explained. 'They're my mum's.' She lay down on the couch behind Rothko and Dionne, legs stretched over the end. 'It's in my blood. We have the gift.'

Dionne fanned them, held them out to Rothko. 'Pick one?'

Rothko looked up, into her eyes. Felt like looking at the sea from the beach on a bright day and seeing all the way to the bottom.

'You have to ask a question,' Rosie told them.

'In my head or out loud?'

'Don't think it matters.' Dionne held the cards still and watched Rothko over the top of them.

'You can do it in your head if you want. You have to think it clearly though.' Rosie turned onto her side. 'So the cards can hear you.'

'What kind of question though?'

Rosie reached out, touched Rothko's hair from behind. Made Rothko pull away. 'Just something you want to know, that you can't figure out on your own?'

Will I ever make it out of here?

'Got it?' Dionne asked.

Yeah, Rothko had it. They moved their hand in front of the deck, looking for a feeling coming off a card. They settled on one. Pulled it slowly. *Am I ever going to get myself out of this place?*

'Nine of wands.' Dionne was looking at the image.

Rosie peered over her shoulder to look at the card in her hand. 'What do you think it means?'

Rothko laughed. 'I thought you had the gift?'

'I'm *learning*.' She stuck her tongue out. Dionne went looking through the booklet that taught the meanings and read out: 'Courage in the face of attack . . . A stability that cannot be removed.' She tilted her head to one side. 'Make sense to you?'

Rothko seemed unsure.

Dionne tried to unpack it for them. 'Think it's saying you've got a big fight ahead of you. And that you shouldn't give up. Maybe?'

Rothko looked, and she showed them the image of an exhausted fighter, still standing. 'I don't give up,' they told her. 'Got that part right.'

'What's your star sign?' Dionne asked.

'I know mine,' Rosie said. 'I'm a Pisces.' But Dionne stayed focused on Rothko and didn't acknowledge her friend. 'Pisces is the fish.' Rosie explained, reaching over Dionne for the Amaretto and bringing it back up to the couch with her. 'Fishes are creative and go with the flow. But how can I go with the flow, when things with Mark are so fucking *dramatic* all the time.'

'What day were you born?'

'April second,' Rothko told her.

'That's *tomorrow*!' Dionne turned her body a bit more towards them. Her head rested on Rosie's hip. Her eyes were calm, but they were fixed on Rothko and Rothko felt the heat of her fixation, the power of her attention to create a moment from whatever it landed on.

'It is tomorrow.'

'Aries,' Dionne told them. 'Fire sign.'

'Is that good?'

Rosie turned onto to her back and dangled her feet off the arm of the couch. Rothko reached into their sock for the draw and held it towards her.

'Here's your drugs, you criminal.'

Rosie caught Rothko's hand and took the wrap. She sang Cypress Hill: 'I want to get *high*. So *high*.' Opened the wrap and smelt it. 'Mmmmm.' She leaned down to Rothko. 'Moley? – Can you skin up for me please?' She draped her neck across Rothko's shoulder. 'You're so good at it.'

Rothko tutted at her. 'I know it's all you want me for.' They grabbed a cushion from the couch to make a table and set up to roll. Happiest when put to use.

'Aries people are honest. And passionate.' Dionne closed her eyes to remember the other things. 'Independent.' Rothko nodded along happily. 'Also impatient . . .' She opened her eyes again. 'Impulsive. Short tempered.'

'Oh what? It was all going so well.'

Rosie burrowed her face into the arm of the couch and said, 'I can't stop thinking about him.' Moaning in protest at the unfairness of the pain she was suffering, she dragged herself up and wandered out of the room and Dionne and Rothko were alone.

'Why does she call you Moley?' Dionne asked.

'My name's Molly. So.' Dionne nodded.

'But you like Rothko better?'

'It's just what people call me.'

'Why?'

Rothko licked the rizla gently. Smoothed it all down. 'You ask a lot of questions, don't you?'

Dionne shrugged. 'Only when I'm interested.'

Rothko smiled at that. 'Good to know you're interested.'

Rosie came bouncing back to the couch, lay down again, sighing. 'He didn't pick up.' Rothko examined their roll, it was alright. They put it down and started the next one. And they felt Rosie playing with the ends of their short ponytail again. 'Don't you ever take your hair down? You'd be so pretty if you took your hair down.' She was pulling her fingers through their tangled ends.

Rothko pulled their head away. A rigidness went through them that Dionne noticed. 'Get off,' they said, smiling. But there was fear in the smile, and they were starting to blush.

'Can we see? Can you take it down and just let us see? Don't be so prang!?' Rothko felt themself shrinking. 'Come on! Let me see! Dionne wants to see, don't you Dionne?' Rosie started to move as if to take Rothko's hair out.

Dionne reached for her leg and said, 'Can't you put some music on, I've seen this film so many times. It's getting boring.'

Rosie's attention was diverted but her hand stayed in Rothko's hair. 'What do you want to listen to?'

'Put that Skiba and Shabba one on?'

She let go of Rothko's ponytail and went over to the stereo. Kneeling at the tape player.

Rothko peeked out at Dionne, over the top of their blush. 'You like drum and bass, yeah?'

'I like the Darkside stuff, aint really feeling the Jump Up shit though.'

Rothko was impressed.

Rancid came blasting out the speakers. 'This is the tape Mark made for me,' Rosie danced over, hands in the air, twisting her body in a clumsy approximation of dancing that she'd learned from TV. 'He used to be so *sweet* to me. You lot don't *understand*.'

Dionne rolled her eyes. Stood to stretch, smiling down over her body at Rothko. 'Want a cup of tea?' Rothko shrugged for *nah, I'm alright*. Dionne left the room. Without realising they were doing it, Rothko turned their head to watch her go.

FOUR

The next day, they were older.

Sixteen. But what did it mean? They didn't know what they wanted from life. Just to get through a day was enough of an ask.

Coming up three p.m. and Rothko was perched on the railings at the bottom of the steps, watching the road. Soon enough, there he was.

Sean.

They felt their cheeks filling up with a smile as their best mate came bopping towards them, checking himself out in the windows of the cars.

Rothko admired their friend as he approached. In his black jeans, black Vans. Gold ganja leaf round his neck. He was letting his hair grow out and it was still at the awkward stage. Sean saw Rothko on the steps and quickened his pace.

He had a gloriousness about him. His big, thoughtful eyes, his clear, brown skin; everything *healthy*. Like it all accentuated the goodness of his energetic boyhood. He uplifted Rothko, the way he bought energy to whatever he engaged with. And Rothko loved him.

Sean had a lot of friends and was popular with girls. People didn't understand what he was doing hanging out with Rothko. How a boy and a girl could be friends like they were, without sex. But Sean liked Rothko. Always had, since they met one day round the back field blazing. He liked that she was who she seemed to be. He knew she was a weirdo. But Sean liked weirdos. He was one himself. It's just that nobody expected it of him. Too straight to be weird. Too good looking for the other kids to think about his personality. Apart from Rothko.

They jogged up the steps. Sean doing his fast feet from boxing practice, Rothko having to take two steps at a time to keep pace.

'Happy birthday, cuz!'

Rothko smiled into their collar.

'Where we going?' Sean was jogging backwards. Fast arms cutting at his sides.

'You're going to trip over.'

'I'm not.' He went faster backwards up the steps. Double time. 'Circle? Who's about?'

Sean tripped over his feet and fell backwards, catching himself just in time and skidding. The two of them locked eyes and bent double. Fell into a bout of rowdy laughter.

'Nooooooo,' Sean was clapping himself. 'Shame!'

'Ratings though. You didn't drop.'

They took the mud path that cut through the fields, heading to the meadows, the open hills that formed the borders of the town, where the misfits and wreck-heads assembled.

Edgecliff.

Rothko had grown up round the seafront clubs and bars, the ice cream parlours and fish and chip shops. Spent their summers dodging the pissed-up weekenders, fresh off the trains for a kiss and a dance and a vomit. Dug in for the quiet winters and the howling winds, stood around watching other people stand around, outside the pubs and dead ends and boatyards. They'd spent a lot of time alone, where the light was absorbed into the wet stone walls and the crates swayed in the teeth of the cranes and the wild rushes of the coastal path sang and the sheer cliff edge threw clumps of itself down on to the rocks below.

Sixteen years of it.

And they were lonely for a different kind of life.

Things for Rothko weren't as simple as they were for Sean. They couldn't just meet someone and see what happened. There was always this moment where they had to work out if a girl was into them or if she just wanted to be their friend. And then they had to work out when to tell them, and how to tell them what they were. However they played it, they couldn't deny it was *something*, and it was exhausting; the constant internal negotiation that was necessary for Rothko to exist around other human beings.

But it hadn't felt like that with Dionne.

School was a nightmare. And home was sad. They were spending more and more time just kicking around. It was Edgecliff that kept them, and they loved it for that. It was like a third parent to Rothko, as dysfunctional as their actual parents. But more predictable at least.

They reached the clearing they were aiming for and found a bunch of kids sitting on crates or skateboards or slumped against the low wall that bordered one side of the path. Fist bumps and brief hugs before they sat down. Rothko started skinning up, noticed Dionne a few people away and pointed a finger at her in recognition. Dionne grinned and winked.

'Oi, oi!' she called across the space between them, 'it's the Aries. Happy birthday!'

Dionne Troy.

There she was.

Even more beautiful the second time seeing her. Gemstone in her belly button, exhaustion in her eyes. Smiling at Rothko. Rothko smiled back and it felt like dancing. *She remembered.* She stretched over towards them with a can of K cider. Rothko reached and took it.

'Thanks Dionne,' they said. Dionne blew them a kiss.

'Is it your birthday?' another girl asked.

They nodded it was.

'How old are you?'

'Sixteen.'

Everyone laughed and blew smoke out of their mouths and Dionne said,

'You're a little baby!' Rothko smiled at her.

'That's not what you said last night.' And everyone laughed again, and Dionne threw a lighter at them. Rothko ducked it and picked it up and said, 'Mine now.' Dionne got up and wrestled them for it.

'No, it aint yours now.' She got it out of their hands. 'Better luck next time,' she said as she walked back over to her cotch, swinging her hips in victory.

Sean nudged their side, 'I think she likes you.' Rothko blushed.

'Nah man. It's not like that.'

Sean clutched his heart and fell backwards to the floor.

'Allow it,' Rothko pleaded with him.

'That you, yeah?' He got up onto his elbow and pushed Rothko's knee. 'How do you know her anyway?' Sean asked quietly.

'I just met her yesterday.'

Sean looked down over his nose as if he had glasses perched on the end of it. He was trying, in his own way, to give his friend some confidence. 'She likes you,' he nodded.

A few kids rolled up with a speaker in a trolley. Rothko swapped a draw for a couple of pills and some mushrooms. Sean dug around in his bag and pulled out two bottles of screw-top rosé. 'What? They was on offer. It was all I could get.'

Some of them were dancing by the speaker in a little group and some of them were skating the railings but most people were just sitting around. Dionne kept smiling over at Rothko.

By the time the sun was going down, everyone was battered. Rothko downed a massive glug of rosé, burned half a zoot in one fierce puff and held their breath while Sean lifted them up in his arms and spun them as fast as he could, arms wrapped around Rothko's chest. Round and round and round. When he let go Rothko fell on the floor, laughing and rushing hard. Coming up fresh from their pills and the smoke, nodding their head up and down to the music and kicking their legs out behind them, laughing. Everyone was laughing.

A few of the skateboard kids were stood in a line, taking turns to jump over a pile of beer crates, and they kept falling on the floor and rolling into each other and knocking the crates over and getting up and doing it again. Rothko turned on to their side in the grass and watched as the bodies jumped and kicked the crates, and they felt the strands of the dark grass in their hands as they pushed themself up to standing. Stood. Watched Dionne, the other side of the crowd. Ripples of laughter still on their breath. They walked over and came to a stop next to her. She was stood with her weight on one leg, hand on her hip. Smoking a menthol cigarette, drinking her cider, looking so pretty and so full of trouble.

It felt good to stand next to her. She looked sideways at them, held their eyes in hers. Then looked away. She reached for their hand and started playing with it, running the tip of her index finger along the lines of Rothko's palm and the force of the feeling from Dionne touching their skin was so strong, it was like passing out.

The night came on. A couple of the older lot built a fire. Two of the skaters that had been jumping the crates started trying to jump over the flames. Screaming when it burnt their legs. Laughing. Doing it again. Everyone laughing. Little Peanut; curly ginger hair, skinny as a blade. In her bra and trackies, her beanie hat pulled down to her eyebrows, had the trolley with the speaker in it and was running it round in a big circle and dancing with it as it went. Shy FX. 'Original Nuttah'.

Rothko followed Sean and a few others, away from the main group, talking in a low buzz, drinking their wine, looking at the stars. Everything was dripping through a fine mesh.

Out of the firelight and moving bodies and spouts of laughter, Dionne walked towards them. She stopped in front of them, and they faced each other for a moment. The voices around Rothko dropped to a single tone. They lost themself in the ink of her eyes, the run of her neck and her chin tipped up like she was getting the measure of them. She stepped closer and Rothko felt their bodies touching. Hardly touching. Touching again.

'You're too cool for me,' she said. And then she kissed them. Caught their lip in her teeth and pushed till the world made sense. The softness of her body giving as Rothko pushed towards her pushing. She held their shoulders and their neck in her hot, blunt fingers, pulled them into her. Rothko in two t-shirts, two hoodies, trackies underneath their jeans, wrapped against the world, felt naked. Stood there in the kiss not knowing how to return it, not knowing how not to return it.

FIVE

That's when time changed for Rothko.

Days went by in a daze of Dionne. Every afternoon, Rothko waited at the meadows to see if she'd show up. And when she did, they stayed beside each other the whole time. And the weeks rolled into each other like the verses of an endless song. They'd only just met, but they got each other. And everything was theirs.

She was a couple of years older than Rothko, but only one school year above them. She'd had to retake after problems at home, and her eighteen-ness gave her status among her school friends that Rothko understood was something she didn't want to jeopardise by being seen hanging out with them. She never said that herself. All she said was, it's nobody's fucking business, but whatever the reason for it, at school, they acted like they barely knew each other.

Up the meadows it was a different world with different rules. They could just be two more bodies in a crowd of bodies piled up, jumping over things. And most nights, when it was time to roll, Dionne liked Rothko walking her home.

Some nights, though, Dionne didn't want to be walked home, she wanted to stay out with the older lot, who took her to clubs that Rothko couldn't get into and raced their bangers down the coast road. Or some nights she'd leave in one of the older boys' cars without saying goodbye and then she'd just disappear, and Rothko would notice too late she was gone. And sometimes, when they were up the circle, Dionne would go off in the bushes with one of the boys. When she did that, Rothko waited for her. Kept guard so that no one interrupted. Face hot and red. They wished it was them in the bushes with her. Then she'd come out, wiping her mouth and pulling her skirt down and she'd giggle and take Rothko's hand, and they'd run very fast together and fall down and she'd curl up in their arms and hold them tight.

It was love in a way. Or at least, something like it.

But back behind their desk at school, the love they felt for Dionne was music through the walls. Somebody else's party. Rothko waited out the painful minutes, staring into space. They knew her timetable by heart. Skipped class to wait around in the corridors, for the moment when they knew they might catch a glimpse of her.

The year 12 and 13 bit, where Dionne spent her days, was based in its own separate block, separated from the main school building by a bleak concrete yard. People in her year didn't have to wear uniform or be in at the same times as the rest of the school. They occupied their own airspace. Supercharged. If Rothko played it right, their paths might cross at break times. Or in the minutes between lessons.

Rothko, in year 11, was almost done with school. Just the exams left to get through. But no one expected much from them. Least of all themself. They swam through the building, smoking the days down in hasty cigarettes, cupped in grubby fists, kicking a tennis ball around behind the science labs, knowing exactly where to be to feel her wash the day in golden light as she passed them without slowing down. That tiny smile was enough to make the world exist. For the pulse that passed between them when Dionne walked towards them and Rothko, against the lockers, looked up and watched her coming closer. They didn't speak or smile. Just stared, tried not to stare. Their secret world so loud it drowned the real world out. And Dionne looked and looked away and looked again and looked away and the school disappeared and slowed right down, and it all sounded like the lowest note on a piano.

A month into meeting, one night under sweaty clouds, as Rothko walked her home, Dionne stopped in front of the entrance to the flats and said, 'I don't want you to go.'

And so, they didn't.

Dionne lived in the yellow-brick flats. Low-rise blocks, four storeys high. Built around communal grass. Red tarmac behind bent railings. Swings with the chains all knotted. Bright yellow slide coming out of the mouth of a painted caterpillar. The blocks were connected by underpasses and archways. Heavy doors with rows of buzzers. Flower boxes on the railings. Kids' bikes on the balconies. Voices bouncing in the stairwells. Concrete steps worn smooth in the middle.

'Mum?' Dionne shouted as they went in. Rothko heard her mum shout back.

'I'm in the bath. Hang on.' And there were nice smells of bubble bath coming down the hallway.

'I've got a friend here.'

'Alright, babe. Give me a *minute*.'

Her home was unlike Rothko's home in every way. For a start, there were things all over the shelves and pictures stuck up on the walls. Rothko's house didn't have any pictures up. Ezra didn't want the clutter.

Dionne's flat was smaller than Rothko's house, but it didn't feel small to Rothko. It felt colourful and warm.

Rothko knew that Dionne's mother, Agnes, worked at the

ferries and she also made jewellery which she sold. Everything was carefully arranged. Her jewellery-making stuff was packed away in lots of little drawers, labelled in her curly handwriting. There were plants growing on top of cupboards and the leaves trickled down the walls. There were yellow blinds on the windows. A calendar on the fridge with black and white photographs of jazz legends. This month it was John Coltrane.

Dionne led Rothko into her room, and Rothko liked it as soon as they stepped through the door. It smelt like her. There were bunches of roses hanging upside down, drying. The walls were dark purple. She had a make-up bag and perfume and a big mirror. She had a print stuck on the wall of two women kissing in stilettos and a huge poster of Tupac.

Above the bed, she had a framed A4 photograph of a handsome, smiling man sitting in a big flowery armchair with a newborn baby in his arms.

They fell back on to the bed. Next to each other. Dionne kissed herself close and reached under their t-shirt to touch their skin. Her hands found Rothko's bra. Seemed strange to her. Light purple, little bow in the middle. It looked young and not like it belonged to Rothko. Her hand moved over their belly and pushed underneath the waistband of their joggers, she felt the little bows on the top of their matching knickers. Big, childish pants with a frilly edge. Rothko was not enjoying Dionne's exploration of their body. They liked touching her, but they did not like being touched. They felt exposed by it. Vulnerable. They looked down from above, at themself on a bed with a girl's hand going over their skin, and discovered as Dionne did that they had a body.

'Do you like these?' she asked, touching the top of their knickers.

'Never really thought about it.'

'Where did you get them from?'

'Dad's girlfriend. Wendy. She buys them and leaves them in my room.'

'Why?'

Rothko was looking at Dionne's hand as it sought them out. Hating it. Dionne looking at the truth of them, forced them to see it too. But they buried their discomfort. They were good at doing that. 'Don't like going shopping.'

'What's worse though? Shopping or these knickers?'

Rothko laughed, squirming. 'You're right, yeah. Sorry.' They looked away from the terror of Dionne's hand, stared up at the ceiling instead, trying to settle their nerves. She was watching them with an interest that Rothko found painful. They blushed so hard Dionne could feel it in her own cheeks.

Agnes knocked, the two pulled apart and sat up, away from each other. She peered her head round the door and saw them scurrying to opposite sides of the bed.

'Hello. I'm all clean.' Agnes was a wide-hips, knowing-laugh and easy-movement kind of person, comfortable in her own skin. She wore tight trousers and little strappy sandals. 'Bit early for bed, isn't it?'

'This is Rothko, from school.'

'Hello Rothko from school.' She had a knowing look in her eye as she surveyed the two of them.

'Mum? What?'

'Nothing. Me? No. I know when I'm not wanted.' And she went back to the other room.

Dionne rolled her eyes. But Rothko thought it was a lovely thing for her mum to have come and checked on her like that. 'Let's go outside and bun one.'

Outside, the sun was going down. All day it had been salty and hot and now the evening light was calming the sky. They sat on the swings in the playground outside the block. Next to each other, facing opposite directions, so they could watch each other, pushing their swings back and forth.

'Is that your dad in the picture by your bed?' Rothko asked, lightly. Dionne nodded. 'What was he like?'

She lit the zoot. Inhaled. 'He was funny. Like you are.' She smiled it. The smile sweetened her voice.

'You think I'm funny?'

'Yeah.' She put her head on the side when she said it. Temple resting on the chain of the swing.

'Like, funny laugh *at* me or funny laugh *with* me?'

'Both.' She stopped swinging. Toes on the tarmac. 'He'd have liked you, I think. You remind me of him.'

'Do I? In what way?'

'Something.' She took another draw. Let the smoke out between her teeth. 'Something about you.'

Rothko leant their head on the chain of their swing, mirroring her. 'How did it happen, D?'

She spoke in a measured way. 'Car crash.' Aimed her words in a straight line out of her mouth. 'Someone stole a car and was driving it the wrong way down the fucking. You know the big roads by the saver centre? Fucked.'

They were quiet with their thoughts a while. She carried on.

'I was messed up bad after it happened. That's why they held me back a year. I'm better with it now. Sometimes I get a whole week where I haven't thought about him. Then I feel guilty.' She pushed her hair back, out of her eyes. 'Worst thing of it is. Like. I just think, in the moment, did he know? How long did he have to think, like . . . there's nothing I can do? Do you know what I mean? Like, that's the *worst* part of it. To think of him scared. Or sad to leave me, or. Like the last thing he felt. You know what I'm saying?'

They passed the zoot. Deep draws in and slow breaths out.

Rothko's voice was low and smoky. 'I see this thing on telly. About near-death experiences.' They scratched at their cheeks, held on to their chin. 'Like, about people coming back from like, heart stopped, dead. And they come back.'

Dionne was listening, waiting for them to keep going.

'*All* of them, right? Whatever it was. One got shot. One had a heart attack. Fucking. One of them woke up on the fucking table. Like, operation gone wrong – don't matter *how* scary it was. What's it? Parachute failure one of them.'

She liked listening to them describing things. The way they picked out the important syllables with a pointing finger.

'Anyway. Point is, they *all* said the *same* thing. Like. They felt this deep sense of peace. Just, bare *peaceful*. Wherever it was they went. They felt a *lightness* they'd never known in their whole lives up to that point.'

She breathed out through her nose. Flicked the lighter a few times and watched the flame. 'Thanks for saying that,' she said. And Rothko nodded, pleased for having said the right thing. 'I've still got his texts in my phone.' It felt so final.

Rothko reached for Dionne's hand. She gave it to them. And they sat like that, holding hands, feeling the details in each other's skin. Pushing themselves backwards a little. Forwards a little. Slowly. Until loud voices came rattling down the street and Dionne pulled her hand away.

Big bunch of kids, kicking a football between them. About their age.

'Alright Dionne,' one of the girls greeted her. Dionne reached out to spud a couple of them, as they stood around them by the swings. A space opened between Rothko and Dionne that hadn't been there before.

'What you lot doing?' Dionne asked.

'Going down Andy's.' Rothko felt eyes on them. 'You coming?'

She shook her head. 'Nah, I'm going in.'

The boys were screaming high-pitched laughter as they kicked the football as hard as they could at each other's heads. One of them had lost his trainer from the effort and was running round in his sock.

'Don't try it,' he was saying. 'I'll fucking . . .' Hopping in his socked foot towards his missing shoe. But someone else got there first and threw it over the fence.

Rothko smiled vaguely. As if they were a part of things.

'Where *you* from?' one of the boys said, looking at Rothko. Gold Nike tick in his ear. Tramlines in his eyebrow.

'Round here,' Rothko told him. Looking up and out from under their forehead.

'Where, round here?' The boy came closer. 'What block?'

Rothko looked to Dionne. 'What you looking at her for, I'm talking to you.' The switch in energy engaged everyone's attention. Rothko got up off the swing. The boy pushed them back down. 'What you standing up for? Pussyhole. What you got for me?'

'Leave it,' one of the girls said.

'Who you talking to?' The boy frowned at her; chest puffed up, full of cartoonish power.

'It's a girl, you dickhead.' The girl tutted at him, and the boy covered his mouth with his hands.

'*Whaaaaaat*?' He jumped back, physically shocked. 'Don't lie!' Rothko tried to hold their nerve but it was short-circuiting. 'Are you a girl?'

'Yeah,' Rothko told him.

'I was going to bang you out!' the boy said. 'Sorry. Nah. Sorry.' And he started laughing, high-pitched pretend laughing. 'Bruv, I thought it was a boy you know.' Gesturing like it was the funniest thing in the world.

'He thought it was a boy!'

Dionne stood up. 'Come,' she beckoned Rothko. 'See you later, you lot.' She walked out of the playground. Rothko following behind. Whole face red. Limbs not behaving normally, too heavy.

'Bye,' the girls shouted after them. Laughing.

'It looks like a boy though, innit?' Rothko heard one of them saying. 'I was about to jack her up!'

'You couldn't jack your mum.'

'Why you talking about my mum though?'

Dionne and Rothko ducked under the archway that cut through the block. Out to the road. Rothko tried to keep their face under control. They turned left and walked around the flats, pacing it, until Dionne took a turning and they followed her down an overgrown alleyway that ran between the back gardens of the ground floor flats of two adjacent blocks. It was a few foot wide. One side had wooden fencing, the other was green chain-link. The alley was full of weeds, unpaved. The weeds grew tall, thick with little blue and white flowers. A few boughs drooped over the fence from the gardens beyond. There was a concrete patch of ground about halfway down where rubbish had been left. A few palettes stacked against the wooden fence. An old tapestry couch. Tassels hanging off the bottom. A big sack of local newspapers. A splintered TV table with a leg missing. A couple of old car tyres.

Dionne looked back at Rothko, who was walking a foot behind. 'Sorry about them lot.'

Rothko laughed it off. She brushed a few leaves off the couch, and they kicked back. It was upholstered in a heavy, patterned material. Might have been grand once, but not anymore. Curved wooden arms and legs.

'I hate everyone.' Dionne rested her head on Rothko's shoulder. 'Everyone can die, except you.' She held their arm and ran her fingers up and down it. Rothko turned their face to the side and gave her their full attention. Time hung gently from the chain-link fencing and music came through the open windows above. It was almost dark.

'I like it here.' Rothko spoke quietly.

'Me too.'

Dionne mapped shapes on Rothko's face with her fingertips. The world shrank down to the barest movements. All things began and ended in the touch. She moved herself closer towards them and opened her mouth against their lips and she kissed them like there was nothing wrong with them.

But underneath their clothes were their stupid pants and stupid bra, and underneath those things, worse, was a body. Not theirs, really. Didn't have anything to do with *them*, who they were. But there it was. It was the thing they lived in, that stood for their spirit out there in the world. But it had got them all wrong.

Rothko broke away from the kiss. 'I've got to go,' they told her. She seemed upset.

'I don't want you to.'

'I know.' They started getting up. 'But I need to get home.' They left the quiet of the alleyway and said goodbye on the main road.

'Next time though, will you stay the night?' She was

looking at them for an answer. But Rothko didn't want to be looked at anymore.

Walking fast. Past the football pitches and steel fabricators, down under the railway arches, past the empty shops and the long blank roads of post-war houses that backed on to the allotments. They weren't going home. They didn't want to sit in an empty house and watch TV.

They turned onto a beige cul-de-sac and whistled at the window round the back of Sean's until he stuck his head out.

'What you doing?' Rothko shouted up.

'Nothing. I'll come down.'

Sean opened the door, and they spudded each other, and went upstairs to his room. Sean's stepdad Derek was cooking something in the kitchen. He was a sweet man. Built like a bouncer. Bald headed, bearded, smiley. He didn't speak much but when he did, his voice was kind. He liked to cross the kitchen floor by sliding in his socks when his missus wasn't looking. He had the oven open, he waved at Rothko as they climbed the stairs, his attention fixed on his roasting pan. Sean's baby brother shouted happily in his highchair.

Rothko felt calm in Sean's room. Big posters up. Bruce Lee in *Enter the Dragon*. Lara Croft in *Tomb Raider*. An alien making a peace sign, saying *take me to your dealer.* And a black and white print of Mohammad Ali, gloves raised, and across the image a quote, in capitals, *the best way to make your dreams come true is to wake up*.

Rothko lay down on the little couch they had helped Sean drag in from the street last year and kicked off their trainers. Sean was playing *Grand Theft Auto 3*. A lava lamp blobbed away in the corner. He slid a big pub ashtray over the low table towards Rothko and Rothko lifted the half spliff out and putted away at it gratefully. Ten minutes went past.

'Mind if I kip here?' Rothko asked through smoke. Sean paused the game and stood to rifle through his wardrobe. He grabbed the sleeping bag that was wedged in the top and chucked it over. Rothko caught it and Sean settled himself back down to restart his game. 'Badman, yeah?' he said to the screen. 'Shut your mouth.' He tapped on his control pad and made the character he was playing hold up a passing car, drag the driver out. 'Want some?' he was saying. 'Have some of *that.* Pussyhole.' His character got into the car and started driving. Sean flicked through the radio stations. Found The Pointer Sisters, 'Automatic'. Got into it. 'You come on a good night,' he said. 'Del's cooking. He always makes loads.'

They ate in front of the TV with Sean's two sisters and Sean's mum, Debs. They watched game shows and Debs got all the answers right. Rothko barely spoke a word. Just sat there feeling like they shouldn't be there and like everyone wanted them to leave. After dinner, Sean did the dishes and Rothko dried up while Derek had a smoke in the back yard. Sean's sisters did their homework in front of the TV, Debs left for her nightshift and Rothko thought, *this is what a family feels like.* The baby woke up and Sean went to comfort him. Derek popped his head in through the back door, his body still out in the yard.

'Sean went to get him.' Rothko said.

'Ah good.' Derek came in and closed the back door behind him, listening at the baby monitor; he heard Sean shushing the baby in a sing-song voice. 'You can stay as long as you like, alright? You're welcome here.' Rothko started to blush. 'There's already enough of us, we'll barely notice another one.'

The kindness of it made them feel ugly.

Morning came through the curtains. Rothko blinked and rubbed their face. Sean had gone out early for boxing training. Left Rothko sleeping in his room. They woke up strange.

Downstairs, no one was in. They walked slowly through the front room. Left behind as usual.

They felt like everything was speaking. The roller skates in the corner. The schoolbooks on the table by the telly. The big gold heart picture frame with Derek and Debs arm in arm, red cheeked and smiling at the finishing flag of a sponsored run, in matching Cancer Research t-shirts. Rothko opened a few drawers, looked inside, thinking *this is what people's lives are like*. One of the drawers was full of medication. Boxes and boxes of pills made out to Deborah Hammond.

Rothko knew she was sick; she had been for a while. Sean didn't go into details. But that day they'd been sitting down by the pier, just the two of them, and Rothko had wrapped their heavy arms round Sean's back and held him while he cried about it.

Rothko picked up some of the boxes. Read the complicated names and it hit home that it was real. That maybe she was going to die.

Sevredol, they read. *Morphine sulphate.*

They weighed the box in their hand. Tried to feel it's power. But could not.

This little white box of pain relief, that looked so clean and efficient, how could this be the same thing as the darkness that lived inside their mum?

Can cause addiction.

This was what she'd chosen over them.

It came in shadow scenes that played around them as they stood in Sean's quiet front room. All the times she'd got clean then gone back, then got clean then gone back and all the lies. Betrayals that Meg would not acknowledge as betrayals. Promises that never came good. All the pretty dreams she weaved and how Rothko loved to watch her weaving. And the sadness of knowing who she was in her heart, and who she was in the world, were so far apart. And never knowing which one was real. The mum who said she loved them, or the mum who did the things that Meg did when she was using.

And it was all for this.

They didn't choose to, or mean to, or even know they were going to, it was only as they pushed the box of pills into their pocket, that they realised they had.

They closed the drawer. They looked around the quiet room again. And then they left.

Back at home, in their room, they swallowed one of the pills and waited to feel different. Felt like ages, but nothing much was happening. So, they swallowed again. And time tied them to its anchor and sank them to its bed. Time held them by the ankles and filled their swimming head with the tangles of its thread. A warmth that choked them as it spread, they relinquished. Their body going slow. Going inwards. Growing old. Growing limp. Going down. They saw themself reaching, chubby little fingers, taking hold of Mum's hand, at the crossing, blowing kisses to the people as they sped into the distance. Is it real, or isn't it? Can't figure the spinning out, the ground is the ceiling, but the ceiling is a moving mouth. Swerving the corners, saying smile like it's summer, at the border of a different life, everything is gorgeous if you want it you can move your moving hand but nothing's moving and the ground is all consuming and it's swallowing their throat, they can see a darkness looming and they want to stop the booming in their ears but the wave breaks over their boat and overturns them. Diving, sinking under weights, down deep. Underneath. Shadows and teeth and slow movement. No music down here, no weather no people no measure no need to keep feeling just ease into dreaming and

'Home.' Ezra shouted as he came through the door. But no one replied. He picked up the bills from the mat and headed to the kitchen, where he opened the cupboards and stood for a while, looking at the nothing inside them. Maybe he'd treat her to a takeaway. Watch some big dumb action movie.

He jogged up the stairs to her room. Called her name a few times. Knocked on her door and pushed it open. 'You in?'

But what he saw sucked language right out of him. She was passed out face down on the floor. He tried to rouse her. 'Rothko?' She wasn't responsive. He shook her shoulder. Turned her face towards him. His heart was stuck with dread, it wouldn't beat, the terror of the feeling was complete and overwhelming. He picked her body up into his arms, shouting her name. She was so heavy. Eyes closed, he opened them, slapping at her cheeks. 'Roth, please?' Calling the ambulance and talking to the woman on the phone, saying *but how long will you be? Come now. You have to come now. I don't think she's breathing. I could get her in the car but won't she be safer in the . . .* He dragged himself to standing and pulled her, with his hands underneath her armpits, down towards the car.

Stroking her face as he went, saying, 'You're just fine, sweetheart. You'll be ok.' But the woman on the phone saying *stay there* and him saying *how long?* and his heart was a scream, and it hurt all through him and the scream said *that's my baby*, and *she's not breathing*. And *how can I protect her from a thing I can't see?*

*

Waiting it out on the hospital ward, sick with adrenaline. Shaking. The shock. He stopped himself pacing. Forced himself to sit down.

He could still feel her, a year old. The warmth of her, asleep on his body.

He could still remember every detail.

It had been pissing it down the night she was born. This very hospital, two in the morning. Two in the afternoon before she'd finally arrived.

He'd been through it before with Sarai, but he still wasn't really prepared to witness the effort it took. The more pain Meg was in, the less sound she made, but he could see it in her face. Laid out on the bed, her hair black as print and her silent mouth hanging open on the pillow and the thinness of her skin and the smallness of her when she wasn't towering over him, full of despair.

He kept telling her how well she was doing. He had this wracking fear she was going to die. She was calm, he was panicking. She told him to piss off for a bit. He went to get coffee.

In the waiting room, the TV was on. It was the riots in Strangeways. He watched those men on the roof. Awestruck. Breaking the place apart with t-shirts wrapped around their heads, hanging banners out the windows saying *We want to talk to MPs*. He stood there in the waiting room for the whole broadcast, neck craned up at the TV hanging from the ceiling.

The footage cut to fire raging through the ugly prison. He felt like it was holy fire.

He had known men who had been in there. Fucking place. He'd heard the stories. Locked up twenty-three hours a day. Routinely beaten. Three in a cell designed for one. Force-fed anti-psychotics. Injected with sedatives to shut them up. No wonder they were ripping the place apart. Good for them.

The news cameras were showing the fire licking through the prison windows. It was a redeeming fire. Just like his baby was going to be. A new life, a new chance to make things right with Meg. If these men could do all this, he must have been able to keep his family together.

He had to get his life under control.

His body was watery with hope as he watched them, ripping tiles off the roof and pelting them down at the screws below. Legs and arms and torsos. Bodies. Such unsurprising, usual things but push them hard enough and they could be capable of incredible feats. Like childbirth. Or ripping steel doors off.

For the first time in a long time, he dropped his head and prayed. The first prayer that came to mind was the one he used to have to say on Yom Kippur. *Forgive us, please. Forgiving God.* Ezra sat in the waiting room, alone, offering God a list of sins. And asking for atonement.

And then she was born.

He held her close to his face, eyes closed, to sense her.

She was his youngest. His baby daughter. Someone he loved more than he'd ever loved anyone. The profound feeling of setting another human being before yourself that Ezra had only ever felt when he looked into the eyes of his children.

But somehow this person who came into his life to teach him what real love could feel like, this child he swore he would never let come to any harm, had drifted so far away from him, he couldn't reach her. He hadn't been there when she needed him.

He remembered her at seven years old, after Meg left, when she had got obsessed with whales for a year or two. She had that big hardback book, full of photographs and diagrams that she used to read from all the time. Spread out in front of her wherever she sat. 'This one is a humpback,' she would explain to him. While he fussed round the kitchen trying to get them all fed. Not listening. 'They travel 3,000 miles each year. Far, far out in the ocean. When the mum one sings to its child, they can be thousands of miles apart, and the child will still know it's their mum by the song.'

How long had she been passed out on the floor like that?

He could see her slumped body everywhere he looked.

He wished he'd listened better to every word she'd ever said.

Ezra dropped his head and prayed, just like he had when she'd been born. 'We have sinned against You through empty promises,' he whispered, and his voice was hoarse and hesitant, 'and we have sinned against You through baseless hatred.' It had been a long time, but he found the words, or they found him. 'We have sinned against You by betraying trust, and we have sinned against You by succumbing to confusion.' His eyes were hot and he was tapping his chest with his hand the way he'd been taught. 'For all these sins, forgiving God, forgive us, pardon us, grant us atonement.'

And God made Himself known in the softly spoken doctor with her glasses in her hand, leaning in to tell Ezra that his daughter had pulled through, and that he could take her home now.

The school had to be notified. The police sent a uniform round and she sat in the front room, ticking boxes on a questionnaire. There were visits from the mental health team. Appointments on the phone with the child-safety people. The atmosphere was claustrophobic. Ezra found himself peering through Rothko's bedroom door at intervals throughout the night, listening for breath. Guilt like a pulled tendon.

Rothko's only escape from Ezra's overbearing presence was to lose themself in schoolwork. They were meant to be on study leave, so they gave themself entirely to revising things they'd never learned in the first place. But since hospital, intrusive thoughts had been accelerating out of everything they looked at. Each day they had to fight harder not to surrender entirely to that itchy sensation, that asked them what would really happen though, if they just threw themself headfirst into the traffic. Or turned a cup of boiling hot tea over their own head. They felt embarrassed and afraid thinking of what they'd done. Didn't want anyone at school to know anything.

Ezra and Rothko spun in wide orbits around their shared secret, two planets, looming. Felt its awesome heat at each swerve of their ellipses. The nearly having lost each other filled the air between them with a new kind of quiet. Ezra hurried back from work in the evenings, allergic to his own thoughts, and desperate not to waste any more time. But after three weeks of it, Ezra was annoyed with the mental health team sticking their disapproving noses in. She had her exams to sit. A future to consider. Seemed to Ezra the best thing for everyone would have been to stop talking about it all the time and let the poor kid move on.

May was an airless chamber. Each movement noticed and logged. But eventually Rothko was allowed out again. They sat their exams alone in the pupil referral unit, supervised by the school counsellor, Gerald. With his ID card hung around his neck, laminated at his own expense. Dressed in the red hoody, faded jeans and scuffed Adidas that screamed out *call me Gerry*. Rothko liked him. He let them take breaks for fags and made them watery hot chocolates.

Friday at last. Five weeks after they went down under the pills, they were up the meadows again, lazing in the grass, scanning the horizon, when they saw Sean's familiar frame on the approach. It was the first time Rothko had seen him since.

Sean didn't know about the overdose. Nobody did. Rothko wanted to keep it that way. Sean just figured Rothko had been skipping school as usual. That's why he hadn't seen them around. They watched him, silhouetted against the setting sun, and they felt the thud of his footsteps travelling through the dirt. He stopped in front of them, but didn't smile. Rothko raised their hand and Sean tapped it, but Rothko knew something was different. They wanted to look him in the eye, but it was hard.

He sat for ages, keeping quiet. Knees pulled up to his chest. Felt like he was working himself up to saying something. Eventually, the others they were with moved on and the two of them were left alone together.

'You've got the shakes, mate.' Sean pointed to Rothko's hands. They were pulling up clumps of grass and fiddling with the stems.

'I haven't.' Rothko flicked the grass away and put their hands in their pockets.

'What's going on with you?'

'Nothing.'

Sean sat back on his hands, stretched his legs out in front of him. 'I know it was you.' He stared at them, confusion in his eyes, waiting for a confession. Rothko held the silence. 'Just own up to it?'

'Own up to what?'

'You're making it *worse* man.' The tone of his voice was the hardest thing for Rothko to take about the whole exchange. He was speaking to them so gently. Even after what Rothko had done, Sean was still taking it easy on them. 'You know my mum's sick . . .' He gave up. The conversation wasn't comfortable for him. 'She's in pain. All the time. Those pills are for the pain. You think she wouldn't notice them just going missing like that?'

Rothko clenched their jaw. They felt their head start going. Their skin was prickling.

'Ever since you been knocking around with that Dionne . . .'

Sean turned so he was looking directly at Rothko, but Rothko couldn't bear to see their best friend's face looking at them, in so much pain and with so much disgust. 'You stole from my family.'

Rothko's hearing went funny. A high ringing in the left. The rest a slack net. Thudding lapse of sound that consumed their inner ear. They said nothing. Better that, than try to explain it away, and have Sean think they were playing him for pity.

They didn't want to talk about the overdose, the hospital. It had been too late to explain for ages, how that little box in the drawer had felt like the only way out of the years spent waiting for their mum to stop lying to their face. A direct line to her heart. They hadn't thought about who or what the pills were really for. Until right now.

Sean couldn't handle it. How could they just sit there, ignoring him? He waited it out as long as he could. Until finally, he stood up. Sighing loudly. 'If that's how you're being.'

Rothko squinted up at him. Swallowed. Found their voice. 'Sorry,' they said at last. But there was nothing else they could think of to say.

'What, that's it?' He waited, loudly, for Rothko to take the weight off him. But Rothko had gone back to looking the other way. They wanted to tell him so many things, but they didn't know how to. Everything jammed shut in their head. Rothko had learned it was possible to still love a person, even if you hated what they did. They were waiting for Sean to stop being annoyed about it, and for things to go back to normal. But the more they ignored him, the angrier it made him. Until he thought he might hit Rothko if he didn't get away. 'You stole from my family.' He said it again, but this time there was less fury in his voice, and more sorrow.

He walked off. And Rothko was left on their own.

It was their first heartbreak.

And they'd done it to themself.

SIX

Rothko didn't want to be alone after that. They attached themself to a group of kids they kind of knew, and stayed out, drinking until things felt interesting. There was always something going on somewhere. Waiting for Dionne on the midnight beach. Listening to the waves. Until there she was. Arms crossed, fag in hand. Smiling down across her body, blowing smoke out of her sideways mouth.

'So, where we going?'

Rothko led Dionne through the heavy doors into the vast storage unit where the party was: concrete floors, steel girders holding up the plyboard ceiling. A roaring lion painted on the wall in gold. A heavy sound system warmed the corners and all the white crusties stood bouncing foot to foot drinking dark bottles of imported stout and smoking pungent high-grade.

They went straight to the speakers and stood facing the music. Soaking it up. There were only a few places where they felt free enough to kiss the way they wanted to. They never risked it in places where men could watch. Not in places they didn't know everyone there. Not near packs of normal people or school people. Or religious people. Or old people. Or young people. Not in the pub where Dionne worked. Not at this dance.

They had got very good at holding each other without touching each other.

But three hours in and they were stoned, moving slowly, listening to the sound inside the sounds, and Dionne led Rothko by the sleeve of their hoody to the toilet block and they entered a cubicle together. Alone at last. Dim, shifting light.

They ached for each other, in the corner of the cubicle with the rattling subs down the hall. The bass beyond the bathrooms shook the floor and the vocals sang out, high. A whistled melody. A choral part, chanted. And the chugging depth of the sub stacks and the brightness of the scoops. Maybe it was the music that made them brave enough to feel. But when Dionne unbuttoned their jeans, Rothko stopped her.

'What's wrong?' She pulled them into her. Lifted Rothko's shirt to print her kisses on their body. And rather than answer, Rothko took her and turned her, kissing her neck and pushing from behind with reaching, heavy hands that found their way in definite strokes, their mouth reaching for her mouth, her face reaching round to kiss as they pushed hard and harder still, and as Dionne shook against their body, shook and tipped her head back, breath catching in her throat, Rothko felt the deep fulfilment of knowing exactly how to bring a person to their pleasure. Dionne turned to face them, sent her hands down, but Rothko stopped her again. Denying her the fulfilment they had just enjoyed.

'You never let me.' She frowned, hurt by it.

Rothko's eyes were troubled. They fought to make Dionne understand something they did not understand themself. 'I just want to be . . . with my *body*. I want to be.' Caught in the headlights of oncoming truth. Laughing at themself to make it easier. 'Feel like an idiot.'

'Tell me?'

They looked away. Rolled the back of their head against the cubicle wall. 'Just wish that we could fuck. That's all.'

'We just did.'

'No. Like, get it out and fuck you. I mean. I wish that I could . . .' And the words out loud were funny and embarrassing and Rothko's smile was sad.

Dionne held her hand up to her belly button. 'I feel you *here*,' she told them. 'Just from the way you look at me.' She put Rothko's hand over her own, pushed it against her stomach.

Back at the speakers, they moved until morning and left in the sunshine.

The music had cleaned their spirits, and they came out into the day fresh from the dub. The dancing made them light on their feet as they walked in step. Rothko sang the bassline they could still hear in their ears, and the two of them skipped as they walked.

'I want to watch the light,' Rothko said, looking up at the morning covering the sky. 'I know the spot.'

Past the corner shop for two Ribenas and a pack of slims. Down the coast road and out along the cliff path until the town was behind them. Jumping the breakwaters, feet in the wet sand, still swampy from the outgoing tide. The light charged the beach and bounced off the waves. Rothko led Dionne into a little cave in the chalky rock and they stood in the mouth of it, climbed up on the flat black stones that had warmed in the sun. The beach dragged the light out to sea, detritus washed up in the wake. Driftwood and pieces of rusted machinery. Seaweed and chalk. It was beautiful.

They watched the water for a sleepy hour. Holding each other and talking in murmurs. And then it was morning,

'Come.' Dionne stood up, started walking back down the beach.

'Where we going?' Rothko jogged to catch her up.

'Shopping.'

Back in town, they were heading down the high street, Dionne a step or two in front, Rothko hanging back, enjoying the feeling of being led. As they walked, they passed a girl that neither of them knew and neither of them noticed. Young teenage girl, something lunar about her. Something nocturnal. White hair, dry lips and an aching face like a blank page, waiting. She noticed them when they went past. Turned her head to follow them. Equally impressed and repelled by the feeling coming off them. She studied their clothes. Heard their voices, talking low. What kind of freedom was this? She didn't like it.

Angel Douglas wore the same clothes as the other girls in her class. Fitted jeans with squiggly embroidered bits and pink gemstones stitched up the seams. White *Tommy Girl* jumper. All-white Air Force Ones. She held on to the straps of her backpack as she waited, watching the road. But her eyes kept going back to the grungy freaks with their baggy jeans and their battered jackets.

Rothko and Dionne hadn't noticed the girl who was watching them from across the road, hunched into the recessed window of the charity shop. They were walking in step now, laughing behind their hands. Angel jiggled up and down on her toes. Annoyed with them. Blue for a friend like that.

Angel had never quite managed it. Never quite worked out how. Never been chosen as *best friend*. Something about her, she didn't know what it was, scared girls away.

Somehow, they sensed she wasn't a natural. Wasn't carefree enough, too much gloom in her. Angel's friends were boys, who she had to out-boy to earn her place. She loved the grudging feel of their respect. Earned in going further than any of them dared to. Like only a girl could do. She just hung around with them though, none of them were close.

Dionne and Rothko disappeared into a shop. And Angel's eyes went back to the road.

She had been standing on the high street waiting for her dad for the last ten minutes. She felt twitchy and like she needed to sit down. She lifted herself up to sit on the narrow edge of the windowsill she was waiting against but couldn't get a proper purchase on it and slid off, awkward, rumpling her clothes. She jumped forward to clear the wall but landed funny and felt a sharp pain snaking up her ankle. Annoyed with herself, she pulled her sleeves down over her hands and turned to look the other way. The wind was making her blink, and she didn't know what to do with her face.

What if he did turn up? What if he didn't?

Angel could see people coming out of the church down the road in hats and pointy shoes. They were all making the kind of noises that people make when they are walking around with their families. She could hear loud, exaggerated laughter and fragments of conversations as people went by, like *I don't usually think much of the portions in places like that, but no, it was lovely. Brunch, it was. Buffet brunch . . .*

Kids were walking with their dads and holding their massive dad hands and climbing on their backs and the mums were pushing the prams and drinking hot drinks from polystyrene cups and everyone seemed to have a normal family. But she didn't need one. She'd never had one and she didn't need one anyway. Because her one wasn't like all these ones.

And she wasn't like them either, so she didn't need what they had. She leant back on the wall. Leant forwards again. Her legs were long in her jeans. Too long for her body. Her mum said she'd grow into them but that's when he pulled up.

Out of nowhere.

Suddenly like that.

She'd waited all this time and then he just pulled up in his silver sedan like as if it was completely normal and he wound down his window and said, 'Hello princess.'

Angel smiled down into her cheeks and held onto her rucksack straps with her hands and walked over.

'Jump in?'

It was a new car. It was very clean. The seats were brown and smelt good. And there was a little scroll page hanging from the rear-view mirror that said *O Lord; I will walk in Your truth; let my heart be undivided in reverence for Your name*, and between them was an armrest. Padded. And her dad smiled at her but kept looking at the road and Angel sat still and felt his deafening presence. Like standing next to an aeroplane taking off. That's how it was to sit next to him in his car while he drove and it smelt like fresh soap, like plants and spice, and it smelt like new car, and spicy chewing gum or something like that. And he was chewing so maybe it was that. He was wearing a smart shirt and grey jeans, and his body was slim and long like Angel's was, but he had more to him because he was an adult and Angel was a child. Angel was his child. But Carl was not Angel's adult. Angel's adult was Mum and Mum had wide hips and a tired face and swore all the time, and Carl was smart and clean and polite and he had a new car, and he'd promised her mum that things were going to be different from now. And that he wanted to be around.

*

Rothko was plodding along behind Dionne. Hanging their head as she navigated the rails. She held a basket over her arm as she looked through the sale racks.

'What is it that you hate so much about these places?' She looked at them, directly into their soul in the way she always did.

Rothko shrugged and looked away. 'Just don't like it.'

Dionne took them by the arm. 'This way.' She led them past skirts and dresses and tops and jeans into the men's bit where she went wafting through the aisles, until she came to a stop. Rothko stared at the floor. Blushing.

'You ever worn boxers before?'

'Dionne?' Rothko felt aware of every other person in the shop. 'What you *doing*?' They whispered it. Desperate.

She picked up a six-pack of navy boxers with a black waistband. Rothko couldn't meet her eyes. 'These will work,' she told them gently, and put them in the basket like it was the simplest thing in the world. Sean's face if he knew, Rothko could just imagine him, frowning and scared. *Why, though? That's weird.* Boxers were for boys. Knickers were for girls. 'You'll look fit as fuck in these.'

An attendant sailed over. Stood close by and observed them, fluttering a false smile. Straightened hair, down to her shoulders, make-up so perfect her face looked digital, not even one crease in her work shirt. Dionne lifted her eyes from the boxers and acknowledged the woman.

'You girls ok?' The attendant was looking at Rothko, trying to work out what it was she was looking at.

'Yeah.' Dionne fronted it out with a deadly smile. 'Are *you* ok?'

Raising her palm to indicate how to be normal. 'Ladies section this way . . . if you need anything.'

'We're fine.'

Rothko felt a tension in the back of their throat. Hated how their presence in places like this made normal people so uncomfortable.

The woman seemed on the edge of saying something else. But instead, she walked off. Looking back over at Rothko a few times as she did. They felt Dionne's hand reach for theirs. Felt her thumb stroking their knuckles.

She led them towards the glittery socks. Stopped at an aisle of workout clothes. Picked up the plainest sports bras she could find. One in black. One in white. 'These are good for you,' she said. 'You'll feel less . . .' And Rothko nodded.

'Yeah.'

'They're tight. So they'll.' She flattened her chest with her palms to show Rothko.

It wasn't until the items had been through the till and paid for by Dionne and put into a plastic bag that Rothko carried in a swinging hand, back out on the street where the light was real, that they felt like they could breathe comfortably.

'Dionne?' Rothko stopped her as they walked. They looked around the street for the words they couldn't find in their own mouth.

'What is it?' she whispered. Rothko checked up and down the high street, *fuck it*, kissed the things they couldn't say into Dionne's dancing mouth, and felt the kisses coming back that told them she had understood.

In her dad's car, still held at the roadwork traffic lights, Angel saw the two girls kissing in the street and felt twitchy and exposed.

Carl saw them too. He tutted loudly.

'I don't care what you do in your own home. But why do

they have to do it out here in the street in broad daylight? There's kids about.'

The girls showed no sign of stopping, and the lights at the roadworks were stuck on red. Carl beeped his horn at them, loud long beeps, until they pulled apart, like *what*? And saw the bleat of disapproval on the staring face behind the wheel.

'Stop looking then, pervert.' Dionne stuck her fingers up at him.

Carl wound the window and shouted back, 'Behave yourself. What's the matter with you?' But the girls were skipping off. Leaving Carl stuck at the lights, chewing on the un-specialness of his fear.

'Look at the state of them.' He laughed at them to ease it. Put his shame on them, the way he'd learned a person was supposed to. 'Why are they dressed like that?' He looked over at Angel and Angel laughed beside him. 'Don't they look stupid? Look at the fat one, there. You look like a tramp, love.' His laughter ebbed.

The lights were still red, but Carl couldn't be held any longer. Drumming the wheel, he checked the road both ways and made a break for it. Speeding round the roadworks. Beating the system. Affirming his status; he was nobody's fool.

Dionne linked Rothko's arm, and they were away down the high street, far from the beeping car and the woman in the underwear aisle with the eyes that said *this is not how we do things here*. Bathed in the light of each other.

A crowd of drinkers stood outside the cash converters ahead of them. One was in a pirate hat. Black hair tufted out around it. Little denim skirt. Camo print army jacket, sleeves rolled up.

She turned around.

'ROTHKO?' she shouted, waving her arms. And Rothko's guts dropped. They felt their mother's arms wrap them in a stifling embrace. Her collarbone digging into them as she pulled them at an awkward angle. She kissed them on both cheeks and looked to Dionne. 'Hello my darlin',' she said, 'who's your lovely friend then?' And Rothko's face went dark, dark pink. A rash of shame.

'Dionne.' They straightened their back. 'This is my mum. Meg.'

And Dionne was so excited she said, 'Oh my god I'm so happy to meet you!' And Meg grinned at her. Rothko saw the gummy gaps in her mouth where teeth should have been. It made her face look like a skull.

'Well I'm very happy to meet you my darlin'.' She took Dionne by the arm and skipped her round in a circle. And Dionne was laughing, spinning with Meg, who took her pirate hat off and put it on Rothko so she could look Dionne up and down. Meg's skin was tired and her eyes were dull but Dionne could see her beauty, in the delicate bone structure, the long black hair. The bright, impressive freedom of her.

'You're so beautiful!' Dionne told her and Meg said,

'Oh, I like this one, Rothko. Can we keep her?' Rothko laughed along but wanted to shoot themself point blank range in the head. 'What are you two doing then?' Meg's voice was raspy, oily. Up-all-nighty. Her skin was sun and dirt. Rothko took the hat off.

'Not much. Just on our way home.'

'Well don't let me hold you up.' She grinned. And her little wrinkly face lit up and she took Dionne's face in her hands and said, 'You gorgeous thing, you look after this one won't you? Very special, this one is.'

And Dionne said, 'I know. I will.' And Meg stared deeply

into her face, for what felt to Rothko like an impossible amount of time. But Dionne just stared back, and she did not seem disgusted or freaked out. In fact, Rothko watched as Dionne took Meg's face in her hands the same way. And they gazed into each other's eyes.

'We've got to go now, Mum,' Rothko said. And Meg smiled at Dionne, exposing the gaps, the big black holes that sucked the world into her gums, and she nodded.

Turning to Rothko she said, 'Hold on, hold a minute.' And she went rifling through her pockets for something and pulled out a crumpled note. 'Here,' she said. Rothko wouldn't take it.

'No, Mum. You're alright.'

'No. Take it,' she said. Her smile falling away. Suddenly stern. 'Take it. Take it.' Not wanting a scene. Rothko took the twenty pound and put it in their pocket. 'You take this lovely girl to the pictures,' Meg said. 'And you make sure you buy her some popcorn.'

'Thanks,' Rothko said. Whole face red. Neck red. Underneath their clothes, they could feel their back was red. 'See you later.' They gave her back the hat and Meg hugged them to her. She was shorter than Rothko and she hid her face in their shoulder and squeezed them with her thin arms and it was like being jumped on by a frightened animal. 'Take care of yourself please, Mum.' Rothko said into her hair.

SEVEN

Rothko had been working hard. Ezra had noticed the effort. But couldn't let go of his doubt. They both knew how useless it was to hope.

But tonight, they were out for a Turkish, huddled round the corner table, combo meal and mezze for two. It had been a smooth week. And Ezra's thoughts had turned to the possibility of a future. And under his supervision, Rothko was allowing themself to wonder if maybe they could have one after all.

'Look, no matter what happens in these bloody exams, you know.'

'They make you think it's life and death.' Their eyes met briefly, pulled by the weight of those words.

'I mean, it's important. Sure. But. If it doesn't go your way. It doesn't mean you can't do what you want.'

'What if I don't know what I want?'

'You just got to give it some thought, that's all.'

'Did you know what you wanted to do?'

Ezra's cheeks were full of food. He pointed his fork. 'I was just grafting. One job I hated after the next. So you wouldn't have to.'

Rothko wasn't convinced that they wouldn't have to. 'I'm not good at anything, though.'

'Not true. You're smart. You've always been smart.' His eyes were kind and full of pain. Under his words, he could feel the real words pulsing, the ones he held back in his chewing mouth: *Gave my whole life so you could have a better chance. But there's no point to any of it, if you don't want to live.*

'Look. I know it's been hard on you. With your mum and . . . I have tried. I hope you know that. And Wendy too. We've both tried to give you a bit of . . . stability.'

Rothko hunkered down over their plate. Nodded.

'But it's not been the easiest time for you.'

He watched a glimmer pass over Rothko's face and was smashed briefly round the head by the image of her, slumped unconscious. That face, dead to the world, pressed into the floor.

'We can turn a corner. Ok?' His smile was convincing. 'Just scrape a pass on the important ones if you can. And if you can't. Maybe you can learn a trade. Something with your hands. You can take a trade anywhere once you've got the skills.'

'I do want to do well, Dad.'

'I know you do.' Ezra raised his beer. 'You will. You've just got to want it.'

He took a big swig. Wiped his mouth on the back of his hand. Happy in Rothko's company.

'Feels like a new start.' Rothko admitted, careful not to mean it too earnestly. In case the world heard them. Ezra was proud of his youngest. She seemed older than she used to.

'It is,' he told her. Believing it could make it real. 'For both of us.'

Maybe the hard days were behind them.

They were lonely. Separated from the other kids at school. Sitting their exams in an empty room behind the science labs. None of the excitement of filing in behind the others. They could see them when they went for fags, waiting in lines outside the assembly hall, pushing each other, and they felt left out.

They missed Sean. But it was too painful to miss him, so they hated him instead.

Even Dionne left them cold. They were getting sick of the confusion they felt around her affection for them. It was one thing having her buy them boxers in secret. But it didn't change who Rothko was, or how difficult being who they were made everything.

It was Wednesday. Sickly afternoon, hot and heavy. Rain coming. July creeping closer. Weird green light pushing out of low cloud. They'd promised themself they were going to stop running to her every single time she called. That was a week ago now. And they were out of patience.

Fuck it.

They dipped out to smoke at the bus stop. Watching the normal kids teem in their happy packs, screaming into their lunch breaks, arms round each other's shoulders like nothing had ever been wrong.

They stood against the bus stop bench, slipping down the plastic seat. Hood up. Hands in their pockets.

There she was.

Dionne.

Walking past, the other side of the gates from the sixth form block, with her little black skirt and her diamond check tights and her red and white Nike Cortez. Dark lipstick and her bra strap through the neck of her t-shirt. Baggy white one with the *In Utero* album cover across the front. Jacket over her shoulder, green parka with the fur round the hood. She was walking beside a tall boy with a fresh fade and a smart grey tracksuit, cheerful grin. Heading for the back field, maybe for a zoot. Dionne saw Rothko through the railings and broke away. Rothko dug their feet in. Braced themself against desire.

'You annoyed with me?' Shoulder against the school fence.

'No.' They looked away.

'Wanna go somewhere and talk?' Rothko nodded and started walking. Dionne followed a few paces behind, caught up to them the other side of the high road, and together they jogged down the steps to the maze of underpasses beneath the busy junction.

Dionne walked backwards in the dark tunnels, smiling at Rothko. Damp concrete smell of skunk and piss and spray paint. Then out into a patch of scrubland. Bottles and cans. A suitcase spilling baby clothes. Garages where people stored the broken things they dreamed of fixing. Rothko sat on the low wall that bordered the scrubland, against the corrugated iron door of a lock-up. Dionne walked to the edges and looked around, then wandered back, coming to a stop in front of Rothko. She prised their thighs apart with her knee and stood between them, pressed up close, stomach to stomach. Breathing. She rested her elbows on Rothko's shoulders. Looked down into their face. An age passed, gently. The gold stud above her lip caught the sunlight.

'What is it?'

Rothko looked away, and back. 'Nothing.'

'Come on,' Dionne pushed them with her body. 'What's happened? Why you not answering my calls?'

If they were normal, like everyone else, maybe they could have had a girlfriend like everyone else did. Maybe then liking someone wouldn't have to hurt so much.

Dionne studied them, her head cocked to the side.

They hated the part of themself that made everything so complicated and impossible. The physical part.

She pushed a slow kiss into their mouth. Lips unfolding. Rothko wilted. Kissed like they were drinking. 'I'll get the car, wait for me at the top of the ramp.' She pulled away, laughed warm breath. 'You want me?'

'No,' Rothko smiled. And she was gone.

Cruising through the neighbourhood in Dionne's opalescent Mazda, Rothko felt themself relax. The car had been Dionne's nan's for a hundred years, and still carried the feeling of her, rising from the beaded seat covers. Perfume, fags, iced doughnuts, dog shampoo. She'd worked at the groomer. But since she had finally admitted she was too wobbly to drive, she had passed it down to Dionne. And now it was her ticket to the world. She loved it hard.

Rothko watched her, sitting low in the driver's seat, elbow resting on the window, sucking on a weighty spliff with wide, damp lips.

Even if it wasn't girlfriend. Maybe didn't matter what it was or wasn't. All that mattered was it felt good to be with her.

'Go then,' Dionne said to a person trying to change lanes, waving her hand impatiently. 'Go on.' And then tutted. 'Prick.'

She put her hand in Rothko's lap. Started pushing at their thighs. She stayed focused on the road, but she smiled at them. Rothko took the spliff from her and sucked two dull pumps off it. Exhaled thick smoke through the gap in the window, balanced it in the ashtray. They moved their weight over in the seat, so they were right next to her. They started to kiss her cheekbones, her neck. Took their time. They felt her body becoming heavy. They ran their hand under her clothes. Their fingers struggled to dance under the restrictions of her jacket, t-shirt, seatbelt. So many barriers.

Dionne turned off the main road and parked on a side street.

'What you doing?' Rothko whispered.

'Pulling over.'

'Why?' They kissed with gentle teeth; their bodies rose and fell together. Dionne pulled away and fixed Rothko with a look that Rothko read as a challenge. They moved towards her, but she got out of the car.

'Where you going?'

'Come,' she said. Joyful.

Rothko chucked their bag on the floor under the seat and climbed out the passenger side. Stoned. Tripping over the kerb. Legs like somebody else's.

'I've wanted to take you here for ages.' Dionne took their hand. Out in the street where the world could see them. Rothko was buzzing off it. Trying to act natural. 'Every time I drive past, I want to take you inside.'

'Where we going?'

'You staying with me tonight?'

They were supposed to not be running to her every single time she called. But . . . 'Course, yeah.'

The sky was blank and thick. Perpetual mash. All the way down to the pavement. They stopped at a shopfront. There was nothing in the windows. The sign above the door said *ADULT*.

They pushed through. Dionne's breath was way up in her chest the way it got when she was excited. Fluttering. Inside, a second door, strips of cream fabric hanging in a curtain. The woman behind the counter looked up; she was in her sixties, thin bracelets jangled down her wrist, her hair was piled up on top of her head, spilling out. She was wearing a long black cardigan, open at enormous boobs. Dionne waved; the woman got something out of the back of her mouth with her fingernail. Looked back down at her magazine.

'What are we doing in here, Dee?' Rothko asked through a closed mouth. Dionne swallowed a giggle, led them through the aisles. Bulky men browsed at either end of the store. Rothko was aware of the men but kept their eyes on Dionne. They came to a stop. 'Look,' Dionne said. And Rothko did.

Tiny ones. Massive ones. Rubber fists. Double-ended glass ones in horseshoe shapes. Vibrating ones with a range of settings. Foot-long ones, curved at the tip. Little purple ones. Flexi ones with spiral ridges that could be bent into different shapes. Butt plugs and anal beads. Leather harnesses with studs and buckles. Ones with ball-sacks, ones with foreskins. Ones with suction pads, for fixing to chairs. Sparkly ones. Rainbow ones. Matte black ones, as thick as an ankle.

Dionne held their hand tightly. Rothko's throat was dry. 'You want to fuck me with one. Right?' she said quietly, into their ear. They cleared their throat as Dionne pushed into their body and looked up into Rothko's face. She caught their eyes and whispered, 'I can't wait.' And Rothko felt their guts drop down to their shoes.

Racks of DVDs and cheap nurse's outfits on hangers. Everything fizzing. Because, yeah. Of course. But Rothko hadn't realised that this was how. You just walked into the sex shop round the back of Burger King and bought one of these things and that was it. They felt big and nervous, their face had gone red. Their hair was uncool.

Dionne, no shame, was smiling. She picked one after another off the shelves, opening boxes and pulling them out to look at them properly. 'Too rubbery,' she said, reaching for

Rothko's hand, turning it palm upwards and slapping a long purple one across it. 'We want one you can wear.' Same calm energy she always had when they were doing things that made Rothko forget how to breathe.

'What about this one?' She held up a cardboard box with a photo on the front of a man and a woman in a bedroom, her wearing it, fucking him from behind, him looking back over his shoulder, mouth open. On the back a picture of two soft-focus women, one on top of the other, in a state of intense animation. They laughed at the pictures. Inside, veins and balls and everything. A beige strap, 'flesh toned'. *Whose flesh?* There was a raised mound of nobbled silicone to stimulate the wearer. Rothko felt like they were going to faint. They laughed. It looked alien. It looked un-magic. It didn't make sense. They wanted to put it in their pants and wear it and take it out for Dionne.

'Yeah, I dunno,' they said. And Dionne took it to the desk. Rothko, silent at her arm, feeling like a farmyard animal, couldn't look up at the woman in case she asked for ID or knew their dad or something. Dionne bought lube and two bottles of poppers. The woman put everything in a thick black plastic bag. 'You'll have plenty of fun with this won't you, girls,' she said. Dionne grabbed Rothko's arm and they ran out of the shop, bursting for air.

Inside the car, the engine turning over, DJ Brockie playing RAM Trilogy. Dionne pulled out into the traffic, laughing a smile towards them out of the corner of her mouth, reaching for their hand, lifting their knuckles towards her lips. And Rothko landed in the present. Finally, a person.

They pulled up at Dionne's flat, got out of the car and looked at each other. It was enough to make them both sink beneath a wave of laugher that almost floored them as they climbed the stairs, bent double, trying to fight their way up to the surface so they could catch their breath.

'Hi,' Dionne shouted as she opened the front door.

'I'm in here,' Agnes shouted back from the kitchen. She walked through to the front room and met them in the hallway. 'How are you two?' she asked, saucepan in her hand. Stirring. Turquoise tracksuit bottoms, baggy Prince t-shirt, *Sign o' the Times*.

'We're fine. We'll be in my room.'

'What? That's it?' She pouted at Dionne, who sighed and gave her mother a loud kiss on both cheeks. 'Thank you!' Agnes said. 'Did you eat?' Dionne nodded.

'Yeah, we got something on the way back.'

'Will you be hungry later?' She addressed Rothko, who loved to eat her food. Rothko leaned towards the pan for a look. Dionne pulled them back.

'No, we're fine. Thank you though, Ma. We're going in my room now. Ok? Love you.' They walked down the hall to her room.

Agnes went back into the kitchen, turned up the music. Brazilian falsetto, guitars.

Dionne dropped her things on the floor. Beers and fags from the offy, pencil case full of make-up in her World Dance record bag. They fell backwards onto Dionne's bed. Lay there for a while. Rothko was looking at Dionne's face in profile. Blinking.

'You're always looking at me.'

'I like looking at you.'

She turned her face, her left eye obscured by bed covers. 'What do you see?' She squashed the covers down. Laughed.

‘You.’ Rothko watched her till it hurt.

Dionne rolled herself off the bed, lit two candles, and closed the curtains on the street below; it was dark out.

She took a box from her wardrobe and opened it on her desk. Sat down and started rifling through packets and baggies. Pulled out a wrap.

‘Want a line?’

‘What about your mum?’

Dionne shrugged. ‘She won’t know.’

Seemed like it was all they ever did together, and Rothko wasn’t sure that they wanted to get on it. Maybe they didn’t want to be up all night on drugs with her. Felt like everything was slipping away from them. Would have been nice to go to the cinema or something. Stand around outside McDonalds. Like all the other kids, who Rothko thought were fucking stupid and had no minds of their own.

Couldn’t have it both ways, they supposed.

‘Go on then,’ they surrendered.

Happy with that, Dionne rose from the desk and took her clothes off for Rothko. Expectant little frown on her face. Rothko stared, as they understood they were being invited to. She took the stare and danced with it. Closed their open mouth with a fingernail beneath their chin. A performance of rehearsed sexuality learned from a Hollywood bombshell, metabolised through two little queers in Edgecliff. Dionne handed them a beer and went to sort the lines.

Rothko lay across the bed on their front, reached for the black bag at the foot of the bed, took the box out and looked at it. Cheap cardboard. It barely held. The thing itself in their hands, firm and soft at the same time. Thick, clean smell of new plastic and latex. Like the Ken dolls Sarai had, that Rothko used to strip so they could see what was underneath.

The funny picture on the box again; they turned onto their back. Dionne, busy with the lines, didn't turn around. They held it over their face, right above their nose. Little piss hole in the top. A hot, low feeling thumped in the pit of their stomach as they measured its weight. They slid it into the waistband of their trackies, holding it there, feeling its current, as they ducked next door to the bathroom.

They locked the door and pulled their trackies off, wriggled out of their pants and socks and sat on the toilet seat naked from the waist down looking at the straps thinking *how the fuck*? Nothing else for it. They climbed in. One big slow leg at a time, awkward. They were too tall and big in this bathroom for small people and when they stood up, they could see their stupid tits in the mirror. Awkward interruptions. Not theirs.

Mirrors were weird. Who they saw reflected in them, felt so far away from who they were. It always spun them out, to have to face how they appeared to the rest of the world. The way they felt it, they walked through life without a body. They had so little sense of it, day to day, that when they saw it standing there, as if it belonged to them, it felt like looking in a funfair mirror. Who they felt themself to be had been stretched out or squashed up small, distorted beyond recognition.

They shook it off. Bent down and around to tighten the straps, pulled them so tight they cut into their legs. They looked down and saw it. Let out a little giggle. They pulled their pants up over it, watched it bulge like porno. Touched it through the fabric. Theirs. Their own. They pulled their joggers up and picked their socks up off the floor. When they bent down, it poked them in the belly and it made them laugh again. They crept out of the bathroom and back to the bedroom, listening out for Agnes in the kitchen at the other end of the flat.

Dionne was grinning when they came back in. 'Hey sugar,' she said, her eyes drooping. Relighting a dense spliff that had been sitting in the tray. Dionne passed them the note. Bigger one was hers. They sank their lines. Turned the music up. Stupid, funny dancing. Rothko air drumming. Feeling faster. Spinning her, giggling. Dionne's face buried in their chest. Until she slowed the pace. Ran her tongue over Rothko's mouth. And they fell into the spell of it. The way they did it, just the two of them.

Rothko escaped their body when they vanished into Dionne's.

Her pleasure was their victory over the world that made them ashamed and never enough.

They lifted her up, sat her on the bed so they could pull off her fancy knickers, not laughing anymore but measured, laying her down, tracing shallow kisses over her thighs and down her legs. Moving up again and up. Dionne, stroking Rothko's back and shoulders, lifted their shirt, but didn't pull it over their head because Rothko couldn't be naked. Kissing down around her belly button, and down again, tracing the line of her hipbones, until they found what they were kissing towards. Sent their breath ahead over the folds and swells of it, held their open mouth just above the surging pinkness, dancing with the tip of their tongue, gradual with it, tentative, until they felt her forcing the back of their head and they gave her the full warmth of it. Sucked her up into their mouth, lapping heavily and gently, slurping on it, faster until her juice had got thick enough to slosh around their cheeks and then slow again, back up to the surface then deeper, into the swell of it, sipping it, kissing it, feeling it grow in their mouth.

Playing Dionne like an instrument, hearing her body sing and vibrate, Rothko wasn't less than. They were more than.

They lost themself in guiding her towards the drop; relented, built her up again, relented, built her up. And as her body bloomed towards its shuddering conclusion, Rothko kept conducting the swell, pushing with their wrists, with their shoulders, twisting their knuckles in, quicker with their lips and tongue, radiating frequencies, massing one into the next, crescendo on crescendo until it was too much to bear and she was out the other side of it, swearing, pushing them back to climb on top; she felt it through their clothes, and it was the first time Rothko had seen that look.

They held themself above her, watching the pleasure paint her face, and dissolved into the other world. The one that opened to them sometimes, when they were alone together. Where everything about Rothko was perfect. A world of held breath and microscopic vision. Touch that reverberated into eternity. Where every little thing that had happened in either of their lives had happened perfectly, in order to create this atomic moment.

Three a.m. and Dionne held her hair back, picked up the note and inhaled a fat chunk of shock that numbed her brain to fizz.

'I love you,' she said. 'You fucking pervert.'

Rothko was complete.

Four a.m. and all the majesty had done one. They were fucking inanely. Lube and lube and Rothko's empty guts were sore, and Dionne was blank in their arms as they rode each other numbly, fiercely, without end. The pleasure was in the loss of pleasure. Close but held at bay. Dionne, gulping air and breathing ragged sound. Her face against the edges of things; her back against the shelves, the door, the wardrobe. Rothko's head against the radiator.

Five a.m. and it had all slowed down, Dionne pushing into

them, and Rothko's eyes were closed against the tears in the back of their throat. When Dionne said their name, it was like they'd just been given it. Just learnt that it was theirs. She was steady with them, gritted teeth, no going back and Rothko giving in to her and letting her, and this was real. It had to be.

Six a.m. and there was no such thing as sleep.

They watched her. The blocked pores across her forehead from her smudged make-up, and the funny, congested way she had of breathing when she was tucked up on her side.

They loved her.

They were chewing the inside of their mouth and looking at Dionne with their hands behind their head.

'What is it?'

They took the risk and told the truth. 'I wish we could be like this. Out there.'

Dionne's face fell into a familiar sigh. 'Boys round here love to break things.' She spoke sadly. 'Especially beautiful things. If they knew about us, all them lot.' She signified the world outside with a faint point of her chin towards the window. By *them lot* Rothko knew she meant the other kids in her classes, or the ones at school with Rothko, or the ones on the estate. The little boys and bullies that were everywhere around them. 'They'd just try and break it.' Tightening to anger. 'Not even *for* anything. Not even because they want to, really. Just because that's what they fucking do.'

'I'm yours,' Rothko told her. Hands still behind their head. 'I'm not for no-one else.' It felt like a big thing to have said. But she carried on like she hadn't heard it.

'Makes them laugh to piss on people. Pathetic, isn't it? Things they do to make themselves feel big and strong.'

Rothko grew solemn, decided to stop asking stupid questions. Dionne noticing their withdrawal, turned towards them, 'No matter what anyone else thinks, you're the only one who knows me. The only one.' She kissed them with a wet mouth that Rothko found oppressive.

Seven thirty a.m. and they were in the shower, Dionne washing their back, their armpits, the soles of their feet. Attentive and methodical. Rothko let her take their hair out of its tight band and she went through half a bottle of conditioner, trying to work a brush through their matted curls. The silent focus of their intimacy, their grooming ritual. No one had ever taught Rothko before: *this is how a person has a body.* No one else in Rothko's life even knew they didn't know.

Eight fifteen a.m. and they were saying goodbye to Agnes who looked up from her handbag, in her bra and skirt, her work shirt on the hanger above the ironing board, her body so much like Dionne's it turned Rothko red and Dionne, two pieces of toast in her hand, kissed Agnes on both cheeks and Agnes said, 'Ok then, you two. Have a good day, girls.' The TV was on, and the iron was steaming and she didn't notice the blank pits of their eyes. Their stuck jaws.

EIGHT

Rothko didn't know what they were going in to school for. Couldn't remember if they had an exam that day or what, but they wanted to be with Dionne for as long as they could, and she had classes to take. So they walked at her heel. It felt good to be led.

Waiting at the bus stop, Rothko could see particles. The spark of a smile on Dionne's mouth sent waves through their legs. She sang along to slow jams on her headphones. Rolling her hips and shoulders. Jodeci. Ginuwine. Aaliyah. It was that kind of a morning. Snapping her neck from left to right. Other people going to work, looking sweetly tired from bed, all done up as clean as fish. The violent norm and Dionne singing the wrong words under her breath.

The bus pulled up, they shuffled to the back. Dionne in the window, Rothko, legs apart, kicking their ankles down the gangway. Up front, purple braids in a B&Q uniform shirt was looking for something in a shoulder bag. Ankle-length silver puffa coat and heavy fringe slept against the window. Smart, scuffed shoes tapped at a chunky laptop. Crochet hat and an ironed t-shirt sat with knees together and read a holy book.

A bunch of lads got on: school shirts, precision hairstyles, bleached white trainers. One girl with them, blank white slicked hair up in a bun. Two gelled strands hanging down either side of her face. It was Angel Douglas. She eyed the girls as she took her seat.

Rothko didn't recognise any of the kids. They were from the other school. They sat on the seats just in front, in fours on either side of the gangway. Rothko clocked them but Dionne was laughing, cuddling up to their arm, holding their leg at the top of the knee. It was unusual for Rothko to receive this kind of intimacy in public.

Rothko heard a voice inside their head, speaking to them from another place. You alright? It asked them. They didn't know if it was their dad or their older self or what it was. They could only watch Dionne. The movement of her throat as she sang along to Mary J. Blige. Dionne noticed Rothko's eyes on her and felt beautiful because of them. She inched closer, pushed her body around and up to touch her nose against Rothko's, and she let her slow kiss ease over them both. They got lost in it.

'What?! Do that again!' Loud shrill voice. Schoolboy. Tyrannical in his usualness. Flicking his hands up and down.

'What did she do?' A taller, deeper voice. Stiller boy. Bigger frame.

'She kissed her,' the shrill one, more excited. 'That's *gay*!'

'Don't lie.' He turned to the back of the bus, so did the whole pack. 'Did you just kiss?'

'Do it again,' another voice, laughing.

'Kiss her again!'

Dionne moved a couple of inches away from Rothko. Looked out the window. Rothko felt her change and wanted to protect her from it.

'Go on!' The low pitched one. 'Don't be shy.'

'She's blanking you.'

'What you blanking me for?'

'Just kiss her, man!' Laughter like nothing was ever funny until now. 'What's the matter? I know you was fingering her last night.'

To Dionne, 'Why you with *that* though? You aint that bad looking, babes. You could get a man.'

Rothko stared through them. Sitting high in their chest, their hair a mess, their unfashionable coat looking tired and weird. Their boxy frame, square jaw, thick bones, the whole vast mass of them feeling like a freak next to these clean, neat, slim, easy, fashionable teenagers.

'Why you staring?' Small one, voice like a mis-lit firework, dug their shoulder into the ribs of the tall one. 'Look at her staring.'

'What you looking at?' low voice said.

'You fancy me, innit?' Patches of bored laughter. 'Don't worry I aint got no standards. I'll fuck you so hard I'll cure you.'

'Urgh man, she's *butters*. How could you even *say* that? She's *bugly*.'

'Won't be no lesbian after me, babes. You'll be my wife. I'll have you cleaning my kitchen.' The laughter caught, flared, died.

Rothko didn't respond. Just stared them down. The shame was alchemising, becoming rage. Dionne kept looking out the window, but she pushed her leg as hard as she could against Rothko's, trying to push them both back into the other world where everything was theirs.

Angel felt her body growing rigid. She hated Rothko. For sitting there, looking like she looked and not caring. Everything about the way Rothko was felt too bright, too close. Angel just needed to stop this ugly girl from shining. To put a fucking stop to the part of Rothko that didn't know you couldn't be like this. Like who she was. You couldn't get kissed like that. She deserved to get smacked in the mouth. She had to put the fire out. The one in Rothko. The one in herself. Her skin was all hot, her hands were hot. Her cheeks were hot. Her vanished face, white as the core of a flame.

Adrenaline spun inside her, clenching her little fists. Hocking up a mouthful of phlegm and holding it in her throat. She pulled herself away from where she'd been sitting with her back against the window, two rows in front of Rothko and Dionne.

'You're nasty,' she told them, her voice hard. She knelt up on the seat and spat at Rothko. It landed on their knees. Rothko watched the place where it had landed. Their hearing tunnelled to pulse. The spit slid off their trouser leg, landed on the floor. The boys laughed, taking pleasure.

The people in the front of the bus turned to watch. Frowning amongst themselves. 'What can you say though? Can't do nothing. They could have knives on them for all I know.'

The low-voice boy covered his mouth in shock. 'Are you going to have that?'

Rothko's face was dark red. Their voice was level. 'I don't care.' The boys narrowed their eyebrows at each other.

'She said she don't care!'

Angel hocked again. Spat again. Aiming higher this time. It landed on Rothko's sleeve. Rothko wiped it on the seat beside them. Dionne was staring at Angel. Breathing rapidly. Holding the edge of Rothko's other sleeve in her fingertips. She wanted to knock this girl out. But there was too many of them and she didn't want to make things worse for Rothko.

'You don't care, yeah?' Angel asked.

'I don't care.'

She spat again.

'I like it,' Rothko said.

'Urgggggh.' The boys erupted into a chorus of distaste. 'You're *nasty*.'

'Why are you dressed like that?' Angel leered over the seat. 'You look like a tramp, love.'

The tall one, his hand in the waistband of his school trousers, was stretched across the seat like the sun was out. 'Is that your girlfriend, yeah? So kiss her!'

'Dirty dykes,' Angel said. 'Come off the bus.' All the boys laughed.

'Fight!'

'She wants to fight you.'

'No,' Rothko said. The boys stood for their stop and walked down towards the doors.

'Come off the bus and watch me beat you.' She was pale, sharp boned. Tall. Her body held together at the shoulder blades. Tired face, craggy eyes. Fast, hard hands that accentuated her skinny words.

'No,' Rothko said.

'Cos you know I'll beat you, innit.'

'Yeah,' Rothko agreed with her. 'If I come off this bus, against all of you.'

Angel walked to the doors as the bus stopped but kept staring back over her shoulder. The boys got off and started walking. Rothko allowed themself a performative laugh as the girl approached the doors.

'What you fucking laughing at?' she shouted down the bus. 'You think I'm joking?' She charged back down towards them, ready to fight. Spiky little face full of hate. Squaring up. Rothko felt their blood thicken. Sick and fucking tired of it, they stood as she came towards them, walked two paces down the bus to meet her. Raging. They drew their fist back and threw a hard short punch at the side of Angel's head as she raised her own hand. It sank right into the temple, the ring on their middle finger opened the skin. Angel fell into the seats and inside Rothko, it went black. Their body moved of its own accord, into the blackness.

Both hands gripped the handrail, so they could launch both feet at the girl's chest. Stamped their entire weight on her thin body as she lay sprawled out in the seat. Stamped again. One foot and then the other. Angel pulled herself up, holding her head, and barged past Rothko for her boys. Rothko was vivid with adrenaline. Rushing from it. Swallowing rapidly. Their balled fists ached from clenching so hard. They stepped back and found Dionne, who unclenched their fist with her fingers and held their hand.

The colour was returning to their vision, light prickling into the blackness. The corners first. Things regained their edges.

Angel scrambled off the bus, shouting for her boys; 'Oi, you lot. *You* lot.' But her boys were a few paces away. The driver closed the door as soon as she stepped through. The others hadn't seen what had happened. By the time they realised there'd been a fight, the doors were closed. They couldn't get on. They surrounded the back of the bus, punching the windows where Rothko and Dionne were sat, shouting to come off the bus. Calling them gaylords.

The driver pulled away. Dionne stuck her finger up out the back window as they drove off. The three people at the front of the bus were still muttering.

'They're all feral.'

Rothko's face was red. Up to their temples and down their neck. They stared at a fixed point, seeing nothing, their stomach churning rage. Dionne traced spiral patterns on their arm with her fingernails.

'I never seen you like that,' she told them. Worry on her face. They gripped their thighs, looking at the place where the spit had been. Shaking. They jumped their knees up and down and leant their head back into the seat, breathing out.

Dionne bit the skin at the edges of her thumbnail, kept looking behind her out the back window. 'You should have just left it.'

Walking fast on wobbly legs, in the crush of her boys, their arms round her shoulders, Angel felt the bliss of their attention. She was a part of something strong. A pack of feathered warriors, who respected her for violence. She laughed along, as they all shouted louder than the others, about how they were going to find those dirty little lesbos. And what they were going to do to them. And Angel was special. Brave as a girl. One of the boys.

But later, in the quiet of her front room, with her mother's frowning eyes going over her skin and Eileen's worried voice, demanding, 'Who did this to you?' 'What happened?' Angel didn't feel like one of the boys anymore.

NINE

'That you home?' Rothko heard Ezra's voice from upstairs as they dropped their bag in the hallway.

'Me,' they called. 'Hi.'

The hallway was warm and the light from the kitchen windows fell across the walls, as Rothko watched the dust whirling in the rays, stuck on it, spellbound before lowering their body onto the bottom step of the carpeted staircase to pull off their shoes. They heard Ezra's footsteps as he left the bedroom at the front of the house and stopped at the top of the stairs, looking down. He'd been in their room.

They stared at their knees. All day they had felt it there. The phlegm on their trousers that told the world who they were: someone that sat in silence while boys said things to their girl like *why you with that though?* And the way Dionne disappeared as soon as they encountered other people.

Rothko walked the halls staring through the glass at the people in their lessons, going classroom to classroom to back-field to smoke, with this spit stain dripping off their clothes. They left school half an hour after they arrived and spent the day sitting in a record shop. Listening to other people listening to music. While it lingered on their clothes. The mark of a ghost. And now they were home, and it was still eyeballing them. Haunted patch of fabric just above their knee.

'There you are.' Rothko turned to look up from where they

sat fading on the bottom step. Their dad's face seemed embarrassingly old. 'You look a mess,' Ezra said.

'Thanks.'

'Where've you been?'

'School.' Ezra picked his way around Rothko, walked through to the kitchen, and waited. Rothko followed him in. He stared at them. Rothko tried to feel out what trouble this was. But Ezra just frowned at them and waited. It wasn't clear to Rothko what was going on. Deep furrows consumed Ezra's face. Eventually, he pulled two cups down from the cupboard, flicked the kettle, turned back to them. 'Miss Shoffa called me.'

'About what?'

'You tell me.'

Rothko rubbed the back of their neck. 'I don't know. You spoke to her.'

'Did you get in a fight this morning?'

Rothko shrugged.

'What, you can't remember?'

'No, it was just . . . I wouldn't call it a fight.'

'What would you call it?'

'Nothing really. Just some kids.'

'Kids?' He scoffed. 'Thirteen-year-old girl. In her school uniform. With two fractured ribs. Because you kicked her in her chest.'

'It weren't my fault Dad, honestly.' Rothko's tone was sluggish. The consonants merging.

Ezra shook his head in disapproval. He mimicked Rothko's tone, '*It weren't my fault.*'

'I'm serious. I didn't mean to . . .' But Ezra interrupted them.

'You punched her so hard in the face, she was bleeding. You must have really swung for her.' Ezra was beginning to shout. 'You're lucky her mum only called the school and not the police. That's actual bodily harm. *It weren't my fault?*' His voice filled his chest. 'You can't go around behaving like this.' His eyes thinned. Rothko watched blankly. Waiting to see what was going to happen. 'Can't you hear me? Hello?'

'I can hear you.'

'Tell me what happened?'

But where were they supposed to begin? At the kiss? Or at the voices of the clean, normal boys telling them to do it again? Or at the blackout that swallowed them up when they felt the rage overtaking. They didn't know she was only thirteen.

'First, I find you face down on the floor. Barely fucking breathing.' Hurting from it. Lashing out. 'Now you're beating up little schoolgirls?' Rothko felt tired. Everything moved in circles. 'I thought we were turning a corner. What happened to starting again?'

Things started to circle and lurch.

'Miss Shoffa said she can't help you any more than she has. She's throwing you out, and to be fair, I don't blame her. They don't want you coming back to sit the rest of the exams.'

'Do we have to do this now, Dad?' Ezra, cut off midstream, was annoyed at the interjection. 'I'm tired.'

'*Why* are you tired? What have you been doing?' Ezra dropped into the chair opposite. They faced each other. Rothko's head was heavy, and they stared at the floor. Piled on the chair like wet washing.

'What are we doing? We've got to do something. You can't just behave like this, and think it's not a problem. You stole a pack of pills off your friend's mum who's got cancer. You nearly fucking died on your own. In your bedroom. What do you think that would have done to me? To your sister? Sean? To Sean's mum?' Rothko shook their head, thinking *Sean wouldn't care if I died.* 'Just *think* about it. Think about what you're doing. You beat up a little kid so badly you fractured her ribs. Can't you see? It's not ok. This is not ok, Rothko.' Quieter now, sadder. 'Where've you gone?'

Rothko took their cap off. 'I'm here.' Held on to the back of their head. Ezra felt trapped, caught under something heavy. Desperate to get out. To get them both out. But all Rothko saw was the self-satisfaction. The raised eyebrows. The loud out-breaths. Looking at things and then looking away. Until Ezra slammed his fist on the table, then put it to his mouth. Rothko found the dramatics of the situation surreal and forced the laugh that filled their mouth back down their throat. They felt some pity for Ezra, fists clenched on the table, sweat prickling at his temples, eyes bulging in self-righteous despair.

'You're going to end up just like her.'

The pain of it was grit in Ezra's eyes and mouth and nose. He dropped his head and pushed the heels of his hands against his eyelids. The silence of the room engulfed them both until Ezra, blinking, lifted his head to see Rothko gathering strength from the table they were slumped over and lifting their body up slowly.

'Sit down.'

But they didn't.

'What about the new start? You were working hard. We were turning things around?' It was so confusing. How was Ezra supposed to be handling this? He didn't know.

Rothko kept their silence. There was nothing they could say. Ezra's stare was getting itchy and they wanted to be alone. They turned towards the door. They had to get out of the room and the pressure and his eyes on them.

'Where are you going?'

'Out.'

'You just got in.' Ezra pushed his chair back, jumped up to slam the door shut before they reached it, and he held it shut as Rothko tried to pull it open.

'You're not going out. To do what?' Rothko pulled against the door; Ezra pushed it shut. He grabbed Rothko's shoulders, trying to pull his child away from the things he knew he couldn't protect her from, but Rothko pushed all their weight against the restraint, and got past him.

They ran up to their room. Ezra following behind them. They grabbed a few things. Change of clothes, stash from under the bookshelf. The little wedge of cash they'd made from serving up that they kept in an old film cannister. Then Ezra was with them, following them as they left the bedroom, pulling at their clothes; they shook him off, on the landing at the top of the stairs.

Rothko turned to face him, batted his hands away and squared up. Chest to chest. Breathing hard. Their eyes were dull as old coins as they threw two punches. Ezra blocked the fists, absorbed the blows, and slapped Rothko, five, six times around the head with an open hand. 'What's the matter with you?' he was saying. 'Stop it.' Trying to get them to calm down. But Rothko was raging, punching hard till Ezra fell back, holding his jaw. And Rothko stumbled down the stairs with Ezra grabbing at them from behind.

'If you leave here now that's it.' He was shouting it. 'You can't come back, not after this.'

He didn't want her out there, where all the trouble was. He wanted her to stay home with him. Where he could keep her safe. But instead, he was pulling Rothko's hair and grabbing at their clothes as Rothko pulled away from him, and Rothko was shouting too, 'Get off me. You better get the fuck off me.' Then they were chest to chest again and Rothko's burning skin the rage like falling rocks, halfway down the stairs, below Ezra, punching up into his guts with all their sorry might and Ezra bearing down. But Rothko kicking at him with their awkward legs, trying to keep their balance.

'Fucking do it again. Go on.'

And the hardness of their voice was a shock to him. He was trying to hold them, keep them, but Rothko was throwing knees and elbows and pushing with their chest, as Ezra held their arms, thinking he was trying to stop the violence. He lost his balance. His full weight fell against Rothko and the two of them went down the stairs and sprawled across the hallway and Rothko hit the back of their head against the doorframe and their shoulder smashed against the door. Ezra with them, still gripping Rothko's upper arms as hard as he could, a terrible pain in his eyes and Rothko was pushing the hands away, and kicking out against him with their knees from underneath him as they scrambled, which made it worse and worse and then finally, they were standing up and Ezra was still trying to hold them. Trying to stifle their punches into his hug. Trying to keep them in a world they didn't want, but it was their only option. 'No more chances,' he told them. 'I mean it. If you leave now. You're on your own. Stop it. Just calm down.' But it wasn't working. Rothko's head went veering backwards away from Ezra, right through the stained-glass panel in the front door. Coloured glass smashed all around them. Ezra let go then and Rothko turned and wrenched the door open, their eyes wide with stress, and fell onto their back in the front garden path. They wriggled backwards, away from Ezra, who stood at the open door. Rothko, climbing sorely to their feet, in their socks, checked the back of their head with an accusing hand, but there was no blood.

Ezra threw their trainers out the open door, and they hit Rothko in their head, face. Rothko grabbed them, put them on. Stood in the front garden and screamed.

'You think you can survive out there without me?' Ezra watched his youngest walk away. 'You can't do this.' But Rothko was gone.

Ezra shut the door. Held it closed. *The fucking neighbours.* Stood in the hallway, glass all around, dizzy from the sudden lack of Rothko. The aftermath of conflict left a tingling in the air. He went and sat on the couch, like *what now*? He felt as if he were being observed, by himself, from above. He was so tired. He lay down on his back, aware of each corner of the empty room pressing towards him. His anger subsiding. Confused. In the family home. Without his family.

The only way she'd learn what she was losing by going the way she was going, was if he cut her off completely. That would shock her into focus. That would bring her back to him before it got too late.

He'd rather it was him that taught her the hard lessons than the world out there.

If he let her behave however she wanted, unchecked, how would she learn that actions have consequences? What kind of a parent would he be?

No.

This was the right thing to do.

She'd soon realise her mistake.

It was the only hope he had of her returning.

TEN

Rothko walked the empty streets towards the meadows. But no one really hung about up there since the police got called to break up a fight and everyone got their drugs confiscated. They took the route that cut through Dionne's estate, stopped at the off-licence by her block. They could feel the ache in their head from going through the glass door. Their hand kept going to the tender places on their limbs where the blows had been absorbed. Testing for bruises.

They read the notices in the window till they spotted a couple of the older lot; Kathy and Jon-Boy. Lost ones. Could have been in their twenties but it was hard to tell. Gristly headed space cadets, drifting in the wake of too much acid. Kathy was curled up laughing, sat on the wall outside the offy, bag of glue in her hand. Permanently sunburnt face with bright, clear eyes and sores round her nostrils. Little zip-up hoody and rainbow-patterned laces in her boots. Jon-Boy was stood next to her, beatboxing terribly and chanting to himself. *Om Shanti.* Rat's tail and a shaved head. Black jean jacket with the sleeves cut off.

Rothko greeted them with a raised fist. Spuds. Touched shoulders. 'Can you buy me some beers?'

Kathy leaned up from the wall and shouted, 'No, we can't. You shouldn't be drinking.' Rothko didn't say anything. Just looked at her. 'She don't know what to say!' Kathy laughed. 'Don't worry, I aint going to tell on you.'

'Leave her alone,' Jon-Boy pitched in. 'She's my mate, she is.' And he passed Rothko his bottle and said, 'here you are, dread. Have a go on that. I'll get your beers, what d'you want?' Rothko peeled a fiver out their pocket.

'Six for a fiver, whatever's on offer?' And Jon-Boy bounced off, walking on his toes.

'Quick, give it here to me.' Kathy reached for the bottle, but Rothko waved it away from her. Swigged it. And she laughed at that, clapped her hands. 'You're alright, you are. Little nutcase, aren't you.'

Was this their life?

Still sitting out here in twenty years like these two? Like Ezra was afraid they would?

Jon-Boy returned victorious, patted the wall beside him. 'Come chill.' Rothko looked over his head and saw the three of them reflected in the dark window of the shop behind the wall. Felt like looking at a memory of the future.

'Nah I'm gone, anyway. Laters, you lot.' They passed a beer to each of their elders. Paid the toll that bought release and took the steps up to the meadows.

They crossed the fields. Alone. Plotted on a tree stump. Caught the last glare of the sun disappearing between the gaps in the trees. Thirsty for something. They poured a whole can of lager down their throat. But that didn't quench it.

They called Dionne, but no-one answered. She'd probably left her phone in her bedroom or something and now she was watching TV. They pictured her, barefoot on the couch, curled up with her face on a cushion watching *EastEnders*. Eating Doritos. Agnes on the armchair, twisting wire with her pair of tiny pliers. Her glasses making her eyes look huge, saying, 'I don't know how you can watch this nonsense.' And then two minutes later, saying 'No! Is she trying to kiss *him*? But isn't that her brother-in-law?!' And Dionne saying, 'I thought you said it was nonsense?' They looked forward to being snuggled into that scene. Dionne's head on their lap, her arms around their body.

They couldn't call Sean. Not after what they'd done. They hated him for taking himself away. Where were they going to go? A stab of inspiration. They called Sarai.

'Hello?' She sounded confident. Laughy.

'Hello.' Hearing their sister's voice made them cry.

'What's happened?' Sarai was in a noisy room, sounded like a pub, Rothko heard her walking away from voices and clattering. 'Rothko? You ok?'

'Yeah. Nothing happened.' Rothko stopped crying. Wiped their face with their dirty sleeve.

'What you been up to?' Sarai, outside the student union, sat down on the kerb and pressed her phone to her ear. Nokia 3210.

'Not much. Just seeing how you are. How's uni?'

'It's fun, yeah. It's funny. People are weird.'

'What kind of weird?' It was nice to think about somewhere else existing.

'Like. I don't know. People play guitar and stuff.'

Rothko laughed despite the misery in their cheeks. 'Weird.' Rothko listened to the sounds of traffic on the other end. Imagined Sarai standing on a street in Glasgow. What did Glasgow look like? They had no idea.

'Are you sad today, Roth?' They hadn't slept the night before. Their jaw was hurting. They could feel the fight all over them like sunburn.

'No, I'm alright.'

'Did you hurt yourself?' Sarai's voice was slow and quiet. Rothko pushed the phone in close to their ear. 'You haven't taken anything again? Have you?'

'No.'

'That's good.'

'Saraiah?' They never used her full name; she didn't miss the significance. 'Can I come and stay with you?'

'Up here?'

'Dad's kicked me out.'

She murmured sympathetically. 'Ah mate. Why?'

'Had a fight with this kid on a bus. Got chucked out of school. It's long . . . I don't even . . .' They were so tired of being who they were and doing the things they did. So tired and so stuck.

'Just tell him you're sorry?'

'But can't I come up there?'

'I would but . . . We've got more people than we're meant to have, and the landlord's already on our case about it. I'm sharing a single bed with Scott as it is.'

'Just on the couch?'

'We don't have a couch. Every room's a bedroom except the kitchen and you couldn't make a bed in there.' They listened to each other, standing still in different places.

'Ok. Don't worry.'

'What about Sean?'

'Yeah, I'll try him. Good shout.' They tried to sound cheerful. 'Listen, I've got to go now.'

'You sure you're ok?'

'I'm good yeah. Honest.' They sounded convincing.

'Alright, shithead. Thanks for calling.'

'I miss you,' Rothko told her.

'I miss you too, mate.'

They hung up. Stared at the little brick phone in their hand but didn't know how to make it connect them with other people.

They called Dionne again. No-one answered. They gave it one more and still couldn't get through. They could just go round and knock on the door?

If she was out, they could sit in the alley on the old couch back there and wait for her. It was quiet in that alley, out of the wind. They sat there together before when things were good. The memory of it was comforting. They just wanted to sit down on something that wasn't a hard brick wall and wasn't out on the street where everyone could see them sitting on their own.

They called again, without meaning to. Found themself listening to the phone ringing. Hadn't even noticed their hand going to the button.

They sent a text: U indoors? X

Nothing came back. They waited as long as they could, then sent another: wot u up 2 2nt?Xx

Nothing.

The air was darkening around them, thickening to indigo.

They cracked another beer, swigged this one slower than the last. Drank half and got up from the wall. They picked up their bag of beers, their rucksack, their open can and carried it all awkwardly, into the lowness of the night. Out of the fields, and back down the steps into the sparkling dark of the seaside town. Strange fog in the air, like a gag in their mouth. Close as a pillow. Sometimes the mist came off the sea like this and made the whole place feel like it was under water.

Maybe she'd fallen asleep.

Their bag dug into their shoulder. It was hurting from where they'd gone into the door. They rang again, holding the phone in the crook of their neck while they carried the beer bag in one hand and the open beer in the other.

The ringing became hypnotic, they forgot what it was. Just a sound that they were listening to as they stamped down empty roads. Lights on in the houses. People in kitchens. And Rothko alone in the dark.

Then suddenly it clicked and picked up. There was music playing, laughter. Nobody said anything.

'Hello?' Rothko said.

'Hello?' said a low voice they didn't recognise. 'Who's this?' the voice asked, more laughing.

'It's me.'

'Hello, me.' They heard people chatting loudly, someone singing along to music. *It's not right. But it's ok.*

'Where's Dionne?'

'She's busy, mate.' And the phone went dead. Rothko stopped still on the street, looking up at the shop fronts. The phone still pressed between their ear and shoulder. They felt like they were about to wet themself.

They called back. It rang off. They called back. It rang off. Their breath rose. Their head got tight. They called back. It rang off. They called back. The voice again. Rowdy now.

'What d'you want?' Laughing at Rothko. 'Go away.'

'Where's Dionne?'

'She'll call you tomorrow.' Sounds of lots of people talking, rising laughter, people shouting over each other. Dizzee Rascal. 'I Luv U'.

'Put her on the phone. I want to talk to her.'

'Just go home. You little weirdo. She don't want to talk to you.'

'What? Fuck off.'

'Alright. I'll fuck off.'

'Wait. Who is this? Where's Dionne?'

'Go home you fat dyke. Stop calling.'

His words were hard to wade through. They rose up from the pavement, knee deep. Rothko stopped walking so they could finish their beer. They threw the empty can into someone's hedge. Started walking off but felt bad about it and tried to retrieve it. It was too high to reach, and they got scratched by the hedge and fell into it like an idiot. Their head was loud with questions as they hurried on, feeling short and hoping they hadn't been seen.

Who was he anyway? Was he trying to fuck her?

Maybe Rothko hadn't done it right last night?

Where was she?

It was still there, in the box by the bed. What if that boy on the phone had found it? The toy Rothko had to use because they weren't complete. What if she told him all about it? *No.*

They reassured themself. They were being mental.

It was love.

It was only a few weeks ago, they were sitting on the beach in the morning after the dub rave. Blazing in the playground outside her flat. Sitting in the alley on the couch. Kissing. Listening to Tupac. *Me against the world.*

Rothko bowled on. Slow, wide strides. Shame like a bone in their throat. Until they came to a stop. Stood in the street outside her block. Looking up at her windows.

The lights were on and the front door was open. Rothko could sense the movement of bodies inside. Two people were leaning over the streetside balcony, smoking. They had their hoods up. Arms round each other's shoulders.

Rothko lit a cigarette. What's the big deal? Dionne's got some friends round. Nothing wrong with that. Didn't hear the phone going. Some dickhead's picked it up and just said them things for a laugh. People say stupid shit all the time. It's probably nothing to do with Dionne. And so what? It's not a party they haven't been invited to. She's just been out with some people, and decided to bring a few back to hers. What was the matter with them? Getting upset over nothing. Why did they always have to be so uptight. It was a secret, their thing. It had to be that way, because otherwise people would get in their business and wouldn't understand it and make it ugly. Dionne had explained it a million times and Rothko got it. They did. They got it.

Still.

Their neck hurt from looking up. They needed to get their head straight, work out where they were going to go.

They walked off round the corner, heading for the alleyway. Soon as they turned down it, they felt less exposed. It was calmer than the street. No cars passing. Hazy light from the windows above. They hadn't been here since last month, with her. But it was the same. The couch was still there. Tapestry cushions ripped and sagging. Big bag of newspapers. Cardboard boxes flattened on the ground where someone had made their bed. They looked at it all fondly. Finally, they could sit down. They rested their arm on the carved wooden armrest, lifted their cap to run their hand through their hair and cracked a fresh one. Two cans pissed on an empty stomach. Hot inside their brain from it. Didn't even want more. But that wasn't going to stop them.

They sat there, waiting for something. But there was nothing to wait for. A long time passed. They must have fallen asleep because they woke up suddenly. Shivering.

They dug around in the earth with their keys. Made a hole. Filled it in. Made another hole. Deeper. Filled it in again. The alley smelt of leaves and rubbish, but Rothko wasn't afraid of it. Even with the flies and the low hanging branches. They had nowhere else to go. It was a sanctuary.

The moon was up there, they could see it through the chain link fence. Hard silver hole in the sky. *Fat dyke.* It hurt them deep down in the back of their guts where the darkness lived. It hurt worse than the bruises on their arms or the side of their head. It made them fidget.

Slow tears threatened their eyes but they blinked them away.

Fuck her.

Fuck all of them.

They'd been sitting on the swings just over there. Holding hands until the kids walked up. The shudder that went through them when she'd pulled her hand away.

Visions of Dionne, her body like a snake with breasts, tipping Rothko back and how they had let her open their legs, even though Rothko went cold and didn't like it, holding onto her back while she pushed inside.

They thought it was different with Dionne. If they'd been a boy, none of this shit would be happening.

They dug through their bag for their roll ups, their lighter, their hands found their can of deodorant and pulled it from the rucksack. They sprayed a long plunge of it into their mouth, through their t-shirt, woozy from it, dizzy and giggly. It melted things. That's all they wanted. Just to feel something different.

They lifted their head with great effort and rolled a cigarette, swigging from their can in sloppy jerks. They put the unlit roll-up to their lips and bit it gently while they held up the can of deodorant and shook it. They held the lighter up in front of it and sprayed and watched it burst out like a blow torch, PFFFFFFFF like a roaring machine. They smiled.

They lit their cigarette and puffed it so fast they felt queasy. They pulled their phone from their pocket and rang again. It rang off. They rang again. It rang off. They sat with their knees far apart, their trainers in the rubbish, their coat splayed out either side of them, head back, cap tipped up. They felt more and more tense each time the phone locked off; it was like they were being physically held back. They needed to do something. Break something.

Sometimes, ok, sometimes, it was true, they couldn't get hold of Dionne. That did happen. Sometimes Dionne managed to get an eighth of chang off a man from the bar she worked in, and she'd sell a few bits to the kids in her year so she could keep the rest for free. They all thought she was their friend, only Rothko knew the truth, that she was playing them. Scamming them to get her bit. It was like she'd told Rothko; they were the only one who really knew her.

And sometimes, when all that was going on, Rothko couldn't get hold of her. A few days later, when she would be back in touch, Rothko would ask her what had happened and she would say, 'It was just *long*. you know what them lot are like. Thick as shit. Anyway. I got two g for us, so who's laughing.' And it made sense to Rothko, but they wished the other people knew that Dionne didn't really like them. That she was just playing them. And that really, she liked Rothko best.

Ezra throwing their trainers at their face while they lay there on the front path, and Dionne on the bus after the fight, her fingernails tracing patterns on their knee, saying *you should have just left it* and Sarai on the phone saying *did you hurt yourself?* and Meg underneath it all, crying in her anorak, crouching in the alleyway, and Sean up the meadows with his guard down, saying *you stole from my family* and Meg clutching their shoulders with her smiling hands, dancing deep into their eyes but her own eyes gone, and the voice on the phone saying *she don't want to talk to you.*

They got up and kicked the bag of newspapers as hard as they could. Kicked it open and the papers spilled out. They grabbed handfuls, stuffed them down the back of the old couch, punching them down inside the cushion covers, all the coils springing out of the foam while they stuffed it full. They picked up the deodorant again and sprayed it all over the screwed-up newspaper. Sprayed it down inside the cushions. They held their lighter to the spray, so it torched, and they torched the newspapers.

In control of something.

They kept spraying until the can was done. Most of the newspaper burnt away to nothing, but the heavy fabric was fuming black and it smelt of burning hair and burning plastic. The whole thing yellow and melting. The foam inside, coming alive with fire. Transforming. The frame of the couch started to take. The wind whipping through the alley and the flames getting bigger. They fed it more cardboard. It was licking at the palettes stacked beside the fence. They heaved the palettes down so it could get to them more easily.

It was really going up.

The top flames were orange, but underneath those flames were other flames; bluer, greener, pushing up from under the orange ones, bubbling the material inside the couch to oil. The foam, the threads, the fabric took. The palettes on the floor all took. The whole thing took.

They swelled as it did, all the fierce colours were theirs. Liquid. Solid. Gas. All things at once. They coaxed it, praised it with what they could find to treat it with; branches, rubbish, slabs of rotting MDF. Devouring force that created itself. It was huge and like an animal. A living thing. More living than this fucking place. This was life. The essence of life. Eyes blazing, reflecting it back at itself. It bore down on them, and they became aware of its magnitude too late. Its heat, its smoke. They stood before it, spellbound. A child in front of a speeding train.

ELEVEN

They pressed their body back against the fence on the opposite side of the alleyway. They swallowed more beer, transfixed.

They were too hot. The flames were biting into the skin of their forehead and hands. Soon it would be too much. Their clothes were heavy on their body. They breathed into it, felt the closeness of its breath against them. Grabbed their rucksack from the floor, threw the last can inside it and swung it across their back.

The couch was blazing. The rubbish beside it had started to crackle and glow. They were still backed up to the chain-link fence, laughing without moving their mouth, just their breath and their teeth were laughing. Impressed.

They'd never been this close to a fire this big, and they wanted to sit down inside it. Until it spat two long nails from one of the palettes into the ground behind them. And as they flew out of the fire, the nails screamed. The wooden boards of the garden shed that backed on to the alley were starting to buckle. It was too much.

They bombed it out of the alley. Ducked round the back of the blocks. Stopped on the street looking up at her balcony. Feeling the fire all over their skin still. Smelling its breath on their clothes.

Shit.

They heard the sirens.

It was loud in the street and people were shouting and this wasn't good. They best not be seen here. They took off. Sprinting as hard as they could. Trying to sprint their way back to before. The whole town grim as the sea but they ran so hard it boiled their sweat.

Where the fuck were they supposed to go?

They wanted to run back in time to when they were five years old and make everything turn out different. But they couldn't do that, and they had to get off the street because this wasn't a little mistake. This wasn't skipping school or getting caught with a draw. This was bad. Someone might have been hurt. And they might have been seen already, looking shifty as fuck, running like this. And after that thing on the bus, what if the girl had gone to the feds? Maybe they were looking for Rothko already? And if not the feds then that girl and her boys would be looking, if they'd hurt her the way their dad said they had hurt her. It wasn't safe being out on the street. What the fuck were they playing at?

There was only one place they could go. Only one person who wouldn't ask questions.

They swerved up, through the winding passages, past the bowling alley, the cinema. They ran until it was hard going; twinges in their hips coughing up metallic spuds of phlegm.

Down Turpin Road, dipping past the vacant lots and abandoned factories, they passed a pair of heavy steel gates, open, and slowed their pace to peer inside. They saw a man, pushing the gates closed, locking them up with a heavy chain, and something about him. Rothko slowed. Their eyes met. He nodded at Rothko, 'You alright?' That voice. It felt familiar. Like the one they heard inside their head sometimes.

He closed the gate, but Rothko could still see his hands

pulling the heavy chain through as he locked up. Something in the sureness and the sadness of those hands made Rothko look down at their own hands briefly. Ash and dirt. Rothko stuffed them in their pockets and decided to keep going.

Down into the busier streets, where the pubs and takeaways and bars were. Baggy knots of people stood around, lit by neon signs.

Maybe she'd be in a good place.

They could feel someone watching but no-one was there. They could have sworn they heard that voice again. They shook it off. Wiped their face on their sleeve and rang the bell.

And there she was. In her little swingy dress and her mascara and her black tights, saying, 'Hello *you*! Come in then, you're letting the draught in.' She ushered them in, checking up and down the street behind them before she closed the door, and she followed them into the front room.

There were people stood around. Music playing. She rushed them into a scratchy embrace. Her face lit up with pride. 'My *baby*. This is my little baby.' She twirled through the room, and they were clapped on the shoulder with big hands. And kissed on the cheek with giggling mouths.

Two women dancing together. Pulling each other's hips. One had a shaved head, big hoop earrings, barefoot on the shagpile rug. The other was in a baggy knitted jumper, nothing else under it, skin like sunshine.

Two big-bellied, bearded men were sat together, and Errol was there, the little wiry friend of Meg's, tough as a collie, and the red-headed woman named Carleen that Rothko remembered from the pub was there, and a scrunched-up girl, hardly flesh at all, just sad eyes, lipstick and a strip of black denim. Slim and pointy with a slow smile. Rothko liked her. They stayed close to Meg, who was shining, with Rothko there to shine for.

And later, sat around, they were all talking about someone they knew who'd just died, and Errol was saying he'd heard that middle-aged men were more at risk of suicide than any other group, especially ones who weren't well off, and one of the beardy men said, 'Blimey, that's you innit, Gary?' And everyone laughed.

'Ever thought about it?' the slim, sad girl asked.

'Him?' Meg cackled her gravelly laugh. 'He couldn't kill hisself even if he *wanted* to. I've seen him trying to put eyedrops in!' And the whole room laughed long and hard at that, and Rothko felt proud to be hers because she was funny and she made people laugh in that long hard way, where their heads went back, and their mouths opened wide.

What if someone was hurt in the fire?

How long had they been in this room? With these people?

What if the pigs were out looking?

It didn't matter how long. This was where they belonged now. Not with Ezra and his comfortable dreams. But here, with Meg and these lot, who saw through the bullshit.

Ezra grabbing their shoulders while their head went back through the glass panel of the door. And the girl on the bus with her craggy face, closing her eyes as Rothko swung their feet down into her chest.

What if the fire spread through the flats? What if it went up to Dionne's?

Here with these people. Free.

This was more like it.

The curtains are drawn. They're listening to 'Fast Car' and everyone's talking and moving around in small steps and things are not attached to other things and Meg's crouching at the table and Rothko watches her, notices her back is very straight. She's wiping the hair out of her face and her shoulders are bare and she's talking to the man next to her and she's smoking what she said she wasn't smoking anymore but there it is, Rothko can see it, and she is sucking in a focused way, her whole body is sucking in, she is still with the effort, straining into the act, and now she's finishing. Looking back towards Rothko, but Rothko's sense is that she doesn't see them, because her eyes have gone. She is staring. Fixed on a distant point, she's not looking at Rothko, she's looking at something behind them. Rothko turns to look, but there's nothing there.

Their phone rings. It's Dionne.

Dionne.

'Alright, you?' Their voice sounds strange to Dionne. Not like them.

'I'm sorry about before,' she tells them. 'Was a mad night.' She yawns and Rothko listens to the shape of her throat opening, loses themself briefly in the vastness of her breath. It's late. They're in the cold part of the night now. The no-way-back part. The fast road to dawn. 'Some dickhead had my phone, I don't remember. I didn't know it was you that was calling.' Rothko can't really hear her, it's too loud in the room they're in and anyway they don't want to hear her. They don't want to sit around at her feet anymore, waiting for permission to suck the dirt out from between her toes. Or something. *Boys round here want to break things.* They wish they could be angry with her. But her voice in their head is too loud. They want to feel past her. Into themself. But. 'Where are you anyway?' she asks. Rothko blocks their other ear and hunches into the phone.

'Nowhere,' they say.

'Did you hear about the fire? All the fire engines come out and everything.' Rothko smiles at the memory of it, surging. 'I don't know what started it. They managed to put it out, though, thank God.'

Rothko grins, their jaw glitches. 'That's good, then.'

'They had ambulances out there.'

'Was anyone hurt?'

'Don't know. Hope not.'

Rothko is far away. From her. From everything. It's a good feeling. Like finally, her power over them is loosening. And even if someone has been hurt in the fire, it doesn't feel like it's their problem anymore because they are far away in another place with other rules. High stakes. Rough skin. Hard eyes. What fire? This room is the only. Dionne's still talking down the phone. 'Everyone's out on the street. Still now. It's mad. To think. What could have . . . you know? People could have really been . . . do you know what I mean? Could have *died*.'

Rothko hunches over further, lips kissing the phone as they ask her, 'Do you like me?'

They can hear her frowning. 'You know I do.'

'So why do you hide it?'

She seems deflated by the sudden change of subject. But her voice is tender when she says, 'It's *because* I like you that I don't want people to know.'

Rothko drops the phone into their lap and locks off the call with a tender thumb. She rings again. They stare at her name, but they let it ring.

See how she likes it.

They pocket their phone and rejoin the group. Meg's wafting her hands and breathing in fast with her teeth clenched shut, drawing the satisfaction in over her lips. Dropping her head back. She passes the pipe to the man beside her, Rothko watches him with it. Taking a throaty, squinty smoke and frowning into the taste. His whole face clenches. Clenches. Clenches. Opens. Breathes out. And he goes to pass the pipe to Rothko, but stops and asks Meg, 'Can she have it?'

And Meg says, 'No she bloody can't.' But he offers it to Rothko anyway, buzzing, and Rothko looks to Meg, but Meg is leaning back with her hands behind her, her entire body is a tuning fork, conducting the vibration, feeling the tingles in her lips. And it looks nice to Rothko to be that free. To be that dark and dead and free from feeling. To be that stuck and ill and sick and scared. It looks like love.

Rothko takes the pipe out of the man's open hand, he doesn't resist. 'That's my little girl you fucking . . .' Meg says but she isn't looking at Rothko, she's looking at the ceiling, smiling at the feeling going through her. Smiling at it quick while it lasts, there it is.

The slim, sad girl drops forwards on to her forearms and says in a wispy, broken voice, 'Do you know how?'

And Rothko looks at her from under their hair and says, 'Fuck off,' and the girl says,

'Give it to me I'll show you.' And Rothko turns away from her to flick the lighter and heat the rock as if it were a piece of hash, can't be that hard? And everything's already gone to shit, so might as well feel good. In all of this. They breathe it in, suck the smoke off the nasty little piece of spite until the judders come and everything is drawn in scratchy black outlines and their chest expands and fills the room, but they are weightless and not feeling and not thinking and not real at all, but more real. More real. More. *Yes*. And their chest is a fist hammering at a window and the faces are bright and they have nothing inside them but this very moment, the past is obliterated and the future is imaginary and Meg is sat on her feet now, crouching down in her swingy little dress with the pin in her fist and the lines in her face like screwed-up paper like pages turning into this big breath that they share that feels so good it feels like

> Rothko came to and the whole world was carnage. Monsters in the dark sniffing cannisters of varnish. None of it was real. Not the packs of laughing men who stared at them when they passed, or the women sat on walls who talked slow and smoked fast. Not the kids in baggy hoods who beefed each other for a taste. Or the manic little fantasists who gnashed their teeth and flashed their eyes like living breathing magazines, pitched up by the cash machines, trying to get another squeeze out of an empty packet. Incremental change solidified into monumental shifts, new blood for old myths. New grudges. Old gifts. As undeniable as flesh turning sour. Kiss kiss. Every hour was a tower to escape from. Risk it out the window, headfirst through the hailstorm. Bliss before everything else. Living like a fish in a bag at the fairground, head butting the plastic, finally they see it. It's one thing wanting freedom. It's another thing to be it. Pissed up on the clifftop, breathing out mist. Time tunnelled inwards to spirals and drifts. Rothko never had time till they lost time. They were still waiting for the clouds to lift. Sucking on the pipe for release. Running rings round slow police. The wind was everywhere. Cuffing at them like a boxer. Whipping rain. Bullied by their solitude, the town was mean. They wandered through its dirty veins and alleyways. Leading. Following. Their mother's hollow face was the dirge the traffic sang. Rothko sang along with their

hand on their heart, the grand anthem of *I'll do it differently.* But it all fell away to *one light one dark*. Sometimes you've just got to fail miserably. Time had collapsed. There was no way back to the start. Until Rothko felt disgusting in their heart. Made of something not worth trusting, maybe something they'd grow out of, but they didn't and they couldn't, and it changed the world around them. When Rothko looked back and tried to pinpoint the moment the world lost order and time ran away, they pinned it on that grey day when they knocked on at Meg's and decided to stay. They were doing their best against Cause and Effect, when Life jumped from the ropes, landed hard on their chest and started screaming over every word and into every breath. Still, the stupid human heart hopes for miracles that won't come. Miracles, like *take me if you want. But please save Mum.* They let themself surrender to the doss house in December. It was good to laugh at things and not remember. Complex pleasure. Getting some attention from the girls with heavy weather in their eyes. They never said their goodbyes to their old life, they just saw through its disguise. What was truth what was lies? What was loose what was tied? They couldn't decide. They could hear the whispers, whispers didn't mean a thing. They were buds in the spring. Always out on a limb. Let them look, look away, look again. Look within. Wrong skin, wrong bones, hair, voice, hormones. Wrong for them all. Wrong her. Wrong him. But they'd gone too far to retrace their steps. Sometimes it was good to forget. This is how Rothko went riches to rags. Itching for a bag. Things were getting switchy and the picture kept lagging behind the soundtrack. Was Meg setting the pace or was she picking up the slack? Sometimes in the dead of night, they could hear their old life singing in the phone lines, ringing in the wind, but nothing had a shape beyond the foil and the lighter. Nothing was brighter than the vacuum within. When did Ezra stop searching the benches and tents with a photo of Rothko grinning in braces? When he found her again, sitting out with some friends, off her head by the skips round the back of big Sainos. She had the same face, but she wasn't the same though. Her name was a pain in his stomach all day. He prayed she would change or stay out of harm's way. *Please God, keep my child out of danger.* But the third time she raided his house for his Ray-Bans, his TV, his blender, his electronic shaver, he cleaned up the mess and didn't even complain. He'd tried to give her shelter when the thunderstorm came, but enough was enough, the whole thing was insane and he realised no one could save her. Even Sarai stopped turning up. She'd been banging on the doors for months *I want to see my sister.* Traipsing round dirty squats where furtive teens sold rocks to people who were forty odd. Until a thing in her broke. Because her sister told her lies every second that she spoke. Sarai lost Rothko to the fire and smoke. She had no choice but to let Rothko go. It happened slowly. They ran out of road. It was lonely but so's life. She tried to keep close but time goes by and soon the pain's dug in so deep, a whole lifetime can pass in the space between meetings. It starts over one thing but soon it's just like that, the fight is the reason they're fighting. It's just what it is and Sarai can't rely on Rothko for nothing but nightmares. Dionne in the real world was feeling left behind. Like Rothko had betrayed her when they sank beneath the grind the way they did. It's hard when she sees them round town, cos she used to be their everything, but now they're not around. Annoyed to the point she gets reckless out raving, ends up regretful and blaming Rothko for not being strong enough to stop behaving like they didn't have a thing worth saving. Soon it's a stress when they pass in the street. Dee crosses the road and kisses her teeth when she sees them. Now it's just grief left between them. Because how can you help if the person you love isn't helping themself and you're burdened enough? Agnes got laid off and Dee had to change up. Real life kicked in, and Dee had to face up; they weren't from the same stock, or cut from the same cloth, or boiled in the same pot at all. Cos pain is pain. But some people's pain is a story they make up. And some people's pain is a skin they can't take off. The way Dionne saw it, Rothko was cushioned by money; the buffer of having somebody to be there whenever they stumbled. However they crumbled, Rothko didn't really know *Trouble*. How could they run to the gutters, and not make the most of how lucky they were and how loved? It was ugly. When someone's so desperate to drop, there's no point trying to catch. All Dionne could do in the end was detach. Summer found Rothko feeling cavalier; crusties carting sound systems around, parties in the woods and downs. Hitching rides. They'd never felt freer. Sleeping on a tarp under the pier. But summer never lasts. And neither does the gear. In the backlit hours, under heavy hands, strangled and sour, Meg went to work, tonguing the socket for a second of power, until the punters were finally numbed. She dismantled herself for a bag of dread powder. Each stranded encounter, each rancid devouring creature that rutted and drummed on her body. Each *sorry*, each *please*. Filling them softly. She spat on her palm and got down on her knees. You don't get to choose your disease. Dionne was a memory, Rothko didn't deep it. Never thought about the past anymore. Didn't need it. The habit grew. *It's me and you.* Nothing else could reach them. Every day they woke to feed it. Every night they worked to please it. To keep it calm. To feel its breathing getting steady in their arms as they rocked it into sleeping. They wanted things they couldn't name; they wanted rest. They wanted change. They wanted less than all of this; to get out from underneath the shame. They came close to wipeout time after time, but something always pulled them back before the soul began to climb. Wide eyes in low light, the room was a corridor, people got close in the shadow of the abattoir. Some folks don't understand what love is for, live their whole lives too scared to discover more. As soon as they met, they felt safe. Her name was Penelope, Pen was like a local celebrity. Her stepdad was a big money man in the town, he'd bought half of it up, just to tear it all down and sell it on for development. Pen and Rothko were in it together, trying to find their way back to forever. She told them everything, the whole sorry tale, how she could have had it all, but she'd ended up a failure. She pinned it on the day she told her mum it wasn't right, how her stepdad was touching her in ways she didn't like. He kept coming in her room at night. The telling didn't stop it. Mum didn't believe. So Pen left home, she felt safer on the streets. Barely fifteen, she was beyond help, trying to rein in a blackhole by herself. Years of it. Mum was at the end of her tether, scraping her up whenever she dropped, getting her admitted to centre after centre, treatment programs twelve grand a pop. Dried her out for a bit, but they never made her stop. Here she was at twenty-two. Seconds from time's up. Veins fucked. Bowels compacted. She didn't want to die, but she didn't want to live on his paycheck; just another property, something he threw money at, till it responded properly. She'd heard about a rehab in Thailand, a monastery. *This is it for me Rothko, it's got to be.* It was free to do a stint there, just had to get the travel up. The program was hardcore and no frills. You had to really want it, no methadone, no pills. Just graft and prayer. So, she was ending it here, she was starting it there. She'd raised about half the fare. She was doing it. Pen left town soon after, Rothko never knew if she made it or not, but sometimes when a night got hard, they still heard her laughter, and the dream that she had was one they never forgot. And why not? If she could do it, maybe they could do the same? If they could get Meg on a plane. They could see it so clear, a little house by the sea, couple chickens in the yard laying eggs, they could fix Meg's teeth, she could get some rest. New life. No stress. Nice weather. They could do it if they stuck to it, together. And every time they thought that thought it was chased by the thought of Pen's stepdad with his fortune in the safe. With his millions to waste and his relentless power, they could get a few grand in like half an hour. The picture got sharper with every blink. Platinum Rolex lying by the sink. One watch in their pocket and the skies were pink. They could call time on the filth and the stink. They told Meg they were hatching plans. It weren't a dead cert, but it was worth trying. She was either not listening, or didn't believe. *My sweet baby,* she squeezed them, sighing. Eyes never not crying. Hands never not holding, but never quite finding. Rothko was hardly a professional thief, once or twice they'd tagged along for a night, but they didn't have the wits, or the self-belief, you had to have a lot of front to really do a drum right. But there it was. The house on the hill. The big driveway. The fountain with the cherub and the lions on the posts. They were sure it was this one. Two a.m. Friday. Not a sound now Rothko, quiet as a ghost. Jimmying the lock with a comb. Foraging for better luck in someone else's well-stocked home. It was a mansion. Crystal chandeliers. Velvet drapes to draw against the little people full of bitterness and fears. Then Rothko heard a voice out on the stairs and froze. What ensued were heavy blows thrown with blunt aggression. Rothko exploded, Rothko melted and corroded. They were doing it for Meg, for Dionne, for Penelope. For all the things they'd never been, and all the things they'd never get to be. Rage. Bone deep and panoramic; when it came on like this, there was nothing else to see. It swept them out and pulled them in, dragged their bones and tore their skin, it was better to surrender than to try and swim free. And when it cleared, they saw themself stood above him, blood leaking from his ears. Face messed up, disgusting. White hair turning red, his body spread across the rug. They were still waiting for the body to get up. Any minute now, sure he was about to come alive when the judge said manslaughter and she gave them twenty-five. Time inside was different time. It passed, it barely passed. It drifted in, through tiny cracks, and pressurised the air, it moved across them, crushed them, locked their thoughts and stopped their function, it arrived in flashing ruptures and it left behind a glare. Staring through the mesh of their hands, head in their lap, time was the stuck drop hanging from the tap, their mind was a blocked pipe, screaming for release while the hands through the bedsheets covered them in grease. Reaching from the past, stifling and scarred, swimming fingers pulling at them from the shadows, *getting clean*, blood hardening, parting their lips, but too parched to take sips, watching their head roll away. Guillotine. Every follicle and socket aggravated, suffocating, brain pulsating through their temples, agitated and depressed at the same time. Heard the voice saying *you're alright.* But they'd been too long in the dark to even know they missed the light. Lungs full of smashed glass. Each breath dragged them backwards. Crushing from the edges with the dregs, cramps in their stomach, spasms in their legs. Vomiting forever while the sweats ran knives through their flesh. New start. Nice try. No dice. Chewing up the corners with the mice, saying *no paradise till you make a sacrifice.* Time passing. Not passing. Stop asking how long it's been. Keep looking at your hands. Looking at the pangs. No sense to anything, meaning is banned. Time wasn't real. Couldn't feel what they touched. The world was a smudge. There was no point to thoughts anymore. Just walk in a straight line and talk when you're asked to. Be normal. Laugh when it's time to. Bury yourself so that no one can find you. Soon enough, they'll all stop looking, it was sure. Awake in the foetal position, too bored to read. Too scared to play pool. Nuggets on Wednesday. Blank in the lunch line. Nothing beats hunger. Dionne smoking fags in a smile and a sundress. Fuck. It just felt too cruel. Funny how long you could stare at a wall. Waiting for the phone, knowing there was no one to call. Violence erupted like weather events. They tried to be more like the rest. Cos after a while no one wants to be friends with the kid if they're always depressed. It was the loneliness. Weary from knowing nobody and knowing nobody could know them. The girls were so bitter, they learned to steer clear. Heavy hitters on the wing liked to make a big deal from the littlest thing. Nothing worked like it did on the outside. So much to learn and no time for mistakes. Stood like a lump no one wanted on association, tongue tied. Always so much at stake. And no matter how much of it Rothko had taken, there was always much more to take. So, they forgot the past. Banished it. Finished it. Better to be new. Life was survival, and nothing was true. Time was a panic attack bearing down. Second by second. Just trying to get through. Stop crying. Play nice. Be passive. Then someone might love you enough to take care. They wanted a friend, like the others all had. So, they tried giving more than their share. Longing for belonging, better strong it. Reforged in the heat of it, beaten into shape. It was their only chance of escape. They were faster, clearer, louder, brighter, deader. At the end of every tether is the last thread gripped against the fall. And if Rothko couldn't feel, then they hadn't lost it all. Go numb. They learned to satisfy the needs of others. Their own needs were smothered and killed. If anything recovered, it was spilled in fractious anger, punches launched at solid doors, they let the girl they didn't like destroy them in their cell at night. Cos why not? Time was a mass without an outline, pound signs flashing on the slots at chucking out time, blood from their cut legs splashed, made the ground shine. Singalong sessions in the next pad. Bound for the reload. Drowning beneath it. Crowd surfing a room full of demons. The hole in their spirit was getting hard to plug. They wanted God to kill the part of them where all the darkness was. They were dying to live. But time after time, something always pulled them back before the soul began to climb. Bite down on the pillow, let it out in desperate shouts, then pull yourself together, raise your head and close your mouth. People fall apart in front of people. You can fall apart alone, but what good does it do you? Were they going to get through or let it beat them? *You're alright.* Rothko had a word with themself, and kept reaching. Was that another year gone past or just a breath? Shipped out. Meat wagon on the A-roads. Bashed around in the back, going places. Every landing was a sleeping volcano. Same old stories told by new faces. They understood the rules now. They'd had a little taste. Saw the tests they were assigned by dirty screws with restless minds. Who's hurting who? Who's worth avoiding? Who's for loving, who's for spoiling? Cruel as time became, they set themself against the fade and tried their best to get their head down and make everything ok. They had a reason to keep going. They had something to become. For the Rothko that they used to be when everything was young. They learned the power of routine. The strength of clear instruction. Learned the books, the looks, the crooked methods by which people functioned. How to get by without ever getting anywhere, when getting through a minute was infinite; but every ending they achieved was still only the beginning. And soon they learned to count the time in blame. They had been left behind by life, and really someone had to pay. Where was Meg in all of this? Out there in the filth, talking in manic sermons to anyone who'd hear, about her youngest daughter, poor girl taken off her by the courts, like a lamb to the slaughter, till she got enough to score, and made it all disappear. They sent her letters back. But she was still there in the mirror. The smaller they made her, the bigger she loomed. Ringing out forever through the ruins and the fumes, like the last note in the tune. Inside, time was like water through a sieve. They were sure they had more to give. But they had no evidence to prove to themself they could grow out of their smallness and live. Fifteen years of observing time, it was time to return to time. They had served their time. Time was returning. Time to put the work in, to working out if they were a person. *How long were you out there waiting for me? Were you looking, back then when there was nothing to see? Was it you? Did you touch my face when my face was a shadow and tell me you hoped I would learn how to be? Was it you I could hear? When I strayed too near to the edge, was it you that I felt? The soft word when I'd caught the rough end of the belt and I was giving everything to giving up on myself? Was it you?* Fifteen years unleashed on a Monday morning, sky like a ride at the funfair falling; Terrifying. Time was a nutcase, running up behind them. They couldn't block it out. It had found them. Final. Time was a bird in the flight path. Time's up. Time was the first dance. The last leg. Staunch as a dead branch, sleeping till spring for the relaunch. Let the pipes burst. Let it all come unstuck. Bypassed by life, trying hard to remember, this was the beginning not the end of it. *Time*. Time was alright just having the one glass. Time was a high-class brass with a dry laugh, who'd read it in the tea leaves, cashed in, dried up. Put it on red and bought her own night club. Time was a dead end. Time was a fine chance. Time was a butch at a line dance, *get it bro*. Time's come. Edgecliff calling. But were they getting free or were they falling? The truth was in doing. It was either resolve or ruin. Deep breath. No way out but through it. What else could they do? They took the only path that they knew. Going home. But was it the place they'd outgrown or a place to get to? A state to attain, a face in the rain, or the fear that swept through them, sure they'd be caught short before their next move? *Was it you I could hear? When I strayed too near to the edge, was it you that I felt? The soft hand when I'd caught the rough end of the belt, and I was giving everything to giving up on myself? How long were you out there looking for me?* That's when time delivered Rothko, pushed them out into today. Twenty years in freefall in a vacuum of delay. And here they were. The beginning had begun. The same Rothko they used to be when everything was young. They wanted to become. They'd run as hard as they could run, but they could never get clear. They were coming back to life. They were free and getting freer. In the corner of their smile, there was a weight there; the child they had been, the denial and the grief. It's not as simple as transition then relief. Or captivity/release. But Rothko was alive at last. Or they were alive at least. That first morning, underneath the heavy rain that came falling on the roof like it was trying to explain the source and the solution were the same. They saw it, the glory in the mundane, they didn't want luxury or anything as vain as entertainment, they just wanted this moment to last, they pushed the pedal down for sustain. But what they didn't hear, while they listened for the trains, is they were held in the arms of every future, every past, every first and every last, that at any given moment, every present must contain. It was all coming for them, slow motion. This moment. Time had them in its teeth, and it dragged them by the throat until it dropped them in today and said, *atonement.*

Today

ONE

Dreary midnight in a town of limited possibilities, Rothko and Fletcher set out for the cellar of the closed-down carpet shop with the boards on the windows and the walls painted black, known as the Basement. Or Debasement, as Fletcher liked to call it. In the part of town that didn't mean anything to anyone yet. It was October, and the night was damp. Heavy breath coming off the waves.

'But . . . how did you decide on Fletcher?' Rothko asked their friend the question without looking at him. Kept their eyes on the dark shop fronts they passed. Nail bar. Chicken shop. Funeral parlour.

'It's my mum's surname. Before she got married.' Fletch explained. 'I felt close to it.' Rothko nodded. Seemed so simple when he put it like that. Fletch walked with a side-to-side bounce. Rothko swung along beside him. 'I wanted a proper tough guy Stud name. Like fucking Axel or something. Blade.'

'You could pull it off, mate. You could be a Blade.'

'Imagine. Nice to meet you I'm Blade. I'm here to teach your child the piano.' They giggled as they walked. Bumping into each other. 'But then she died and I realised I wanted her with me.'

'That's beautiful.'

'Felt like a last gift from her. Keep me strong.'

They walked on for a while, listened to each other's

footsteps drumming down the quiet road. 'And what about the surgery?'

'Is that something you're thinking about?'

Rothko felt around in the pocket of their soul. Found the truth there, all crumpled up and pulled it out into the light. 'One day.'

Fletcher slowed the pace. 'It's not for the faint-hearted, mate. It's a big, heavy ordeal for the body. Maybe you've seen some before and after pictures of trans guys having the time of their life, back in the gym two months later. But I'll be real with you: you'll be sleeping sitting up for three weeks, you'll be in pain. You can't lift your arms above your head. Your body will be getting over it for a year at least. You know? They put a scalpel to your skin and cut you open and scrape out a load of tissue and sew you back up again. Don't get me wrong, my life is more possible since having surgery. I regret nothing about it. It saved me. But I just want you to know that it hurts. And you might come out of it and look at your chest and think, *fuck*. You might miss what was there before. You might feel exposed walking down the street, like there's this big hole in your chest where something used to be? Or maybe you find yourself walking down the street with your shoulders back for the first time in your fucking life. Or maybe, something goes wrong and there's a little bulge in your chest, or something doesn't heal right, it's not like you have this surgery and suddenly everything's fixed and you don't still feel all the ways you feel now, you know? It's a start. But it's not the finish line. What finish line? Obviously, this shit is lifelong. And it changes all the time. Or maybe your body rejects your nipple graft.'

Rothko pushed him at the shoulder. 'No?'

'Oh mate, yeah. This is what they don't tell you till you're in the room with the surgeon. They cut your nipple off, cut the areola to make it smaller, then they sew it back on! And they tell you not to smoke. Because if you smoke, your body's more likely to reject it.'

Rothko stopped walking and stood, mouth open, eyes wide, hands on their nipples.

'I tell you what, it's a good way of quitting.'

'I bet.'

'Direct trade off. If I smoke this roll up, my nipple falls off.' They were laughing.

Rothko felt a feeling rush them of possibility and Fletcher saw it in his friend's face and melted for them, took them into a hard, strong hug. They held each other. Rothko pulled their head back.

'Wait. Did yours . . .?'

'What? Stay on? Yeah, they fucking did!' Fletcher walked them on, his arm around Rothko. And they came in through the carpark. Down a set of concrete steps, through an unmarked door and then a further door. Until finally.

They were nodded in by a big bouncer butch and Rothko wanted to sit at her feet. She was monumental. Arms the size of Rothko's legs. Shaved head, calm disposition. Gorgeous, laid-back, stonewashed jeans, bomber jacket, two brown moles on her cheek. They felt their body pulled towards her. She reminded them of Kingy, from the jail in Peterborough. They bowed their heads at one another, and Rothko received it as a consecration.

There hadn't been places like this in Edgecliff fifteen years ago. Or if there had been, no one had told Rothko. Before going away, they never went to clubs. They queued for death in crack houses. Or rotted away in old boozers.

But here they were.

It felt like coming *home*.

Smiles, or the lack of smiles.

No need to push.

You could just.

They moved through the dancing crowd towards the bar, breathless from the joy of it. Rothko didn't know if it was ok for them to look or not. There weren't that many people in the room. Low, hard music was playing out of speakers stacked in two corners. A big sound system. Meaty. Thudding. They hadn't heard music like this in so long, too long, and they let it pull them under. Couples moved in circles. Grinding. A red laser and a green laser shone in the blackness. Apart from that it was dark.

Through that room and out along a corridor into another. That's where the bar was. It was brighter in this room. Golden spotlights lit the bartenders. Barstools in front. Low benches ran along the walls on both sides. Purple underlighting beneath the benches. Small speakers rigged in the top corners, directed down towards the middle of the room. The music was quieter in here. Rothko nodded their head. Feeling like somebody's weird dad.

They watched a couple, one of them sat on the bench, shirt open, thick scars out, head back against the wall. The person's lover was stood over them, dancing, pretty hands held the wall either side of their head, black lace bra and the body just moving slowly backwards and forwards, pushing and pushing and pulling away. The one on the bench looked up, not touching, not moving, just watching their lover. A look on their face of total sensation. It was beautiful. The world was soft.

Jail had been a hard place full of hard people who had seen hard things. The kinship that they felt inside was always bristling with sadness and conditions. People came in, went out, went over. Hung themselves with knotted bedsheets. Cut themselves to pieces. Spiked the food with drawing pins or razor blades or blood-soaked tampons. Fought and raped and hurt each other. Laughed at little things. Looked for the world they'd lost in the gym. People were powerful and terrifying. Or disappeared under other people's noise. They felt closer to the part of themself that was hard in jail. But this room was different. There was no violence in this room.

It was the opposite in fact.

Beautiful people. All kinds. Lipstick, long eyelashes. Impressive outfits, everything shimmering. Glamorous. Dirty. Tiny tops or leather straps, tits out and legs out and bums out in high heels. Big shoulders, tight jeans. Thick bodies. Strong and delicious. Rock hard, tough-looking softies, pretty ones dressed up like teenage heart throbs. Shy delight and dark desire. Drugs in their faces. Freedom in the close air. Hot.

Rothko had never known a thing like it.

My lot.

Fletcher got drinks and Rothko leant back, elbows on the bar. Fletcher opened a wrap and dabbed a fat padful. Winced, swallowed. Rothko declined. 'I'm good mate, thanks.'

'You like it here, don't you?' he shouted towards them. Rothko nodded. Hand on heart. Fletcher laughed. 'I got you, my brother.'

Rothko's eyes followed the butch behind the bar, as she controlled the space. Laughing with the customers, in a black vest with block writing across the chest, saying: *Your Daughter Calls Me Daddy* and her big muscly arms and her shoulders back and when she saw Rothko watching, she winked. And Rothko blushed.

Rothko was moving, side to side. *Music*. It had been so

long. They wouldn't have known how to let their defences down if they'd tried, but that's what was happening. And it felt revelatory. They lifted their feet a little higher, pointed out the snares.

Songs became other songs. Rothko was all wrapped up in the sound. They didn't even have to remind themself to feel everything. They knew it was real.

A slim boy with a kind face kissed them on the cheek as he passed. His eyes were sincere. Rothko felt a tranquillity they hadn't known before. It was like all the little Rothkos they had been made sense and were welcome to reside in their body.

They looked from face to face to face. Smiling a dazed smile. Charging up from the proximity to other people, and the vibration from the speakers. And then into this came a person that dulled the whole space into background.

Her face.

It hurt Rothko from a long way away. It did something painful to them and they wanted it. It was immediate. Strong features and those lips like storms at night, like sudden storms in hot summer in the middle of a terrifying night, her cheekbones cutting through the dance. Darkness in her eyes and shining, big still shining eyes. She stood on the other side of the room, dangling a straw, talking with three people who could have been models: angular and well-dressed and all done up like showtime. The people kissed her hands and walked away, and she stood against the wall, alone, dancing to herself. Rothko did not know how long the moment lasted but they were intensely aware of every detail of her body and there was nothing else. They looked away but they did not really look away because there was no away to look towards. There was no room, no bar, no basement club. Their chest felt like they'd been sprinting for miles. Beats turned into other beats; it was the only measure of time.

And then she looked at them and smiled.

Rothko saw it curling and uncurling in the side of her face, but they couldn't be sure. They watched with a smile of their own that belonged to her, and it lasted a long time, this smile between them, playing. Staring. Looking away. Each dancing a little, alone. She was staring. And looking away. Nothing else had definition, the only shape was hers. And now, she was moving. She was coming over. *Is she coming over?* She was. She wasn't. She was passing them by. Maybe the toilets. The bar? No. She was stopping. She was stopping in front of them. There she was. Just like that.

She seemed as tall as the room. Taller. Hips like the tick of a mighty brass clock. Lips all glossy. Her neck lengthening and her lips parting and her voice a rasp of smoke and rum and perfume, as she came up close and said, 'Hello, handsome.' Her hand on their chest and Rothko could smell her hair and the sweat from her skin. 'Do you want to dance with me?' she asked.

And then they were moving together, she was pulling them closer, fingers through the belt loops of their jeans. And Rothko was pulling back to study her face, touching her gently: cheekbones, earlobes, shoulders, wrists. Tender like they'd known each other all their lives. Searching like they'd only just met.

'I could feel you staring, you know,' she said.

'I wasn't staring. I've never stared.'

'Must have been someone else.' She pretended to scan the room for the person. 'Maybe I should go and look for them.'

Rothko admitted defeat, happily. 'Ok, yeah. Maybe I was staring a little.'

'Good.' She smiled. 'I should hope so too.' Rothko watched her hand holding her glass as they moved together. Her hand was rough, the skin was chapped and dry. Her fingers flat, long, blunt, the varnish chipped, the nails bitten. Seemed at odds with the grace of her body, dancing. It made Rothko ache for her. That detail. Those desolate hands.

'What are you doing here?' Rothko asked.

'This is my spot. What are *you* doing here?'

They pulled apart and their faces shone.

'I can't believe it's you.' Rothko could feel the power of her rising from her cheeks as they spoke into her ear. Maybe it was the hot low room and the couples around them, but everything was moving in slow, dark judders.

'I missed you,' she said, teeth glowing in the purple light, stud above her lip glowing. Eyes glowing. Skin glowing.

'Dionne.' Rothko studied her. Tried to read the last twenty years in the lines on her face.

'Rothko.' She laid her head on their shoulder, and she squeezed them, tighter and tighter.

They couldn't stop looking at her. Hot sharp smell of her breath. Crooked teeth and pimpled skin. Ornate script tattoos twisted down her neck, spelled out names that Rothko couldn't read. Her desolate eyes, her little top, her hip bones out, the lace of her bra. Hard as nails and soft as spring and there she was. Laughing, an inch away from Rothko. The long, slim shape of her eyes as she laughed, the dimples and lines that surfaced and were buried as she spoke.

Rothko worried how they must have looked to her after all this time.

'When did you get out?'

'April.'

'That long?' She narrowed her eyes like *and you haven't called.* 'April's your birthday month.'

'I didn't know you were still round here.' And then, moved. 'You remembered?'

'Course I remembered, numpty.' She pretended not to smile at them. 'I left for a bit.' Rothko strained to listen past the music. 'But I come back to be closer to Mum.' The straw went to her lips. She sucked in a guzzle. Swallowed. 'When I had my baby. Fifteen now. Not a baby anymore.' And her long, rough hand went to Rothko's collar, straightened it. She smoothed the edges down while she stared into their eyes.

'What's their name?'

'Joseph.'

Rothko touched their heart. 'Like your dad.' The memories went smoking through them. All those years ago, sitting out on the swings by Dionne's block. Dionne saying how she thought the two of them might have got along. The past clung to everything.

'I see your mum round town now and again. She's always got a kind word to say.' Rothko was grateful to hear that.

The music changed. Computerised. Popular vocals Rothko didn't recognise but people around them were singing along, apparently delighted. Rothko found it harder and harder to dance. Their body slowed to the slightest steps.

'Do you want to sit down for a bit?' She nodded that she did, and they went together to the bar and after, sat down, bodies close. Leaning down towards each other's ears to talk, holding their smiling faces close in the dream of it, weird UV light and the crush of the rattling subs through the wall from the other room.

'You look good,' Dionne said. And Rothko blushed.

'You look good too.'

'No. I mean. You look *good*.' And what she meant was you look clean. You look human. You look strong and like the person I knew before you went down.

'All that time and I didn't come to see you.' Rothko waved their hand like it was nothing. 'No. I should have come. Things weren't simple.' She focused on Rothko's eyes and sent some information that Rothko wasn't sure they had received correctly. 'I was angry with you. For going so far into . . . what you went into.'

Rothko wanted to say *I was angry with me too*. But they couldn't, in case it ruined everything.

'We've got a lot to catch up on, haven't we?' She seemed shy for a moment, and full of wonder.

The tinny songs changed into other, deeper songs. Less persistent. More rolling. Skippy drums and basslines like shovels digging down to the core of the world. Rothko could see Fletcher talking to people at the bar. Every now and then Fletcher cast an eye around for Rothko; satisfied, he dabbed again. Bobbed his head to the music.

'So . . .' They straightened up. Turned towards her. 'Are you. In a family, like, with Joseph's dad? Or other mum? Or.' And they couldn't bear to look at her as they asked that question in case it was the wrong question to have asked. But they forced themself to hold it and act like a normal human being for once in their life.

'No,' she said. 'I'm not seeing no one right now.'

'That's good.'

'Is it?' She smiled. The bass shook the walls.

Dionne traced her fingertips across Rothko's knee, their thigh, their knee again. 'Nice trousers,' she said. 'Nice. Material.'

'Think they're just denim, aren't they?' Rothko glanced down, surprised to find trousers, legs, the room. 'Jeans.'

'They feel so nice,' she said, scratching at them. Until. 'Let's go for a cigarette.'

Dionne got up, bending to get her jacket from under the bench. She picked it up in the same hand she held her drink in. Rothko noticed the play and the stretch of her body in motion and followed, a step behind. As they got to the dancefloor, she reached her free hand back and Rothko took it and they walked that way, hand in hand, natural like that through the dance and up the steps to the carpark where people stood smoking and then Rothko noticed they were still hand in hand and it scared them and they let go, gently.

Dionne rooted around in the ice cubes for a slurp of her rum, and dangled her straw in her open mouth, watching Rothko watch her lips. She lowered the glass.

'Can you hold this while I roll a cigarette, please?' Rothko took it and she looked through all the pockets in her jacket for the bits. Rizla, filter, burn. Twenty years disappeared and it felt so normal to be around each other. Rothko hadn't felt normal around anyone in a long time.

'What you been doing with yourself, then? Since you got out?'

'Working.' They realised they weren't watching from above.

'What kind of working?'

'I'm a handyman. Handy person.'

'Course you are,' she said, her smile a wink.

'Why course I am?'

'Hot.'

'Is it?'

'Yeah. Very hot and butch. You fix things. With your big drill.'

Rothko laughed. 'I do have a big drill.'

'Several I imagine.'

'I do have a couple. Yeah.'

'And all those little attachments.' She sucked smoke in. Blew it out through closed teeth. Round lips.

'I did lots of learning in there. Got my trade. City and Guilds. Passed my driving test.'

'I'm proud of you.' She meant it. 'That's amazing Rothko.'

'Thank you.' The compliment stirred up so much pleasure in them, they bowed their head under the weight of it. 'Yoga. All sorts. Meditation.' They laughed at themself.

'Yoga is God. Shag it.' Dionne told them. It made them laugh. She was deadpan.

'I mean, yeah. I would.'

'I'm not joking.'

'I know. Five fucking thousand years ago, they were like – this is how a person has a body. And you don't need nothing for it. Just stretch your legs out. And breathe.' Their eyes were wide with revelation.

'Rothko. You need to share your discovery with the world. We should be telling people this.' Nice feeling. Having the piss took out of them. They bathed in it for a while.

Dionne noticed the shape and movement of Rothko's face. It all felt so familiar. And so unusual. Rothko caught her eye, watched her watching them, their eye contact had its own gravitational field.

'I was sure this morning I was going to leave town.' Rothko felt themself standing up straighter, shoulders back. 'But I'm not so sure now.'

'I think about leaving all the time.' A hand went up to touch her hair. Her eyes were wide. Rothko had never seen eyes like Dionne's anywhere else. Black as coffee but bright somehow. As if they were lit from within. 'But . . . I don't know. Everyone's fucking dead or gone mad or,' she indicated Rothko, 'gone jail or gone rehab or had a billion kids they can't bear the fucking sight of, or never had a kid and not having one sent them over the edge. It's all . . . fucking . . . Where else would I go? I aint the type. To dream of things I'll never. You know? Fucking New York? Start again. Never going to happen.'

'New York.' Rothko savoured the weight of the words. The possibility of a new city. A new continent. An old dream.

'Or. What? Paris? I just. What for?'

'What for? Paris?'

'Yeah. Why not just be wherever you are and don't. Stop trying to.'

'I don't know, you know. I get it. Start again. I want to. Except maybe not Paris. I was thinking more like Birmingham. Why not?'

'Because what are you starting again?' She flicked her lighter. 'You go to a new place. It's still *you*.' She shrugged. 'I do like Birmingham though, it's good people.'

Rothko instructed their senses to focus. They knew something important was happening and they wanted to make sure they were registering it properly.

'I had a, you know?' she raised her eyebrows, dropped her voice, 'Whole life since we seen each other.' Rothko nodded, *of course*. 'And I just. I think I stopped wanting things to be anything other than. Just whatever's happening is good for me, now. I'm not *there* anymore. You know? In the dark.' She spoke slowly. Her eyes were glowing in the streetlight, Rothko watched them and wished they'd been there to go through it all with her. The force of that feeling encouraged them to open.

'When you get near the end,' they began, cautiously. 'That's the worst part. Gate-nut, they call it. That's when you start getting . . .' They tapped their temple to indicate what they meant. 'The middle bit, it's like, your body knows it can't do nothing about it; something happens to you, after a certain amount of time, like, you just, kind of like, give in to it. But when you get towards the end, when it's weeks rather than years left. You start getting antsy. Like the walls are closing in. Feels like it felt at the start, all over again. A lot of times I thought I was never getting out of there.'

'Fuck.' They knew each other. In the eyes. It was recognition. 'Well, them days are over,' she told them and turned away to focus on relighting her cigarette. 'Cos you did get out, didn't you?' Her eyes looked back at them, over her shoulder. 'Freedom.' And Rothko dropped their head and laughed because yes, they fucking did get out.

'I heard it was a heart attack that killed him.'

Rothko was surprised to hear she'd kept up with details of their case. Dionne saw it.

'What? I had a little google, now and again.'

Rothko smiled. 'Nothing wrong with that.' They rubbed at their shoulder, held the muscle in their neck that had been hurting them earlier, up the ladder in the wind. 'Probably brought on by the shock of it. The violence.' Their face became sincere. 'I've got someone's life on me whatever way you look at it.' A heaviness fell on them. 'But I keep coming back to the same thing.'

They paused before the might of the sentiment they were about to express.

'People do not make it out. Of the life I was in. That life.'

Dionne understood. And all the people each of them had known who had not made it out of that life lingered briefly with them.

'In some ways, I'm glad I went inside when I did. Otherwise, I don't think I'd still be here. I've got another chance that I never would have had. And I want it. I do want it.'

Dionne hugged them then. Threw her arms around them and hugged them and expelled loud air and they both made long humming sounds together, feeling the vibrations of each other's voices through their bodies.

'I feel at home,' Rothko said, looking at Dionne. 'Seeing you again.'

'Me too,' Dionne had tears in her eyes. 'Let it out, let it out, let it out.' She shook her hands and feet and limbs. Rothko rubbed their arms and legs and shook their ankles. And they both laughed and then the laughter ebbed. And Rothko said, 'We were young, weren't we?'

'Little babies,' Dionne agreed in a whisper. 'I've thought about you a lot.'

Rattling around in their own skin for years, they'd given up on somebody finding them. Long-time dead to the idea that there might be someone out there who could open the vent and let the steam out. Wriggling around in the desolate pull towards recklessness. It was unusual for Dionne to stand still with a person. It was unusual for Rothko to move slowly with someone. And underneath it all *just do me in. Please, do me in.*

TWO

In her en-suite room above the swollen Tudor pub, Meg woke with a start.

Where was she?

She was in the rehab.

She was in the clinic in the room in the rattle, and the walls were not walls but were the muscles in her back that spasmed so hard she was sure she was dying, and the shocks that went through her were violent and stiffened her body in seizures, her vision all white as she held herself together and the punishing nurse stuck her head round the door and said *maybe you're hungry*, and waited there staring at Meg with her wobbly eyes like two boiled eggs *no I'm not fucking hungry*, she said it out loud, while the walls caved her skull in with a brick and all she could think of was *Rothko* buried in the dream of it, that was the hardest the death of the dream because they were a pair behind a forcefield with their bond that meant the rest of the world couldn't hurt them and she missed her Rothko but next minute nothing, next minute fifteen years, laying out her nice clothes for the visit, but next minute nothing, there isn't a thing and she didn't care about nothing anymore, that's the whole point, using is its own universe, as complete, it's a galaxy spinning through a body, it's a dead sun exploding through dead veins, it's cylindrical light searching for the ends and running back to the beginnings, it's infinity contained in a person, a person contained in a spoon and the light of a dead star, a sunrise within until it's dawn again and she goes back to the womb. When she was using, she didn't miss anything or care about anything, the end of the world was at hand and two solar systems were colliding in space while she tried to swim back to the womb but how much was left and it was supposed to be over and it was supposed to have lost its power so how did she get back here? She had got herself out of it forever and she wanted so badly to believe in her feelings but instead she was stuck in a room with nothing to believe in but the body and the things it made her do because it needed, she was sick and getting sicker and *I started again the second I met you* the dance of two broken people rebuilding and cleaning the dirt out of the old wounds and how when she held her babies in her arms, her scars were like ribbons wrapped round her wrists, silver under lights not blood or shit or dead and dying anymore not doing it for chocolate bars, not pulling water up from a puddle in the gutter for the works, and then it was Christmas in the lot by the station, remember holding hands remember choosing our tree, Sarai wanted the big one, it was so big it had to be driven round later in the van, it was too big to carry. *I remember*. Meg wakes up, nods out, wakes up following a thin girl down an empty street, going up the stairs to the room where she lies on her face and he does what he needs to, the encounter is nothing to Meg it's less than a handshake but for him, for the man who pays for the pleasure of telling himself he knows what she is. How desperately he needs his useless fuck of a body to be as total for any other person on the planet, as it is for him, poor him, but the fuck is a nothingness. Not even pity. Not pain. Just nothing. Still. Bless them in a way, these deranged little killers who have never known dying, with their alcohol skin and their rage and their futile erections. If only he knew how the person that he beats that he fucks that he pays to submit to his will to act young, to whimper and suckle is not even moved by the dreariness of the routine. Let him laugh at it after, let him tell all his friends what he did to the whore because she is a figment of his imagination and he is a figment of his imagination except that she isn't she never has been, because no matter the exchange the person that he pays remains a full person and fucking is nothing but a bodily function as unspecial as shitting or pissing or standing too close on a train, as daily as dying or healing or changing a dressing especially if you've been fucked since you were a child and you need to get money to score. Raped. Meg can feel them walking through the room can see them in their frilly tops their skirts that swish as they go the hard ones the glorious ones the little girl ones the teenage boy ones the brute force of a body that has survived so much, who has taken the brunt of the world, still standing, in kind little groups outside the meetings, leaning in to light their cigarettes they laugh until they swear. There used to be more of her. Everywhere she went, she had her babies. She was theirs, she was *Mum*, but now she is just on her own, was it really the end of all that was it *Ezra* the way down is a vertical slide slick with grease and the way out is a cliff-face that crumbles in her hands as she climbs and her body's made of diesel and she can feel her body dripping down her back *I'm sorry* how could she be down here again when it used to be *sickness* we used to have so much to *Rothko* following a thin girl across a busy road scoring oblivion again, there it is the great round sun and all of us spinning around it *where are you I can feel you are you with me I'm sorry* that woman in the chair said she was Sarai but Sarai is only little, or she was, how long have I been in this room? She was my little baby, smiling with her big brute arms and her gorgeous love and you're not meant to have favourites but she was, she needed my love, always wanted my cuddles and maybe this is just what it's like to live here, weighed down by gravity or trauma or whatever, it's just one rock one spinning rock not even a dent in the press of eternity and each little *now* is entirely meaningless but it's all that we've got so *Rothko* how can it feel so real so lost so cruel so fix it I'm trying to fix it depressed and fanatical desperately clinging to prayers or diets or discipline none of us, all of us children of a dead regime spinning *where are you,* and most of all *Rothko* how could a thing as weightless as life be so fucking heavy so much of the time.

THREE

Rothko surveyed the thudding room. The dance was tiring. Full of bodies crushing close and parting but they were into the night's last quarter. Gentle, heavy faces, tit-tape and glowing skin. Scars out. Elder butches with short grey crew cuts, hard faces, checked shirts and folded arms. Seaside night out. Young femme girls, kissing. Lifting up each other's dresses. Dazzled couples pulling each other around the room. Two muscle boys with their bodies close. Long deaf kisses that drowned out the world.

Rothko and Dionne, drinks in hand, walked together back to the dark room with the solitary lasers and they sank deep into each other, into the bass and the harmonic vocals, and they were alive in each other's orbit, touching warm skin and hard muscle, deep softness and holding each other and rolling and stepping and how many hours were passing?

'I was so *gay*,' she said. 'But no-one believed me. Or maybe I didn't believe me.' Earnest, talking into their ears. 'It felt like I wasn't allowed to be. Because all the boys. Wanted . . . to fuck. And if the boys wanted to fuck you, it was like you weren't allowed to not want that. It was like what you wanted wasn't real.'

'What?' They tapped their ear to show they hadn't heard. The music was loud, and they missed each other's words but kept going.

'I said, I was *gay*.' She shouted louder. Rothko nodded. 'But I was scared of it.'

'It's ok.' Their lips against her earlobe as they spoke into her ear. Holding her face gently as they tried to be heard. 'I was scared of it too.' They looked around, back to her. 'But look at us now.' She nodded. Her eyes sad with it and brilliant.

'You just wanted me to love you out in the open.' Her voice was trembling as she shouted over the bass. 'But I couldn't make it better. Being you.' Rothko held their heart and listened. The past was everywhere, 'I'm *out* now, you know? I don't care anymore. It's so good not to hate yourself, isn't it.'

Rothko was glad for her. 'Freedom,' they said. And she hugged them as tight as she could.

The night was fading. It was the final moments now, people were stood alone at the bar, wiping their faces, grinding their jaws. Rothko looked up for the first time in ages. Saw her. Saw the room. The lights came on.

'Do you want to get out of here?'

Outside, Fletcher was sat amongst a pile of bodies, posted up against the carpet-shop wall, laughing. Rothko hugged him goodbye.

'You leaving?' he asked. 'Am I coming?'

'Do you want to?'

Fletcher looked around him, thought about the answer. Decided it was no.

'I'm staying.' Fletch lifted his cheeks up to be kissed, Rothko delivered big wet kisses on both of his cheeks. 'I love you,' he said.

'I love you, too.'

'I love them,' Fletcher told the people they were sitting with.

'This Dionne,' Rothko said. 'This Fletcher.' Dionne bent down and kissed Fletcher on both cheeks as well.

'Hello, Dionne. You take care of my man won't you.'

'I will, my darling, don't you worry. I've got him.'

'He's got himself.' Fletcher told her. And Rothko felt it like an arm around their shoulder.

They left the club and walked the hollow streets, the bass rolling in their ears. Walking in step.

'What shoes are you wearing?' Rothko asked her.

'Why?'

'Are they special?'

'No, just my trainers. I mean, not *just*, but not special.'

'Ok, follow me. Let's go this way.'

They turned off the main road onto the overgrown footpath that led to the river. It was scrubby underfoot and full of brambles. Lit by occasional streetlights. The occasional moon. Dawn wasn't far away. Rothko hadn't been outside, in space like this, for a long time.

They loved the way it felt. Like they could *see* everything they looked at.

It was the first night they had been to a rave, without drugs or drink. And experiencing it clean felt like a stronger high than anything they could remember from before. Not that they could remember much.

That whole time they'd been hiding from life in the drugs and the drink.

Then hiding from life in jail.

And now they were in it, and they didn't want to hide anymore.

The music had felt mind-altering. Spirit-altering. After all those years spent trapped in a room, being with that many people and not freaking out, felt like some kind of divine encounter.

They walked past football fields into an industrial wilderness. Strange concrete tanks and pipes, the sounds of water rushing inside vast cylinders.

The point isn't to feel good, the rushing water told them. *The point is to feel.*

Fenced-off buildings. Echoing pathways. Looming silhouettes. Staggered rooves and glass-panelled buildings with blacked-out windows. Workshops and units. Complexes linked by red metal staircases. Chain-link fencing and sleeping factories. UPVC window manufacturers. Steel fabricators. The girders piled in endless rows. Something magical about it all, so quiet, like the world had heard their prayer and run away. Rothko took her hand. Played with her fingers, stroked her wrist. Dionne leaned into their shoulder, rested her head on them, smiling. They passed the recycling centre with the vast skips stacked in towers. She was humming quietly. All the little flourishes, just for them.

A picnic table stood alone on a patch of grass between two factories. A trampoline behind a warehouse. A broken heater. A rusted jerk pan. Miniature football goals without nets. The luxury of unused space.

'This must be where they take their breaks,' Rothko said.

'Who?'

'The people that work in these places. Or, maybe it's squatted? Or.'

'Yeah,' Dionne hummed. Nuzzling close. She had missed this feeling but hadn't known until that moment; The relief of being close to them.

It felt like they were alone in a finished world. Walking past banks of intricate structures built to house invisible forces;

the unseen things that keep the town in constant motion: pipework, units, tanks. Holding on to each other. Letting go. Holding on to each other again. Bright blue storage units. Big glass secure doors. Entry systems that backed on to the dark river that ran to the sea. The tangled bushes that grew at its banks. The security lights from the factory yards lit the surface of the river and the night was thick with breath. They could hear it, gurgling across the fence. Autumn was here. And the night was dense, but it wasn't cold.

This is exactly the thing they had missed the most. Turning a corner and not knowing where the road might lead you. Letting things happen, just by accident.

Rothko saw a gap in the fence and ducked through, and Dionne came with them, laughing, and they were together, out in open space.

A wide field, long grass, a path cut through it. The sky ripening to peach as the new day approached. They pushed very close. Studied each other with their eyes closed, feeling the distance between them with breath, closing the distance, parting their lips and pushing their parted lips together. They kissed at last, and the kiss was hot and thorough, a complete kiss that involved every cell of their lips and mouths and cheeks and chins and hands and entire bodies dancing into, around and out of the kiss, in the dark, in the dim dark light they kissed on and on and their clothes were in the way of the kiss and they had to have skin and body and touch, and so they kissed through the clothes, the clothes were unbuttoned and pulled up and dragged off, so they could kiss deeper and reveal the buried levels of the kiss in all its glory and filth.

They laid their coat for her and they fell down together, undressing each other, Rothko kneeling at her feet, dragging off her jeans by the ankles. Dionne wriggling to get them over her hips. And Rothko sucking gently at Dionne's belly, hips, thighs. Kisses like praise words. Insistent, forever, touching, retouching, a painting of kisses, that wasn't a painting at all, it was music and listening intently; the gorgeous low note, the inside of a person, and playing her music, kissing and parting and pushing their wet mouth down and around and finding her there, little bulb in their lips, budding, and swelling and Dionne grabbing at Rothko and moaning, turning her face to press her cheeks into the earth, her breath digging into the ground as Rothko pushed harder and sucked at it, hard little licks at it, softer and washing it, tasting it, bass of it, base of their tongue pushing into it, loving the feel of it, then panning out wide and glimpsing the whole of it, all of it, the juice and the froth and the delicate weight of the walls caving in, the outside, the inside, the hidden, the seen, and this paradise moment in a desolate field on the edge of the town with the hum all around them of waterworks, steel works, electric and theirs; and here it was, she was thunder in the silent dawn, her gorgeous voice and her clenching body and Rothko's urgent mouth and her hands pushed Rothko back, too sensitive now, and pulled them, desperate, up towards her and she laughed into their neck and she wanted their big body to press her bones into the field until they were both made out of dirt.

'You filthy bastard,' she said. 'I *never* come.' Her eyes were damp. 'I mean it. I never, ever come.'

'You used to.'

'Well,' she said, smiling. 'Not for a long time.'

'How long?' Rothko held their weight off Dionne's body. Supported themself on their elbows. Watched her.

'About twenty years.' She looked them dead in the eye.

'Fuck.' Rothko laughed.

'What do you mean *fuck*?'

'I mean. Fuck. We're in trouble then. Aren't we?' And Dionne was breathing, shining. She held them against her, and she liked them.

'You coming home with me?' Rothko asked.

'I want to, yeah, but I don't want to. Because I'm fucking . . . waved. And I don't want the first time in so long to be like . . . I want . . . I don't want this to be it and then it feels weird tomorrow and then. You know what I mean?'

Rothko nodded. Pushed close to her.

'I don't think I want to just do this the once.' Her head was touching Rothko's, and her lips were quick with pleasure and the dawn was coming. 'So, where the fuck are we?'

Rothko pulled her up to her feet and together they buttoned their jeans and pulled their tops back on and picked up their jackets and once everything was assembled, she took their hand and they started running through the empty field, down the path mown through the middle of the high grass until the field became a yard behind a water tower and a row of garages, looking for a gap in the other side of the fence that led out to the back of the cinema, but finding none, they had to climb.

Dionne moved instinctively, pulled herself up and over. But Rothko was slower, second guessing every hold. Face turning red. They ended up stuck, legs shaking at the top of the fence. Terrified of falling headfirst into the pavement below. But under Dionne's guidance, they found the courage and jumped clear. Landed heavily, the impact stinging through their legs, but the rush they felt was so intense they screamed, like scoring the winning goal.

They were back on the quiet street, like that secret place had never existed and the whole town belonged to the normal people.

They laughed at what they saw. Lines of step-machines in the windows of a gym. Rows of parked cars, facing the same way. It all seemed so unnecessary.

'Everything's changed.' Rothko told her as they walked. 'I don't know if I've changed, but this place is the same. Or if this place has changed. And I'm the same. I can't work it out. But everything feels so . . . fucking . . .' They didn't know how to say it.

'You've been away a long time.'

'But also, *I'm* changing. I mean. I can't stop thinking about. Who I am. Who I *actually* am.' And Dionne, the only human being in the world that Rothko felt their heart beat normally around, walked close to them and listened with an upturned face.

'I'm a man.' Rothko said it out loud for the first time. It felt like all the sleeping people behind the windows that they walked past had synchronised their breathing and were breathing with Rothko as he finally allowed himself to breathe out.

'I know.' Dionne smiled her face into his chest.

It was so new. He was scared he had broken the shell too early and killed this thing before it had hatched.

His arm was around her waist as they walked, and he slid his hand under her clothes so he could feel her skin against his palm. The realness of her. He wanted to log every fraction of the feeling deep in his atoms and never forget it.

'I've never said it out loud.'

He felt exposed. Like he'd made a big deal out of something that was nothing and maybe it was stupid and maybe he should try and take it back.

'Thank you for trusting me.' She squeezed her arms around him.

They were heading to the edge of the meadows. Treading softly, down the narrow steps where Rothko used to sit and wait for a glimpse of her getting off the bus, all those years ago.

Church Lane. Radford Road. Preston Court.

And at the corner she put her number in his phone and said, 'Let's see if you call, then.'

Rothko watched her walk away. Watched Dionne jog heavily up to her flat. To her sleeping son and her mum and Rothko watched the balconies, remembering. He couldn't believe the day, the night. *Dionne*. Back in his arms again.

It felt like everything that had happened once kept happening forever.

Time was pounding in his ears.

He could see himself, running down the road towards his mum's place. Sixteen forever. Terrified forever.

But as he watched, he saw the kid he used to be looking back behind him, and for a second he could have sworn they locked eyes.

FOUR

Meg sat up in bed. There were curtains. There were windows. She got up and opened the curtains and the morning rushed her worried face.

No.

It wasn't the rehab.

It was the pub. The train to Cherry Hill. And the pub. That's right.

She pulled on clothes and went down for breakfast. Dizzy.

The lady from reception greeted her, 'Just in time. I was about to clear it all away.' *Just in time.* 'How was your night?' she asked Meg.

'Good. Thank you.' But Meg was aware of her bandaged wrist, and her strangeness here in this world for other people. 'How was yours?'

The woman reached up and touched the back of her hair, 'Nearly finished now.'

'From last night? That's a long shift.' Meg felt the floor sliding. Steadied herself with both hands on the tabletop. Vertigo rising, up from the carpet.

'Doubles are good for the money.' Meg nodded but felt unprepared for the conversation. An animal supplanted into a human body and set free in a breakfast dining room, expected to get on with it.

'Coffee? Tea?' the lady asked her. But Meg didn't know. The

woman's lowered eyebrows told Meg she needed clarification. But all Meg could do was hold on to the arms of her chair to stay upright. She looked towards the continental buffet table with deep desire. The woman was lingering. Meg smiled at her. 'Coffee please. Be nice. Thanks.'

Meg stood at the buffet and looked at the things. Admired the spread with a hand that reached and touched the bowls and packets, gently. She picked up a pear, held it briefly and then put it back. She sat down again.

When the coffee came, she ordered cooked tomatoes on brown toast and a fried egg from the kitchen. She drank a cup of coffee with hot milk and sugar. Then she went back to the buffet for the pear.

It was as if she was someone else.

Someone who sat in an airy dining room above a pub and ate whatever she wanted and had no life beyond the moment. It was glorious.

The lady who brought the coffee watched Meg closely as she stood. Something about her was worrying. She was acting *off*.

Meg just wanted to walk.

Just wanted to walk in the air and feel the outside.

But she only made it a few paces across the room before she fell backwards. The lady rushed to her side, tried to rouse her, but Meg had gone rigid. She seemed to be on the edge of a seizure of some kind.

'It's ok.' The lady with the stern eyes was cradling her, trying to keep her from hitting her head. 'Can you hear me? You're fine.' She nodded at her colleague who had stopped clearing tables that yes, she should call for an ambulance.

FIVE

Angel Douglas got home, clutching bags of food, as if that made it all ok. It was early morning and the only person out was Kev-over-the-road, who had a body-mounted blowtorch strapped to his torso. He was using it to incinerate the weeds that had grown between the paving stones on the street outside his drive because, as Angel had learned, that was what people like Kev-over-the-road did on a Sunday.

Ruby was in the kitchen talking on the phone. Angel dropped the shopping in the hallway and inspected her blistered palms. Nice little jolt of satisfaction she got from carrying shopping bags that twisted into her skin. Some sign of an hour well spent.

I live here. She thought. *These are my shoes, and I leave them by the door.*

'Are you home?' Ruby called from the kitchen.

'Home,' Angel affirmed.

'Is that you?'

'Yes.'

'I'm on the phone.' Angel bent to pull her work shoes off, pulled her tired hair out of its band, and walked into the bedroom where she wrenched off her clothes and stood in her pants, flicking her hair out of her face like a fighter.

Bound to pass soon. Ups and downs.

Some days she just wanted to explode.

Other days went fine, and she barely even noticed.

There she was in the mirrored door of the wardrobe. Everything about her body was unrelated to her being. She got through life by forgetting it existed.

Maybe they could get a dog. The kid could be Ruby's. The dog could be Angel's.

Or maybe she could learn a language. Maybe she could travel through small southern towns bartering for wine and olives. Maybe she could begin wearing hats and get work as a grape-picker like the beautiful woman she had seen on *The Repair Shop* who'd said that was how she used to spend her summers. *Take her to a pine forest, kiss her with the edge of my lips so she can barely feel it, kiss her until she shivers, kiss her with my breath, breathe over her skin until she comes apart.* Maybe there was another life beyond Edgecliff where Angel could be a person who sold olives at the market.

Or maybe not.

Ruby was still ending her phone call, saying, 'Ok, yeah. Bye. Yeah, I know, I heard. I don't think he meant it, and anyway . . . no, you're right. But . . . Yeah, ok. I will. Yeah . . . no . . . not until Tuesday. Ok. I will . . . I have already . . . It was fine, yeah . . . Ok, love you . . . Bye.' Angel knew this would go on for another ten minutes at least.

She ran the shower so hot it felt dangerous and afterwards sat naked on the bed, feeling like she was about to pass out from the steam coming off her. Looking down at her body like she'd just been eaten by it.

'Did you get food?' Ruby was in the hallway with the bags of food.

'Yes. I got food.' Angel pulled on football shorts and the cashmere jumper Ruby had bought her for Christmas and went to carry the bags into the kitchen, enjoying the feel of the smooth floor under her bare soles. Underfloor heating. Ruby had been adamant about that.

Ruby began unpacking the shopping. Looking at things, then putting them down on the table. She held a mango under her nose. Sniffed it belligerently.

'No point buying fruit in this country,' she told Angel. 'Doesn't even smell. Can't even smell anything.'

'I like mangoes.'

'It's not a mango.' She pushed it into her nose, sniffing loudly. 'It's a placebo.' She put it down, disappointed in it.

'I like placebos. In the morning. With my yoghurt.'

Ruby had put them on a diet. She said it would be good for them both to have developed a healthier lifestyle before she got pregnant. Angel didn't know if it was working or not, but she had been dreaming about cheeseburgers for weeks.

'What are you doing tonight?' Ruby was standing beside her. 'I thought we could go out.'

'Do you want to go out?'

'I thought we could. Go out.'

Angel handled the plastic packaging. Unloaded the rice into the rice jar. 'Where would we go?'

'The pub?'

'You hate the pub?' The way they talked to each other was disorientating. Incessant exchanges of meaningless sound. While underneath it, meaning festered.

'You're not allowed to neg an idea if you don't suggest an alternative.' Ruby reminded her.

'Will we eat there?'

'Do you want to?'

Angel sighed. Because she knew if they ate in the pub, Ruby would get sausage and mash and a sticky toffee pudding and then when they got home, she'd be angry with Angel for not stopping her.

'Don't sigh.'

Angel put away the lentils. Next to the other two packets of lentils. 'I didn't sigh.'

'You did. Don't.' Ruby had her hands in the cupboard, she was re-arranging the tins of coconut milk and kidney beans.

'I can sigh. If I want to. But I didn't.'

'No, you can't. You've just got home. Don't *sigh*. I don't want that. I don't want miserable hard done by. I want . . .'

'What do you?' she interrupted her but there were no real interruptions because they spoke in one continuous flow.

'Oh me and my poor steady job how difficult for me.'

'Go-getting professional brings home the bacon.'

'Much better. Undeniable provider returns home to loving partner with . . .'

'Home from the modern coalface.'

'Back from a hard night at sea, thank god he's safe, returning to his.'

'To my beloved. To sweet Marie who waits for me.' When Angel is sure that Ruby is not looking, she puts the packaging from the vegetables into the wrong bin. Once it's in the rubbish truck, there is no way all that rubbish isn't going in the same hole. But she can't tell Ruby that. She has to get her little buzzes where she can.

Who is she when she is in this house with this woman?

How did she get here?

'I don't want to cook,' Ruby tells her.

Angel speaks like Ruby. Ruby speaks like Angel. But Angel doesn't know where the character they both play came from, where their real selves have gone or when the play even began.

'I've just bought all this food though?'

'I'll eat it, don't worry.' Ruby cast her eyes over the piles of food. People were starving. But not in this kitchen.

'Will you eat it? I hate waste.'

'I know you hate waste.'

'I hate it.'

But Angel didn't really hate waste. She just said she hated waste because Ruby thought she did, and when they were together, Angel was the person Ruby thought she was.

Ruby smiled and edged in towards Angel's body and the two of them embraced in a routine way. Contact and pulse. A shared life. The safe bet.

It doesn't matter that this isn't real. Nothing's real.

SIX

Rothko was alive to the details. He felt so close to life; it was like he was inside it. Everything was real. The rolling surge of time washed the town in suds and bubbles. He walked and he walked, his legs powered by the years spent without space to roam, down to the beach where the tide was out, his whole vision filled with the stretch of the sky and the reach of the sand that gave way to clumps of weeds and pools of cloying water, past the bingo and the snooker room, up into the guts of town, till he found himself back in the old neighbourhood again. Past Sean's mum's place where the shame lapped loudly, and school down there and the bus stop and look, there he was, the teenaged him, smoking into his fist and waiting for Dionne.

He crossed the bridge over the dual carriageway. Lumbered along, watching the cars.

Down the other side and out through the underpass that he used to sit around in. Past the scrubby lots and broken fences of his youth that were new apartments now.

He was still here, and that was something.

Meg was in his body. His movements jerky and assured like hers. Ezra in his head, saying *if you leave now. You're on your own.*

All that time surrounded by people who'd never had family had turned him inwards. Looking for the people who'd raised him in his responses to things. It had made him realise how lucky he was. How loved he had been.

When Rothko was younger, Ezra had disgusted him for giving up on his heart to chase the money, the house, the car. How disconnected and unromantic he had seemed. And Meg so free and vivid. The world had taught Rothko to be ashamed of her. Of how dirty and loud and ruined she was. How drunk. But he had always seen a grim kind of dignity in the way she threw herself so fully into desire and abandon. Into terror, into bliss.

Until that night when he'd turned up at her door, hoping Meg would know the magic words, that somehow, she could make it all stop.

She hadn't been well. It wasn't her fault.

But the things they'd done together, in the mutual hell of using.

It didn't matter if they never even spoke about the things that happened; as long as Meg was out there somewhere remembering, then Rothko didn't have to carry it alone.

Inside, it was Ezra who had come through for Rothko. Evidence of his slow, unyielding care stacked up in letters and birthday cards. It wasn't his fault he had fallen for a woman he could never be at peace with. Meg had been made from rocks and earth and wind, and Ezra had loved her for that. Until he needed her to stay indoors and put away the children's toys. That's when he started to despise the roughness of her nature. To find it showy and immature. She wilted under his central heating. Lost her shape under the tightness of his bedsheets.

He was doing what he thought he was supposed to do.

She was trying her best. But sometimes she went under.

Rothko could see it everywhere he looked; it was in the low sky and the endless rows of little shiny houses, where people assembled families, puzzling over the unclear instructions, left to them by their own parents years before.

Ezra had given up on life in the same way that Meg had. It's just the life he had given up on was the deep life of the soul, and the life she had given up on was the real life of the world. Neither was less hurt by what they'd turned their backs on. It's just the world forgave one more easily than it forgave the other.

Why was he so stuck on the grudge?

Who was it serving?

Wasn't he the one who'd made it out in the end?

He took a side road and pushed through the glass door of a corner café. Blue and white striped. Nautical memorabilia on the wall. Anchors and wheels. He sat in the window and watched the street. The waiter came over, sweet kid in a trucker's cap and ripped jeans that had been that way when he bought them. He looked twelve years old to Rothko but he could have been twenty-five.

'Alright feller,' the waiter greeted him, and the sun shone on Rothko.

'Morning mate.' It was busy with families sitting in silence, annoyed with each other, just another grumpy Sunday. Spoilt kids drinking milkshakes, spoilt parents drinking tea. It seemed so sad. Rothko wished there was something in the world apart from suffering, that could show a family how much they meant to each other.

The entire wall above the counter was taken up with the menu. So many different combinations. How was he supposed to know what he wanted? Fifteen years of eating whatever he was given.

'Please can you ask the chef to make me a plate of whatever they would have for breakfast if they'd been out all night?'

The waiter was excited by the idea. 'What if you don't like it though?'

'Whatever comes out, I'll be happy. I eat everything. I just want someone else to decide for me.'

The night before was sat across the table, and he gazed into its eyes. Dionne in the dance. That closed space that held those open people. The butch behind the bar with the *Daddy* vest on. Fletcher dancing with his arms in the air.

He needed to think.

The waiter bought the food over. Stood eagerly by while Rothko looked at the plates of food. Grinning.

'Looks *perfect*. I couldn't have created a more perfect breakfast for this exact moment.'

The waiter was laughing. 'She's done you a spinach, mushroom, cheese omelette, with salad *and* chips.' He pointed to each item on the plate with great ceremony. 'And then that's your one blueberry pancake with maple syrup on the side.'

Rothko clapped the plates in front of him and blew a kiss towards the kitchen.

'You're happy then?' The waiter laughed. 'Seems like you had a good night.'

Rothko ate his breakfast in a trance, watching the day get going the other side of the window. He could feel the heavy pull of all those years locked away, all the milestones he'd missed, balanced against the pull of Dionne's eyes flashing in the wasteland.

Her body.

Pressing close and the giggle in the corner of her mouth. Looking up across her stomach. The feel of her skin. His own skin. *I know.*

God was alive in the caff and spoke to him tenderly in the

way the kid with the baseball cap and ripped jeans was singing along to the radio. 'One Moment in Time'. God was alive in the meal the chef had cooked for him that he worked his way through slowly, and in the solid ground feeling of the money Meryl had left for him that was still safely in his wallet.

As he ate, he caught himself fantasising about wedding days and old age, the two of them sitting on a swinging chair together on a front porch in a mythical place. Joseph calling him Dad. And he laughed. 'Calm down, mate. You've only seen her the once.' He said it out loud to the tablecloth. Smiling.

He left the caff, bowing to the waiter. Wedged a score under the plate for a tip, he was in that good a mood. Up all night. But without the hangover, the tiredness in his body didn't feel menacing. It felt well-earned.

Sarai rang. Sounded like she was sheltering her mouth as she talked. Her voice was tight under pressure. 'She's turned up. She's back in hospital. She had another fall. But she's ok.'

'Are *you* ok?'

Maybe it was the shock of hearing Rothko ask her that did it. 'Oh mate. I don't know, I just want her to come home and be with us, here. But I haven't sorted anything out. I haven't got her things. I haven't even cleared the room. It's all got loads of. God knows what. George has his judo competition Tuesday night, I'm meant to be helping him, wants to make a video for YouTube, can you believe it, he wants to be a YouTuber, which I didn't even know was a thing you could be until this morning, and apparently we're late because eleven years old is almost too late to start, like he wants to start *now*, and I'm already thinking he's spending too much time online as it is, fuck knows who he's talking to when he's up there all hours and Tommy still needs his outfit doing for the sponsored, fuck, it's dressing up day tomorrow and I haven't even got round to sorting the food shop yet . . .'

Rothko slowed his pace to listen better. Squinting up to watch the sun swell the belly of the clouds like a good meal.

'One kid's bad enough. Three kids, I must be a fucking masochist . . .'

It was one thing knowing right from wrong locked in a room. Much harder to have morals out here in the world, where so much was at stake.

He just wanted to be who he hoped he was. But how?

He had spent a lifetime doing without thinking. Found out too late: it was what he did that made him who he was.

So how could he become a different person?

Maybe he just had to try doing different things.

SEVEN

The van was warm when he got home and Rothko fell asleep in his clothes, cuddled up to Donovan who took up most of the bed. He came to in the late afternoon, woken by the sound of his own voice, shouting, and the rain smashing down on the roof. He was sweating and his heart was pounding. He sat on the edge of the bed, his mouth sticky. Waiting for the dream to leave him. Embarrassed. He peered out at the rain and thunder from under the awning outside the van. He felt too ugly for peace. An interloper who lacked the elegance for something as skilful as existing.

Not anymore.

The van found its own way, he barely had to turn the wheel before he pulled into a parking space on a residential street in the comfortable part of town. He turned the engine off and sat in the pulsing silence for a steady minute outside Sarai's.

He knew her address by heart from the letters but he hadn't been here before. It looked just like the house they'd grown up in. The road felt the same. The maisonettes, the terraced blocks of thirties pebbledash. The green garage doors. The small front yards with their foxgloves and lilacs and roses. Autumn in the air, casting everything in bronze. People in jumpers carried bags of shopping. People on the phone led children by the hand.

This was a neighbourhood of loft conversions and personalised numberplates. Sarai had a red front door. Everything else was shades of beige. Exterior walls, garden path. It had always seemed such a sinister, menacing endless pretence. But maybe there was something in deciding to knuckle down and get on with it. And what right did Rothko have to judge what anybody else had to do to feel safe?

Rothko climbed out, held the door for Donovan, and they loped up the path together to ring the bell.

Heavy footsteps bouncing down the stairs. Sarai opened, presenting a measured face, like *hello how can I help you*? When she saw it was Rothko, her expression collapsed into truth. She looked done in. Rinsed.

'You're here?' Her voice was small.

Rothko's smile looked just the same to Sarai as it had done at four years old.

'Want to go and get her stuff then?'

There was a lot to do. But Rothko had learned from looking down the barrel of all that time, that if you thought about how much there was to do, you just ended up getting none of it done.

It was better to break it all down to the bare minimum, as if each little job was the whole thing. If you stuck at that all day, by the end of it, you would have made progress.

He used to think of the time he had to do, like he was digging a tunnel under a mountain, with a fucking spoon. One that closed behind him as he went.

He couldn't think about how impossible a task it was. If he did, he'd just give up. The walls would cave in, he'd run out of air and suffocate on how useless he always knew he was.

No.

You just had to keep digging. And eventually at some point, if you stayed on task, you would get through it. Out to the light and the air again.

Here he was to prove it.

But you had to dig for the digging itself, not with the end in mind.

Suspended in time, like the planet. Applying his skill. Processing practical challenges released him from his racing thoughts. Making order out of chaos. When he was absorbed in it, his creativity was a prayer sent out to all creation, as he ritualised the myth, the Genesis re-enactment of giving life to new ideas. And when he surfaced from it, at the end of the second day, he saw that he had done it. And it was good.

He was out of the tunnel at last.

He'd built the shelving, varnished the ply and the grain was swimming beautifully through the finish. Now, he was unpacking the boxes. All the things that made her who she was. Books. Black spines and orange spines and pale green spines. Framed photographs of days spent together that Rothko had forgotten he'd forgotten about. A two-tiered musical jewellery box that had belonged to Ezra's mum, Rose. It played Tchaikovsky when you opened it. And the worn-out silk dressing gown, dusty pink, that was all she'd got to remember her own mum Lizzie by. It had two embroidered wrens encircling the sleeves.

Her record player.

He'd had to replace the ancient plug and get a new stylus for it. But the player itself was fine.

He mounted the deck on the surface he'd built for it. Cleared all the cables away nicely, so there was no messy wiring spilling into the room. He positioned the speakers so that the best sound was directed at the bed. It was one of those up and down beds with a remote. He sat in it and lifted the headboard up. Realised that if it was only an inch and a half higher, Meg could see out the window from lying down. So, he'd been out for more timber and built a platform and raised the bed.

Sarai got home from work that evening and found Rothko in Meg's room. It was transformed.

The platform was built, and all the sawdust had been swept away. There was a bedside table and a matching dressing table, with a three-panelled mirror that had a frosted border with flowers curling round it.

Her records were in a wooden crate built into the shelving. Her books were on the shelves. Her pictures were in their stand-up frames, and Rothko had hung a framed Picasso print he'd found in the charity shop. *1948. Mother and Child.* There were white metallic racks along the back wall for all the necessaries of caring, with a thin curtain to cover them; forget-me-nots printed on yellow cloth. A lamp by the bed. A lamp on the dressing table. Yellow lampshades.

'Looks amazing in here,' Sarai took it all in. Hands over her mouth.

'Once I get into something. You know.' Rothko sat on the dressing table stool. Bobbing in the wake of extensive effort. 'I think I've finished now, anyway.'

Sarai opened her phone and went scrolling through. 'Look,' she said. 'Do you want to see her?'

Rothko stood up, took the phone and stared into the image. There she was. Her hands like little claws at her side, her body all spiky and thin as the wind. Wearing a big fake mohair cardigan with tassels coming off it. And blue jeans, cut short above the ankle, all the ragged threads hanging from the bottom of the hems and fluffy pink sliders and

Rothko could see her ankles at the back, where the ring of forget-me-nots she had tattooed around the left one had wilted in the heat of time. She was half turning away from the camera. Walking in front of whoever was taking the picture, through a room Rothko didn't recognise. She was in the middle of a laugh, chin up, mouth open. Deep lines in her skin, and her body all warped and shrunken. It was so real to see her. But it was a shock. Because there she was. That was her. And her eyes were smiling and as fizzy as they always used to be.

'Look, it's a live one. You can press it and it moves.' Sarai showed Rothko that if you pressed the photo on the screen, it became animated; a two-second clip of life that looped. Meg laughing, and walking, and looking away. And Meg laughing, and walking, and looking away.

'She don't look a day over seven hundred and fifty.' Rothko played it down, but Sarai could feel the impact it had had on him.

'I think she looks beautiful in that one.' Sarai lay down on the bed, 'Keep flicking if you want. There's more.' She buzzed the remote so it sat her up. 'Bed's so good.'

Rothko swiped and stared. Meg, at a table in a café with her head turned to the side. Looking out the window, with her hair as grey as the spray off the breakers. They tried to press the photo like Sarai had done, but this one didn't move.

'Scott got it on Marketplace. Amazing what you can find.'

'That's lucky.' Rothko handed back her phone and sat on the dressing table stool again. Spun it a little. *Her face.*

'Honestly Roth. This'll be the nicest room she's ever had in her life.' The gesture felt enormous to Sarai. 'She won't even know where she is!' She couldn't believe it. She seemed so happy about it; it made Rothko worry he'd done too much. Had he gone too far?

She buzzed the bed as far up as it would go. Then down so it was flat. Then up again. Rothko got up to close the window; he'd been airing the varnish out and he stayed there, looking at the street. 'How much did it all cost?' Sarai asked.

'Don't worry about that.'

'Don't be stupid.'

'Honestly. It's fine.' Rothko walked slowly over to the vinyl, flicked through them. Tracing the memories that lived in the sleeves. How he'd spent whole afternoons looking at the pictures on the covers of these albums when he was young. He picked one out at random. Bob Dylan, *The Bootleg Series*. He dropped the needle on him singing 'Who Killed Davey Moore' live from Carnegie Hall. The two of them were transported.

'I've never heard that song before,' Sarai said at the end, as the audience started to clap. Rothko joined in the applause.

'She's got some bangers in here.' He flipped again. Stevie Wonder. 'Remember this?' He put on 'A Place in the Sun'. Sarai danced happily on the bed. Sang along. '*Like a long, lonely stream, I keep running towards a dream* . . . I fucking *love* this song!' she said, and she had tears in her eyes.

'It's so good!' And Sarai's laughing, crying, singing face in the mirror and the deep lamplight and the smell in the room of the cut wood and the lingering varnish. After Stevie, they flipped again through the stack, went for *Speaking in Tongues.* It had always been Meg's favourite album.

Sarai got up and started doing her funny up and down dance, big slow strides. Rothko turned it up and the noise brought Sarai's kids in. George first, he was the oldest at eleven. Then Hayley. She was five. Shyly round the door. They started dancing with Rothko and Sarai, then Tommy came jumping in. He was the middle one. Seven now.

'What is this?' he asked. 'What are you all doing?'

'Ask your aunty Rothko.' Sarai said, grabbing Rothko's hand in an awkward dance, 'It's her fault.' Then Rothko was jumping in a circle with his nephew, holding hands until Hayley broke the circle so that she could be a part of it.

'BURNING DOWN THE HOUSE!' Sarai sang into Hayley's face.

'She loved this one, didn't she?' The joy was wide in Sarai's eyes. 'I haven't heard it in so long!'

The kids were pushing each other and jumping. Tommy went down and was trampled, but got up, unfussed. Sarai was singing along at the top of her voice and the kids were squealing.

Scott shouted up, 'Food! Kids. Food. Now.' And Rothko turned the music down. Sarai ushered the kids downstairs to eat but stayed in the doorway, looking at Rothko.

'She'll be so happy to see you.'

Rothko sat in the chair by the dressing table. Sarai could see the back of him in the three-panelled mirror.

'I've got to tell you something, though.' She nodded for *I'm listening.* 'This is what I'm capable of. And I did it for you, more than her.' He straightened his posture, opened his chest. 'I haven't forgiven her. And I don't trust her. I don't think I can risk being round her. Ever again.' Sarai came into the room and closed the door behind her. Stood against it. 'She's a wounded, vicious, toxic person.' Rothko was holding firm under the pressure of revealing himself. Refusing the urge to backtrack and play nice for the sake of getting along. 'And at the same time, I know, she's also a beautiful, exciting, generous person. Full of love. But whichever version of herself she's being, it's always been about *her*.' Sarai was frowning. '*Her* pain. *Her* joy. We were *her* babies, and then we weren't and that was *her* burden. Didn't matter how heavy it was for us, going without her the way we did. She can't feel it if it isn't her pain.' He looked up to check his sister was with him. Tried to tune himself in to the frequency she was listening with, couldn't quite find it. 'We only went without her that way, because she was so fucked. It's *dark*. If she'd have pulled herself together, it could have all ended up so different.'

Sarai heard the truth in what Rothko was saying, and was grateful for it, but she didn't agree. Since her own kids came into her body, and out of her body, and into her life, she'd done a lot trying to work things out, and she'd forgiven her parents. She saw how complicated it was. How impossible and fragile. She wanted to move on from what had been hard in the family and try and enjoy what remained.

She had seen how much her kids loved being with her mum, and it had done something. Made her realise how little the past mattered, now she had a future to take care of. She had arrived at a point in her life where she cared more about her children than she did about her childhood.

'What I'm saying is, this is what I can give.' They looked around the room again, together. Rothko's eyes misted, blinking tears. 'And after this, I'm done. I can't be here to care for her the way you asked me if I would.'

Sarai pulled him up from the chair by his wrists, and wrapped her arms round him, pressed him tightly to her, rubbing his back. Held him how only a mother knows to hold a person. Felt Rothko let go.

A bang came from downstairs, then screaming.

'Oh dear.' She squeezed his arm as she pulled away, 'That don't sound good,' and she left the room to check what damage had just been done to who.

Rothko stood and flicked through the stacks again. Mad that Meg had managed to hold on to them all, so much else had fallen away.

Roberta Flack.

The music took him, hard, and put him in his skin and draped his skin over his body and fixed it all together and sang in him and gave him life and taught him everything he knew and told him everything was what it should be and that really it was fine that things hurt so much the way they did because some people in this world could take that hurt and make this fucking magic out of it. This music that meant other people could bear it better.

He had got it from Meg, his love of music.

He moved his hands over the shelves. Pulled down the shoebox of letters he'd put away earlier that day. Mainly from people he'd never met or heard of, but right at the back, there they were: all the letters she had written to Rothko, that Rothko had returned unopened. He took the latest one and read.

Hello pigeon,

It's your birthday. Well, it is for me anyway. It won't be for you, by the time you get this. Not that you'll even read it!

30 years old. Don't seem real, does it.

I haven't had a drink in four months or anything else. I know you won't believe me. But it is true.

How's the food? Hope no one's troubling you. I've got my ways of keeping track of what you're up to. I know you're behaving yourself. Everyone's ok here. Your sister's ready to pop. She's fine.

I was walking home just now, and I saw someone who looked like you. It's sunny now. But it's been raining all morning.

I've got the radio on. They just played 'Sound and Vision'. I remember you dancing to it. You used to be a good dancer. You were so cute and chubby.

I know it's not easy being strong. Much easier to fall apart. But that's not your way. I'm proud of you. Keep your chin up.

Love Mum x

He put it back in its envelope. Heavily. Put the box back on the shelf.

Haven't had a drink in four months. If he'd have just fucking replied.

He had packed most of his tools in the van, but did a last sweep of the room for drill bits and chargers. Satisfied, he sat down again at the dressing table. It had scrubbed up nice; he'd found it in the architectural salvage place Meg had worked in six thousand years ago. Rothko had hung around that place for hours, waiting for her to finish her shift till she'd given him that rocking horse to fix and told him he could do it, if he stuck to it. That too-bright summer when everything was still to come.

There was so much of her in him.

Dionne in the rave, shouting over the music saying, *but I couldn't make it better. Being you.*

It was like every Rothko that had ever lived was in the room with him. All the Rothkos that he had carried around for years and stifled and not listened to and pushed down into his feet, they were all there. Stood around, holding each other's shoulders. He lifted the needle on Roberta. Put it down on Miles, 'Kind of Blue', and he himself was lifted. Dropped. Plunged. Carried. Everything was speaking and all the little Rothkos from the past and all the Rothkos that had grown up and all the Rothkos that hadn't and all the Rothkos from the future and all the Rothkos from the right now were in the room and standing with their backs against the bedroom walls, their faces calm, their voices were Miles and John, their hands were out there floating on the wind and he could hear them calling to him, all the Rothkos who had been inside for fifteen years and the Rothkos who had gone down under a heavy habit, and the Rothko who ran to Meg's the night of the fire, and the Rothko who never came back and the Rothko who did.

He loved them all. And it was new to him, that feeling.

The kids were eating in the kitchen, and everyone was shouting at each other as Rothko slipped downstairs. Donovan, asleep in the hallway, stretched himself up to follow him out and they managed to leave without anyone hearing them go.

EIGHT

In the urgent care department at Edgecliff General, Meg was waiting to be seen. She was sitting on her bed, swinging her legs off the edge, with the curtains drawn open, watching the waiting room traffic.

The girls out there reminded her of the days before, when as soon as Meg would wake up in a room like this one, she'd unplug herself and get back out to use again.

Not anymore.

She felt tenderness for them. The whole sorry lot of them. Including herself. And it was new to her, that feeling.

Both her babies had been born in this hospital. But it wasn't her space, any more than it was anyone else's. It belonged to whoever woke up in its beds, terrified, all on their own. Or passed out in its waiting rooms, grateful and overwhelmed.

She saw a familiar face, limping over to the vending machines. Errol looked up from the other side of the room and raised his hand. 'Hello trouble.'

'What you doing in here?' she called out. He shuffled over.

'Just come in to get a face lift,' he said. Meg laughed her boomy cackle.

'Whoever he is, he aint worth it.'

'I saw your youngest. Couple of days ago. Rothko?'

Meg's eyes went wide.

Errol took his cap off and held it in his hand as he scratched at his head. 'She said if I saw you, to tell you she'd come home.'

Meg's face was a flower in the sun. The wrinkles in her forehead melted. She unclenched her jaw, unclenched her fists, unclenched her neck and her back, stopped hunching. She slipped into a state of pure elation, clasping her hands under her chin and closing her eyes so she could feel the feeling better as it warmed her veins like *love you* like maybe it wasn't too late. Like *Mum*. Like, maybe it wasn't too late to be loved.

It was dark out. Angel Douglas was sat on her favourite bench in the park behind the train station. Near where the river dug through the strangled banks, down to the sea. Where the industrial units and storage facilities frayed the edges of the town.

They never used to come to this park when she was a kid. Maybe it hadn't existed back then. Private land or a pledge not yet made by a desperate council. Or maybe it had just been too far from the flat for her mum to have considered it a place that belonged to them.

It felt good to Angel, to sit somewhere that wasn't connected to before. Like maybe she was a newcomer here, like Ruby and her friends.

It was her favourite bench because no one ever sat in it. It had dawned on Angel that maybe people left it unoccupied as a mark of respect. But that didn't stop her sitting there. It was a memorial bench to a dead child, and the family had hung spinning things from the branches that sheltered it. Mirrors and ribbons bounced and caught the wind.

She couldn't really believe that the same space, that only a few hours earlier had been full of families and playing children and wagging tails, had so suddenly and completely changed shape. Become furtive ground for shadows to lay cardboard and hope they wouldn't be broken by the night.

The same stage. A different show. A new cast. The change-over seemed as if it had been carefully rehearsed.

Angel didn't know how long she'd been sat there. Since the football kids had clapped each other, running backwards from the opposite end, saying *unlucky*. Since the old men in winter coats, with their hands behind their backs. But now it was night, they were all gone, and there was threat in the air.

She couldn't move. Her sunglasses were scratched on the left lens. It was too dark for wearing them, but she didn't want to move her hands to take them off. If she moved any part of her body, it would be even harder to decide what to do.

She should go home.

She didn't want to go home.

What was home? Home was this moment, this bench. Alone in this park. Where by day people jogged against their pointlessness. And by night they drank, for the same reason.

She'd told Ruby she was on the night shift again. Maybe she was.

She'll be ok. Everything will be ok.

She never wanted children. She was only doing it for her. That was the whole problem, she did too much for other people. Ruby told her all the time.

But it was all she knew.

As a kid, playing funny to keep Mum's spirits up. Keep Dad from getting angry. Keep the peace at all times, in case of outbursts, torrential moods when the stress of trying to hold their lives together rendered her mum inconsolable. But if Angel could just stay ahead of the weather, lighten things up long enough, the storm passed without breaking.

The person she was supposed to be said what people wanted to hear.

It was pathological, Ruby told her. *Your people pleasing is psychotic.* Angel nodded in agreement. But what the fuck did Ruby know about psychosis?

She'll be fine.

NINE

The low night pushed down over Edgecliff and Rothko could just about make out the moody clouds above, looking like bearded faces as he lingered in the traffic, wondering about the people in the other cars.

He pulled up outside Dionne's.

Even after all this time, the view from the street up to her flat was devastating.

It was ringing. He wanted to hang up, but he forced himself to stay on the line.

She answered in a slow way. 'Hello?'

'Dee?' Rothko asked. But of course it was.

'Yeah?' Her voice slunk low around Rothko's ear as he pressed it to his phone.

'It's me.'

'I knew it would be you.'

Rothko laughed. 'How?'

'I just had a feeling.'

'What kind of a feeling?'

Rothko craned his head back to watch the tops of the buildings. Looked for the moon but couldn't find it.

In her flat, Dionne sat on the carpeted floor of the front room that was also her bedroom and leant against the wall beneath the window. Shuffling her fluffy red slippers side to side with her toes. Agnes sat on the couch with her crochet needles, frowning at the TV, every now and then challenging the newsreaders. Joseph was in the kitchen on his computer. Doing his coursework.

'What you doing?' Rothko asked her.

'I'm at home.'

'Are you busy?' And Dionne let a beat of silence pass between them. Wondered if she should punish him for not having called her sooner?

'Maybe. Why?'

'Erm. I was thinking . . .' But the sentiment was inexpressible. Rothko could hear her smile.

'Do you want to come over?'

'Yeah,' he admitted.

'Come over. I'd love that.'

He had a feeling in his body that began in his smiling jaw and ran the whole length of him; a giddy *yes* feeling that made him turn in rapid circles, too fast. He bowed against the headrush. Waited for the blood to settle. 'I'll see you soon then, Dionne.'

'You do remember where I live, don't you?'

Rothko hummed a little note of pleasure. To be spoken to with such familiarity. To be complicit in a game. 'Think I'll manage. Just about.' He interrupted himself. 'Oh Dee, sorry, but do you mind if I bring my dog with me?'

'We love dogs! Our Diesel died last year; we've all been heartbroken. Bring your dog! Joseph would love to see a dog. Wouldn't you babe?' She called towards the kitchen.

Rothko heard a voice saying, 'I can't hear you?'

'My friend's coming. Going to bring his dog,' Dionne shouted.

Then the voice saying something Rothko couldn't hear and Dionne laughing and saying into the phone, 'Joseph's very excited. To meet you. And your dog.'

Rothko swayed on his toes from the pleasure of the blush.

His.

TEN

Angel hadn't been sleeping for months. She knew tired. But sitting up all night on a bench like this, it was a new kind of numbness. It washed the whole scene in heavy froth.

You're just tired.

Maybe when the baby came, she'd be overcome with maternal instinct, and it would improve things with Ruby.

Every time she blinked, she could see Trish's brown eyes blinking back at her.

Print a little badge with new pronouns? Wear it to work like anyone would give a fuck enough to read it?

Ruby had told all her friends that they were trying for a baby.

Everyone was very pleased and they went out for a celebration meal. Ruby had put her arm around the back of Angel's chair and kissed her on the cheek and neck and said *Angel's going to make a great dad* and everyone laughed. Angel laughed with them. It was funny. And then Ruby was happy with her. But nobody knew how desperately she ached to be somebody's dad. How hard she had to fight to stop herself from knowing it.

At home that night, Angel had been battered from all the conversation and Ruby had said *you never make an effort,* and at some point in the argument, Angel couldn't remember the words, just the sounds and the feeling in her throat of suffocation and Ruby threw the lamp at the wall and it smashed and knocked the wine bottle too and stained the carpet and Ruby was outraged about the carpet.

Ruby loved that house.

She said it all the time, the best thing about Edgecliff was the housing stock.

How would she keep the mortgage up?

She'd ask her dad. Her sisters. Ask her mum.

They'd be crushing round her. *Poor you*, they'd say. And they'd wash Angel's memory out of things, cleanse it with new purchases. Don't worry about the wine stain on the carpet. Get a nice new carpet. For the baby's nice new feet.

All the things she wanted that Angel never knew how to buy. Things like curtains, shoe racks, smart new window boxes. All the things Angel couldn't do.

At first, Ruby thought it was charming. Angel was her little project. Someone to be civilised. But it turned out Angel could not be civilised enough.

How long would she wait for Angel to come home? How long before she twigged it was really over?

Angel had never been dependent before. But Ruby needed more things than Angel needed. Like dinners out. Or vibration plate machines you stand on that are supposed to shake the fat off while you listen to a podcast. Or hotel rooms or drinks on the terrace. So, Ruby gave Angel an allowance, put it in a bank account, said *now you'll have money to treat me*. Spa days. Theatre tickets. Things for the house. She checked the statements every month to make sure it wasn't going where she didn't want it going.

But even then, with clear instruction, Angel couldn't buy the right things. Because Angel lacked the training. The subtle tells of having never had enough. Enough what? Don't say the word in front of Ruby. Don't say *class*.

She said she wanted Angel to surprise her more.

But what she meant was give me exactly what I want, or I will stare off into the middle distance, thinking loudly that I would have been better off with someone else.

Dionne was sleeping, Rothko watched the blue light through the curtains sending shapes across the room. Waves were breaking across the carpet. Massing one into the other. All the nights he'd spent without sleep: too alert, too dead, too scared. Tweaking out, or sick. Too unconscious or too conscious, too alone, or not alone enough. Kept awake by a company of shadows, sometimes real, sometimes imagined. Or the screams of other people in their rooms beyond the walls. Or the loudness of their own ideas about who they were and what they were.

He was done with Meg. He was not going to be on hand to care for her. He couldn't go backwards into the heartache of trying to love her. You could love the person and hate the addict. Even if Meg didn't see it that way, he wasn't going to be prey to her needs ever again.

He studied Dionne's skin, saw the flourishes within it. The freckles, spots and grades of pigmentation. Sensed the expansion of her lungs. The perfection of it all. He didn't want to fall asleep. The moment being what it was. Quiet. Soft. Perfectly blue. So restful. Rich and safe. But he slipped into its pull.

In their own ways, each of them could feel it as they slept in its presence. The deep-down calm that had been buried so long in their bodies; they'd both thought it had never existed. But it was there, and had been there all along, waiting. This calm that was desperate but methodical. Patient. Curious.

Full of compassion. And sleeping in each other's presence, a glowing kind of calm that didn't fade with morning. Loving each other like grown-ups.

Donovan at the foot of the fold-down bed. The light through the curtains was a fanfare. It was warm in the room and Rothko was happy and Dionne was happy, and it was a simple feeling.

'You working today?' Rothko asked, holding her against him, feeling her nuzzle backwards into his body. Her hair on the pillow and her soft skin smelling like sleep. 'Or can I take you out somewhere?'

'No,' she rolled herself over. 'I'm not working today.' She looked at him with her eyes, and then with her kisses. 'Where we going?'

'I don't know. Somewhere nice for a day? We could take the dog for a walk? Country pub? You know? Get the train?'

Dionne liked his way of talking. Shy as a wounded dog. But bold with it, somehow. She admired him. Hot, strange, honest person.

'Yes please.' She went to put the coffee on and wake Joseph and bring Agnes her cup of tea and Rothko packed the bed away, took last night's empties to the sink and washed them up.

He was in the kitchen when Joseph came in for his breakfast. 'Morning,' Joseph said to him as he sat down at the table.

'Morning, mate.' Rothko was bubbly with him. Smiled as Donovan walked in from the front room and laid himself down at Joseph's feet underneath the table.

Morning, Donovan,' Joseph greeted him as he reached down to stroke his head.

And Rothko had never known a feeling like it.

Like ease.

Like morning.

Like nothing was missing.

At some point, the night must have given up trying. Spat the park out and left it for dawn to pick up.

A glum light crept inwards from the edges.

Angel's bum had gone numb. Angel's back had got cold. How long had she been sat on this bench? Had it really been a whole night sat here?

She just had to get up and then what?

There was no then what.

The cast changed again as she watched. It was showtime.

The joggers first, they made their big entrance in neon. Then the people with the uniforms on their way to supermarket shifts. Then the dogs, rolling over each other while their owners stood around watching, smiling with teeth.

Then it was the mums and the prams and the coffees on the benches and the people on the phone having loud conversations and the toddlers walking on leads and Angel was still sat there, watching the trapped light. Things felt greener than they used to feel.

There was a storm coming.

It was changing the air.

Angel watched them all, pulling their collars up as they walked a little faster than was comfortable. School kids. Cyclists. People with shopping. All trying to pull themselves through the tangled reeds of the underwater daylight.

The pressure was building behind the clouds. And Angel was a part of it. Any minute.

It was going to piss it down.

The flies were buzzing round in lazy orbit. She watched

the one in front of her face make the sign of the cross a full three times and then disappear upwards.

How long though? How long had she been sat here?

The runners kept looking up. The park was emptying. And then the thunder.

It was like a cheap sound effect of thunder. Like someone striking an iron sheet with a xylophone beater in the radio plays Ruby made her listen to. But when it came again, it was sharper. More like gunfire. It pierced, then it flattened and the whole sky was full of it. Angel looked up for the lightning. Counted the seconds. Or was it the other way round and she'd missed it?

You're tired. That's all it is.

I am. I'm tired. I've not been sleeping.

Maybe exercise would help. She used to like swimming. She hadn't been for ages. She could join the leisure centre. But her tits and her gut and her hairy legs.

She had let herself get carried away with the maybe-I-won' t-be-alone-anymore of it all. But sat here on the memorial bench in the murk of the emptying park, she knew she was no place for anyone, let alone children.

The thunder was lower. A chorus of thunder for three voices. Ruby's blazing temper. Blood red. Bearing down.

The rain came.

It was real rain. Each drop as fat as a peach, till it hardened like the thunder did and fell out of the sky to rage against the dirt, in bitter platoons.

Angel got up. Took her sunglasses off. Stretched her shoulders back behind her, as if she was preparing herself for flight.

She'd been sitting down for so long that she had got to the point where every single muscle in her body had either gone numb or was killing her.

The rain was warm in the cold air.

The electric concrete smell. Angel breathed it in and in and in. The other people in the park were open mouthed, running home.

She started moving. Walked towards the café at the top of the hill. It was closed, but it had an overhanging roof. That little sheltered bit in front.

And all Ruby's friends would be horrified. They wouldn't know what to say at first and Ruby would cry and drink negronis in the small plate bars that Angel never took her to, and they would comfort her and walk her home and it would all be Angel's fault.

The path curved up, past the tennis courts, the basketball court, the playground, everything was empty and lashed by the falling rain.

Angel got to the café and ducked under cover. Bumped her body right in, back against the wall. Looking out at the rain that was so heavy there were waves breaking on the tarmac.

A little crush of teenagers were sat a few feet from Angel, vaping blueberry and candyfloss, giggling. The lightning in sheets like stop motion. The teenagers didn't acknowledge Angel's presence. They just played with each other's shoelaces and screamed into the lightning.

Angel didn't know when it happened, or who started it but suddenly all four of the girls she had taken shelter beside were singing. Voices in harmony. They were good singers. Church-like precision and un-self-conscious joy. Angel was sure it must have been a church song, or at least a very old folk song. But it wasn't.

I never meant to cause you any pain.

When the sky cleared, the sudden change of tone felt overdone. The sun came out and the birds started singing and the fog lifted. It seemed unrealistic how rapidly the murky light had brightened. The teenagers picked up their bags and ran off into the park. Screaming at each other. Angel felt this particular part of the show had got a little sentimental and missed the gloomy magic of the storm.

Angel Douglas could not even conceive of a time in her life when she wouldn't feel as trapped under cloud as she did at this moment.

She did not know the *why* of it, she was stuck in the *what* of it. She had been living on autopilot for as long as she remembered, and her systems were shutting down.

She got to her feet. She straightened her clothes.

It was time.

She was heading for the train station.

She was leaving.

It was time to leave.

ELEVEN

Dionne and Rothko were walking arm in arm, feeling the strange new beat of another person's rhythm beside their own. Not yet sure where one person's hip met the other person's waist. Donovan padded in front, for sniffs and pisses. Dionne held his rope. Every now and then she spoke to him in a high-pitched dog-voice, 'What you found, you good boy? What can you smell?'

They got to their platform. Rothko wanted to walk right up to the end. He wanted to see as much as he could of the train coming into the station. He was excited about it.

There was only one other person about. White hair scraped back but straggling loose, thin face, skin so pale, there was something lunar to it, craggy gullish eyes set on the ground. Tall but hunching over. All her clothes were soaking wet. Jeans, boots, long dark coat. Her arms were folded. Her teeth were chattering.

Donovan whined as they approached her.

'Think she's alright?' Rothko slowed. Dionne didn't like the look of it.

'Come on,' she pulled him away, and they kept going up the platform. But Rothko kept looking back to check on her.

She was holding herself as if she was hurt, and apart from her teeth, she wasn't moving. She was stood so still it was haunting. Staring down at her feet. Her face a mask of utter sadness. It didn't look good to Rothko. He was the type to notice someone else's pain, and not pretend it wasn't happening just because it happened all the time.

'Sure I know her,' Dionne shivered, holding Rothko's arm. She couldn't place where from though.

Rothko was worried. 'Think she's alright?' He pulled away from Dionne to walk back down the platform to the woman.

'Just leave it.' Dionne hung back. It wasn't their place to get involved.

Angel Douglas had achieved calmness. Things had been decided. And the decision had released her. She heard her mother's voice. *She was a waitress, Angel! Gave her demo to a customer.* Ruby in the restaurant and everybody laughing. *Angel's going to make a great dad.* Things had been decided at last. And that was good. There was an end to it in sight, they didn't have to keep pretending anymore. And then there was a shape with a voice at the edge of her vision. Coming closer. She saw the face swimming through the reeds in the underwater daylight.

'You alright there, love? Need any help?' Rothko called out, as he paced towards her. Her eyes were pits as she shrank from the question.

Rothko set himself on letting this person know she'd been seen. Because sometimes Rothko knew, that was all it took.

Angel didn't want to be seen. She had finally managed to turn the world back on. She didn't want someone coming over and pushing her back under.

Close to her now.

Rothko could see the train coming. He could feel the burst of noise and light as it thundered towards the station.

He saw her see him. He saw her see the train. Then he saw her hands drop to her sides as she ran towards the edge.

Dionne was standing back up the platform, holding onto Donovan. Watching. It happened so quickly. But Rothko felt it happen in slow motion.

The train smashing in closer, filling the air with sound. Rothko could hear it in his teeth. Angel was bolting for the tracks. Throwing her body through space. Rothko moved on instinct. It was like a rugby tackle as he flew against her flight. Launched himself, hard, at the person who was launching herself towards oblivion, and grabbed her, arms extended in a dive, out of the mouth of the speeding train. Grabbed her body in his reaching arms and pulled her with him to the ground as he fell, and holding on to her as tightly as he could, as they sank against the concrete of the platform. Landed. Tangled limbs and heavy torsos. Bodies. Such unsurprising, usual things but push them hard enough and they could be capable of incredible feats. Like pulling someone back from the edge.

Somehow, they were both still on the platform as the train sped past, rattling the station roof. Its noise louder in the presence of the other person that each of them found themself so suddenly close to.

It was a fast train, unstopping juggernaut of metal and commuters. Going somewhere with more to offer to the people in its carriages than Edgecliff.

The faces in the train were looking back behind them, at Dionne running towards Rothko, and Rothko in a heap with the person underneath him on the floor.

And then the person started shouting. *No. NO! NO!* And each *No* lasted a long time.

Rothko scrambled up so they were sitting, and held the

person at the shoulders and she was breathing in sobs and fighting Rothko off saying, 'Why did you do that?'

Dionne crouched to hold the woman, eyes jumping between the stranger on the floor and Rothko's stricken face. The woman opened her eyes and was suddenly heavy. She lay back again, staring. Curled her body up. But people were coming. People with pushy little faces and logos on their t-shirts.

It was over. She was lying on the floor, looking up at the two people whose faces were as heavy as her own.

She wasn't dead.

Dionne spoke to her, 'Sweetheart?'

Angel looked at the woman with the stud above her lip and her big sad eyes.

'It's ok.' Her voice was a comfort. 'You're safe.'

Angel closed her eyes again. 'I'm so tired.'

'I know, darling, but you can't rest here. They'll call the police, and they'll come and they'll take you away.' Angel looked up at the woman who was speaking to her, she was holding her shoulder and stroking her with her thumb. Angel opened her eyes again. She didn't want the police to take her away. She waited for these people to tell her what to do.

'Do you want to come with us?' Dionne asked her. 'We can go somewhere that's safe? You've had a shock.'

And Angel looked at Rothko and Dionne and Donovan, and said, 'Yes.'

And so, Dionne helped her up, and the three of them, unsteady, shaking, walked out of the station together. Donovan brought up the rear. Protecting at all times.

They left the station and Rothko's eye was drawn to the broken benches outside what used to be a strip of rundown shops. He saw himself at sixteen, sitting on those benches outside the bookies, kicked out of class again. And he nodded at the place where he used to sit, and the place nodded back at him.

Maybe this is what it had all been for.

'Let's go to the yard,' Rothko told Dionne.

'If you're going to fuck me. You're too late. I'm fucked,' Angel's tone was matter-of-fact.

Dionne laughed. 'No, babe, we're friends.'

Angel's hair had fallen out of its band and was hanging in front of her eyes, as she looked out at them both through the strands. Winter light glimpsed through branches. Her clothes were wet against their arms. They held her up. The four of them walked in silence past the howling, laughing, eating town, where the shops were stocked with strange apparatus: double-decker pushchairs, wall-mounted singing fish.

Dionne rubbed Angel's back to warm her. Angel stumbled under the touch and Rothko thought he saw the younger Rothko, a few paces behind. Wide steps and a pained expression, walking fast, squinting out from underneath their cap. But every time he turned to catch them in his sights, they'd disappear.

Finally, down Turpin Road and through the heavy gate, into the yard. Rothko saw the younger Rothko peering in. And this time their eyes met. The older Rothko nodded. The younger Rothko slowed their pace. 'You're alright,' the older Rothko told them, before he closed the gate. Out on the street, drawn to something they could only half feel, the younger Rothko watched the older Rothko's hands threading the heavy chain through the gate. Something in the sureness and the sadness of those hands made them look down at their own, covered in dirt and smoke and ash, before they stuffed them in their pockets, and decided to keep going.

'I know it's weird,' Rothko told Angel. 'But you're safe here.'

Angel rolled her eyes and said, 'Oh god, not a safe space.'

Dionne laughed at that, but Rothko didn't laugh. He had a feeling of eternity stopping in the moment. The whole push of time, channelled into right now; even when he blinked it didn't go away. And there was something pitiless about it.

Donovan, Dionne, Rothko and Angel came up to the kitchen where Dill and Eugene were taking turns reading to each other from a paperback. *Hangover Square*. It was warm in the kitchen, and it smelt like cooking.

'Visitors,' Dill said, looking up. Silver slip dress. Silky black hoody with feathers round the cuffs.

'Here. Sit down.'

Rothko got Angel a chair, and she sat in it saying, 'Not that bad, am I?' She was trying to joke, but her face wasn't joking.

Dionne sat down next to her, and Eugene went to the stovetop and stirred a pan.

'Do you want something to eat, sweetheart?' he asked, looking at Angel kindly. For Angel, it was that look that did it. She couldn't hold it anymore. There was too much she'd been pretending not to feel.

Tears came.

Quiet tears that saturated her face and flooded her with steady relief. She dropped her head to feel the force of the moment. She gripped her hands together in her lap to ground herself. Long bony fingers. Pushing hard.

Eugene stirred until he was satisfied, and he fixed Angel a bowl of soup.

'I'll just put it there for you.' Eugene put the bowl down in front of her and sat, crossing his legs, dangling his ankle. 'I thought I could feel a cold coming yesterday, so I made a chicken soup. It's very good.' Angel looked at him from a long way away. 'Swear down, it's better than your nan's.' Eugene was perceptive, he liked working people out. He watched Angel with interest. She had a kind of grace to her, Eugene thought. Bit severe for his comfort, though. Her boxy figure folded over itself, hands clinging to each other. Pale as the bleached driftwood left out in the yard. He recognised the him in her. The her in him. Queerness like a bridge sometimes. This one was an egg, he had no doubt about it. Even if the poor thing didn't know it yet. He saw the hardness that she draped around herself; it wasn't mean. A necessary wall, built to keep the trouble out. But it looked very much like the trouble had got *in*.

'Do you want one?' he asked Dionne.

'No, darling, thank you. I'm alright.'

Dionne, on the other hand, was much more Eugene's type. He looked her up and down and gave her a tick of approval, in the eyes. Wasn't like Rothko to bring friends home. And Eugene's curiosity was easily aroused.

'I'm Eugene,' he whispered. Emphasising his name. 'That's Dill.' And Dionne kissed his cheek. '*And?*' Eugene said to Rothko. 'Who are your friends?'

Rothko said, 'This is Dionne.' And he blushed when he said her name.

'Oh!' Dill clapped his hands. 'It's a love story. How disgusting.'

'Don't listen to her,' Eugene whispered to Dionne. 'She's just jealous.'

'I don't blame her.' Dionne winked at Dill, 'Have you seen my man?'

And Dionne's public declaration hung like a golden bridge between their teenage selves and the adults they had, at that very moment, become. 'And this is someone we only just met. I don't know her name.'

Angel, still crying, swallowed and cleared her throat. 'I'm ok,' she said, head in her hands, hair falling down around her face. 'I just.' But she stopped.

'You don't have to say anything,' Dionne told her. 'You can rest.'

Eugene rubbed a warm hand over her shoulders. She was soaking wet. 'We need to get you a change of clothes.'

Angel lifted her head. Her hands dipped gracefully at the wrists as she wafted her palm towards Rothko. 'Why did you do that? You didn't have to do it?'

Rothko's blush was pounding now. 'I'm going to get you a clean towel and some clothes. So you can have a hot shower. If you want.'

Angel stared at this person who was speaking to her, trying to see what she couldn't see from looking. The feeling that had rushed at her and dragged her to the floor. The giant warmth that had kept her in the world.

Her body was still carrying the storm, the night she'd spent watching the trees. She wasn't supposed to be here anymore.

The colour was returning to her vision, light prickling into the blackness. The corners first. Things regained their edges.

She had got so close to it. Felt its breath on her. Been inches from it. Seconds from it. But somehow, she'd come back from jumping out, alive. All the years of waiting at the edges of herself. All the years of desperate not to feel. It was like they were with her, in the room, crowding close with these too-friendly people Ruby would roll her eyes about.

She'd been waiting all her life to feel a part of herself.

She thought she never could.

But here it was.

A feeling drumming through her, like nearing the surface after holding your breath too long. Lungs on fire. She had to breathe.

Rothko watched Angel as she inhaled through her nose, for as long as she could. Watched her hold it, then exhale it in deep concentration. And Angel watched Rothko. Sheepish face. Sincere eyes. Anxious, fidgeting mouth. The reason she could still breathe in.

'You saved me.'

Rothko squeezed her shoulder. 'You're alright.'

She looked at his hand on her shoulder. Then down at her own hands, clasped in her lap. She could feel the breath travelling through her body, she could see the breath in her fingertips as she held her own hand tightly. Her body. Working for her, even as she worked against it.

Dill leant back in his chair, 'Erm,' he asked the room, 'am I missing something?'

Rothko jogged downstairs and looked around his van in a daze. He hadn't done a wash, and he had nothing to offer her. He knocked on Cookie and Roxanne's to see if they could help rustle up some things for Angel.

Rox was at home; she had her fire going and was sitting in her chair with her wonky glasses on and her socks that went up to her knees. Rothko told her what was happening, and she got some bits together. As Rothko turned to go upstairs, Roxanne remembered.

'Bruv, a letter came for you. I've got it here.' And she passed him the little gold envelope addressed to Rothko Taylor, with the small capital letters that he knew belonged to Ezra. It must have been a holy day. Which one? Was it Rash Hashanah yet? Maybe Yom Kippur. If it was, he hadn't realised. But it was usually around this time. Autumn, like a portal opening to God.

He pocketed the letter and went inside to give Angel the clean clothes and the towel and the shower gel.

But he stopped before he climbed the stairs to the kitchen. Opened the envelope and read the card.

> For you, Rothko. May it reach you on this solemn day of atonement. Today is the holiest day in the calendar; it's a day of repentance, and renewal. Here's a prayer for you, from your old dad. You are in my thoughts. Always. And Shana Tova. It's a new year.
>
> > Our praise of You accords with Your essential nature: slow to anger and easily appeased. You do not desire the death of the sinner, but rather that we change our ways and live. You wait until the day of death, and if one returns, You accept that person back immediately. Truly you are their Creator, and know the nature of your Creatures, that they are only flesh and blood. Each person's origin is dust, and each person will return to the earth having spent life seeking sustenance.

Acknowledgements

I worked on drafts of this novel at two writing residencies. Civitella Ranieri and Residencia Literaria Finestres. I want to acknowledge that time as crucial to this novel, and to thank everyone involved in both, for providing the space and allowing me the opportunity to dig so deeply.

As well as the people behind the selection processes, and the people responsible for running the residencies and caring for us while there, I would like to thank the artists I was in residence with, for the conversation and companionship.

Thank you to the Fellows and staff at Civitella: Adam Basanta, Alper Aydin, Ayelet Waldman, Borys and Liudmila Khersonsky, Brigitta Varadi, Carlo Pizzati, Carman Moore, Claudia Durusanti, Délio Jasse, Diego Mencaroni, Eric Nathan, Francisco Goldman, Greta Caseti, Ilaria Locchi, Ivy Haldemann, Stacy Lynn Waddell, Lotte Arnsberg, Marie Howe, Michael Chabon and Zhu Xiaowen. A special thanks to those who fed me every day: Romana and the two Patrizias; I still daydream about your cooking, years later. And another special thank you, to my dear friend Dana Prescott, for believing so fully in my work.

Thank you to the team at Finestres: Ari and Mike and Imma, Nicolás G. Botero, Matías Medic; and my little family of writers: Irene Pujadas, Mariana Enriquez, and Robin Robertson.

Thanks also to Stephen Bass, Roger and Carola Zogolovitch and Rufus Norris and Tanya Ronder, who offered me space to write in their beautiful homes.

Thanks to my agents Nicola Chang and David Evans at David Higham Associates, for your commitment to these characters and this story, and for your care. It's been revelatory to have your input and expertise.

Thank you to my editor Zeljka Marosevic, for challenging me to go further. Pushing me, pushing the plot, pushing the language. Thank you to the whole team at Jonathon Cape. Also, to all the editors who read the first draft and offered their thoughts and feedback at that very early stage.

Thank you to my management team at Wildlife: Emma Greengrass, Sarah Abbot, Natalia Quiros Edmunds, Jack Bexon, Jack Gould and Ian McAndrew. So much gratitude for all you do.

Thank you, Imani Qamar. It takes a lot of courage to lead by example. And you do. Your current is flowing through this novel.

Thank you Juliette Larthe, for me the way you do. For reading this novel before anyone else. For getting so absorbed in it, you stayed up with it all night. You made me feel like what I had been wrestling out of the ether had found its form and was holding its shape.

I want to thank my community. I wrote this for us. And my family. Who I adore.

And lastly and most importantly; I want to acknowledge the endless commitment to this text that I received from Amie-Faith Francis, who made space to consider every single word of this novel with me, even as she was pulled down to the depths, in the mouth of an illness so complete it swallowed the world. Wherever you are, I know somehow, you'll get hold of a copy. That you'll find a place to sit down where no one can find you, and that you'll open this novel for the first time, breathing in the grandeur of it, the finished thing at last. I know you'll flinch when you see your name written here in black and white, that you'll shake from holding the groan in your throat. I can see you, Amie. Covering your mouth with your fingers, crying into the corners of your eyes. I couldn't have done it without you. Thank you for every day of it. You beautiful nightmare. You're always in my prayers. I still believe that you are strong enough to come alive.